FALL GUY

ALSO BY ARCHER MAYOR

Marked Man

The Orphan's Guilt

Bomber's Moon

Bury the Lead

Trace

Presumption of Guilt

The Company She Kept

Proof Positive

Three Can Keep a Secret

Paradise City

Tag Man

Red Herring

The Price of Malice

The Catch

Chat

The Second Mouse

St. Albans Fire

The Surrogate Thief

Gatekeeper

The Sniper's Wife

Tucker Peak

The Marble Mask

Occam's Razor

The Disposable Man

Bellows Falls

The Ragman's Memory

The Dark Root

Fruits of the Poisonous Tree

The Skeleton's Knee

Scent of Evil

Borderlines

Open Season

FALL GUY

A Joe Gunther Novel

ARCHER MAYOR

MINOTAUR BOOKS
NEW YORK

First published in the United States by Minotaur Books, an imprint of St. Martin's Publishing Group

www.minotaurbooks.com

Library of Congress Cataloging-in-Publication Data

Names: Mayor, Archer, author.
Title: Fall guy : a Joe Gunther novel / Archer Mayor.
Description: First Edition. | New York : Minotaur Books, 2022. | Series:
    Joe Gunther series ; 33
Identifiers: LCCN 2022019724 | ISBN 9781250224187 (hardcover) |
    ISBN 9781250224194 (ebook)
Subjects: LCGFT: Mystery fiction. | Novels.
Classification: LCC PS3563.A965 F35 2022 | DDC 813/.54—dc23
LC record available at https://lccn.loc.gov/2022019724

Our books may be purchased in bulk for promotional, educational, or business use. Please contact your local bookseller or the Macmillan Corporate and Premium Sales Department at 1-800-221-7945, extension 5442, or by email at MacmillanSpecialMarkets@macmillan.com.

First Edition: 2022

10 9 8 7 6 5 4 3 2 1

ACKNOWLEDGMENTS

As always with these tall tales, I am indebted to many others for at least trying to keep me on the straight and narrow when it comes to procedures, protocols, and processes. Those below did their best, I am sure. The results of my heeding their guidance, however, are all my responsibility.

Tom Andrews
Margot Mayor
Greg Davis
Castle Freeman
Tracy Shriver
Sean Eaton
Eric James
VSP Bomb Squad
Sarah Clark

Steven Brown
John Martin
Adam Belville
Ray Walker
Todd Faulkner
Jeremy Evans
Matt Sweitzer
NHSP
Jesse Bristol

FALL GUY

CHAPTER ONE

Joe Gunther crested the hill overlooking a small cluster of flashing, multihued vehicles below. They made him think of a swarm of fireflies, settled untidily by the side of the road, but in fact were a group of cruisers and unmarked cars much like his own. They appeared randomly scattered, as if abruptly stopped by a startling event.

They had in fact been summoned here, in the looming twilight of a fading Vermont winter day, as they often were by mishap or catastrophe, to sort through another mess left in humanity's wake. Their common dismissal of parking protocols was due mostly to this road having been closed to traffic. But, beneath it, Joe recognized a fondness for flouting convention, perhaps because police officers were so often called upon to enforce it. Cops could be rebels that way: trained to the rule of law, obedient to procedure, policy, and authority, they are also drawn by the occupation's spontaneity, adrenaline, and the rewards it offers creative thinkers.

Anyone can mentally retire while still on the job and merely put in the hours. Police officers are no different. But older investigators tend to rise to a higher calling. They are the profession's theorists, and when placed among the right peers, the best of them can be almost termed artists.

Joe was such a man, a veteran of decades of police work, and he was about to join a group of colleagues honed by experience to the same edge. He was the field force commander of the Vermont Bureau of Investigation, and they were all about to lay open the inner workings of an untimely death.

It was late winter—cold, harboring decaying, crunchy snow, and punctuated by surrounding bare-armed trees, their dark branches upthrust in surrender or supplication. It was getting warmer—slightly—the days longer, the lakes melting from their edges, and snowfall more frequently turning to rain. Winter was dying, for which Joe was grateful. He liked New England's seasons, had known them all his life, and cherished living where, for six months at least, nature could be lethal. But it was the variety that gave the place life, and everyone he knew was ready for the coming spring, especially now that the annual maple sugarers were done collecting their product.

Everyone apart from the person responsible for their spontaneous gathering, who presumably no longer cared.

Joe rolled to a stop by the side of the road, the only vehicle not using its strobes.

A man, narrow, intense, unsmiling, approached with watchful eyes. His lame left arm was pinned to his side by its hand being tucked into his Tyvek suit's pocket. This was Willy Kunkle, one of Joe's small special unit, whose injury had been incurred years earlier in a shoot-out, but whose natural talent—and Joe's influence—had kept him employed.

"Hey, boss," he said in greeting, his accent betraying a hint of his New York City roots. He opened Joe's door and stood back to let the older man out.

Joe looked at him inquiringly as he straightened and stamped his feet.

Willy answered the unstated question. "It's a clusterfuck. We're gonna earn our pay with this one."

Joe nodded, looking around. "Who else is here?"

"Who isn't?" Kunkle counted off. "We got state police, sheriff's deputies, our crew, the ME's office is responding, EMS just left, and the local fire department is working the detour. We're only missing the town constable. Even the wrecker showed up early to rubberneck." He gestured toward a shallow ravine running between the woods and the hard-packed dirt road. "But that wasn't what you meant, I know. Sam's down there. Lester's wrapping up a case at the office. Should be here soon."

Sam was Samantha Martens, another squad member and the mother of Willy's child, Emma. Lester Spinney was the last of the VBI's southeast regional team—one of the agency's smallest despite its caseload, which was not something this tight-knit group wanted to change. They'd become family over time and preferred no outside meddling.

As he pulled on the type of white coveralls everyone else was already wearing, Joe indicated the roof of the abandoned car he could see from this angle. "Looks fancier than your average used pickup."

"By about a hundred grand," Willy agreed. "Mercedes four-door. Crap car, in my opinion. All flash for a lotta cash. You could do as well with a GM. Course, that's just me. It's registered in New Hampshire and was reported stolen five days ago."

Joe was beginning to grasp his colleague's point about complications. "Therefore not belonging to the dead man I was told was inside?" he asked doubtfully.

"You wish. Let's just say the word *inside* is a matter of interpretation. He's in the trunk, which they made way too small, natch."

"Stolen five days ago?" Joe asked. "No one traced its GPS? They should've found it within hours."

Willy hitched one shoulder. "Beats me. Supposedly, they tried but got no signal. Who knows?"

Felony crime scene reconstructions tend to be oddly leisurely paced affairs. Perimeter and access avenues are established and roped off, vehicles come and go on assorted tasks, tents are set up, specialist teams delicately work around one another like dancers of a minuet, and quiet conversations occur in small clusters, with hands cupped around paper cardboard cups of hot coffee. In some instances, as here, the natural daylight gradually yields to a spindly forest of powerful LED lamps, a growling thrumming of generators adding to the already running car engines.

Thousands of images are taken throughout, by patrol officers, investigators, medical examiners, and a special crew manning a FARO 3D digital camera designed to preserve the whole scene as a form of hologram—this to be available long after the surrounding reality has been dispatched to the morgue, the wrecker's yard, or fed into VBI computers for analysis, consolidation, and distribution.

At some point, state crime lab investigators arrive in a large truck and collect, bag, and inventory anything from cars to computers to footprints and finger smudges. Collectively named the CSST, or Crime Scene Search Team, they catalog and store bag after bag until, finally—many hours later—the ant-like activity slows and dissipates, the cruisers, vans, tow trucks, and SUVs thin out, and at last, the reopened road and surrounding bare trees get to witness once more the gentle creaking of cold branches in the quiet breeze, and the rare passage of a car whose driver has no idea of the theatrics preceding his appearance.

Having arrived long before that end point, indeed at the height of the activity, Joe stepped off the road and gingerly worked his way downslope, following one of the staked-out avenues to the rear of the thoroughly stuck four-door sedan. He ended up beside a slightly built but wiry, intense young woman who was aiming her camera at the interior of the car's trunk.

"Hey," he greeted her quietly.

"Hey back," Sammie Martens replied, still shooting.

"We have an ID yet?"

"Course not. Can't be that easy." She lowered the camera to study the curled-up body before them, nestled like a sleeping stowaway resting on his side, one hand tucked under his cheek.

"The ME hasn't moved him yet," she added. "He might have a wallet."

"Despite your having already checked."

She cast him a look. "That would be a breach of protocol, boss. You know I'd never do that."

Her voice lost its hint of playfulness as she indicated the young man's blue-jeaned hip. "I'm betting it's gone. You can see the faded outline of a billfold in his back pocket. He was probably relieved of it before getting shoved in here."

"To steal his documents and money or to hide his identity?" Joe asked.

"Questions to be answered, for sure."

"When you weren't checking for an ID, did you also not notice how he might've died?"

Sam tapped the side of her head. "Don't know what's going on under his clothes, but he caught something hard with his temple. It looks ugly enough to be fatal."

"We know who the car belongs to yet?"

"One Lemuel Shaw," she offered. "If you can believe that. I hope for his sake he has a nickname."

"Old New England moniker," Joe said. "Where from?"

"Gilsum, New Hampshire, between Keene and Marlow," she told him. "On Route 10. If the car's any sign, I'd say Mr. Shaw eats high on the hog."

"How do you know this isn't Mr. Shaw?"

"Wild guess? There's about a fifty-year age difference, according to Shaw's DMV photo."

"Willy doesn't think much of the car. I overheard somebody say it looked like a teenager's bedroom."

Sam led him to one of the rear doors, open to reveal a lightly stained and dirty back seat. "Most of what was in here's been removed for inventorying, but you can still see how it was all just tossed in. There wasn't room for our friend, even if that had been an option."

"So what's your theory?"

She answered immediately. "I don't think it was moving day. It all amounted to easy-to-carry tech toys, booze, silverware, and a piece or two of jewelry. And money, just thrown in. A real jumble."

"A magpie nest," Joe surmised.

She nodded. "But is our dead man the magpie?"

"And who were the drivers?"

"Drivers?" she asked, before catching herself. "Right. Dumb. The one who drove here and the one who picked him up after."

Joe made light of it. "He could've driven a corpse here and then stuck his thumb out to hitch a ride. Not a stretch, considering some of the people we've arrested."

Sam accepted his kindness. "True, but unlikely."

"How 'bout foot or tire prints?" Joe asked, moving on.

"Yes on the first, cast and photographed, not that I'm putting much faith in them. Negative on the tire marks. The first responders didn't totally destroy the scene before they left, but the road still had nothing to tell us. CSST did a complete exterior sweep; they have yet to do the car's inside, just so you know. They're waiting till they get better lighting and more heat. And they haven't grabbed the electronic black box."

"Speaking of which," Joe said, "Willy told me nobody got a fix on the GPS after it was reported stolen. What's that about?"

"I was told they got no joy. Maybe something short-circuited the unit."

"How many times did they try?"

"Beats me," she replied. "Nor do I know which agency was asked."

A waving flashlight beam caught their attention. Willy was above them, signaling from the edge of the road. "Got something interesting up here."

"Maybe the driver *did* stick his thumb out and got run over," Sam commented.

"We could never be so lucky," Joe replied, joining her in the steep but short climb back up.

On top, Willy indicated the open rear doors of the CSST truck, whose glaring interior was equipped in part like a mobile office, complete with stools and workbenches.

"Jim found something you'll love," Willy added, his tone thick with irony.

Jim Collins was the CSST leader, whom they found seated near the front after clambering into the truck. He was situated before a rectangular container with a glass viewing window cut into its top and two holes into which he'd thrust his hands to work on something inside.

"Joe, good to see you. Sorry I can't greet you formally." He nodded toward the box holding his hands. They knew what he was doing. Standard search protocol regarding electronics dictated that officers first and foremost protect all phones, tablets, and computers from possible self-destruct signals sent remotely by their owners. They do this by using so-called Faraday pouches, designed to shield devices from outside impulses until they can be delivered to the lab. However—given the unlikely yet fortunate circumstance of a computer lab readily available by the side of the road at night, complete with an even larger, full-fledged Faraday box—an initial quick peek was too hard to resist.

"There were only six phones recovered from the car," Jim was saying, "so I thought, what the hell, right? This being the only one without encryption, why not take a look? You might be glad I did."

Joe peered over the top of the man's Tyvek-hooded head to look into the lighted box. The portals Jim had used for his hands were fitted with gray metallic gloves inside, making the box's interior as secure in its way as a miniature biohazard vacuum room, and Joe could admire how Collins's fingers were expertly manipulating the phone's controls to reveal its contents.

"Kiddie porn," Jim explained, scrolling through images of pale, hairless, exposed young flesh. "Found it in an email where the sender said that if the recipient likes what he sees, there's more available, quote-unquote, the usual way."

Joe straightened, sadly not surprised. "Swell," he said darkly. "Just what we needed."

Blessedly, Vermont was no hotbed of child abuse, but it had enough of its share to make these images depressingly familiar.

Willy was standing within earshot. "It might be. Jim says the phone's also from New Hampshire. All this—the car, the body, the contents—is looking more and more like a dump job, although there's no saying the guy in the trunk wasn't killed over here."

Joe turned toward him. "Keep going."

Willy indicated the Faraday box. "That email could legally give us cross-border access to New Hampshire. Underage porn is a federal rap, and those photos are date-stamped recently enough to maybe make them an ongoing crime, not to mention the peer-to-peer implications of the text, which point to trafficking. We could use all that to mother-may-I the AG's office and get the ICAC task force activated. Keep us involved, regardless of jurisdiction."

Collins spoke without looking up. "If you do cross the river, Fred Houston's your man—he's ICAC out of Cheshire County and a federal task force officer, to boot. Incredible resource. Nice guy, too."

Joe listened without responding, processing Willy's suggestion. ICAC stood for Internet Crimes Against Children, the umbrella organization representing dozens of task forces across thousands of police agencies nationwide, all aimed at interdicting and prosecuting the offenses advertised in its name.

Meeting this form of criminal activity on its own terms, ICAC overrides the usual limited local jurisdictional reach by creating units trained by Homeland Security, armed with federal laws, that travel where they're needed.

There's little regional pushback. Local cops are more than happy to have ICAC task force officers—also called TFOs—take these often costly, always technical, and certainly viscerally unpleasant cases away.

What Willy had suggested, however, went beyond handing over the sex crime aspect of this investigation to ICAC. Joe, Lester, Willy, and Sam had received special training several years ago and were themselves certified as TFOs, qualified to interact with Homeland Security not only in internet child sex offenses, but drug investigations and other crimes as well.

Given the disparate layers they were already facing here—a hot car from New Hampshire full of stolen electronics, some of it containing pedophilia, and equipped with a dead body—the option of maintaining jurisdictional control was very appealing.

"It's not like we get to play our TFO card very often," he said softly.

"The ME's here," a trooper called into the truck's interior. "Wants to know if she can have at the body."

Joe turned, smiling broadly. "The ME herself? The chief?"

"I didn't ask for her ID, but yeah," was the answer.

Joe was delighted. That meant Beverly Hillstrom had made the trip from Burlington to Rockingham township in person, to support her local investigator. This was a rarity, and only seen in major cases. There were but two forensic pathologists for the entire state, and they usually stayed put to conduct the hundreds of autopsies called for every year. A trip across the state by one of them happened once or twice a year, at best.

None of which had anything to do with Joe's reaction. Beverly also happened to be his romantic other half, whom he got to see once a week if each of their schedules allowed it. He suspected her arrival tonight had less to do with the importance of the case and more with their not having seen each other in a fortnight.

Willy, unknown for his subtlety, laughed, stood back, and ordered everyone in the truck, "Make a hole. Special Agent Gunther needs to show proper respect."

Sammie scowled at her partner and said, "You are such a dork," as Gunther made his way toward the exit, unconcerned, already used to Kunkle referring to the chief medical examiner as Joe's "special friend."

He returned to the ditch-bound car to find the scene considerably altered. Now that the search team had finished with the vehicle's exterior, a tarp had been laid out at the edge of the trunk, lights repositioned, and a half dozen people summoned for the body's extraction and examination.

Beverly, tall, athletic, her fair hair tied back, gave Joe the smallest of half smiles as he came into view, not an expression she universally wore. Her decades-long renown for following procedure, bordering on severity, preceded her within the ranks. You minded your step around Hillstrom.

Not breaching that aura, Joe merely sidled up beside her, barely bumped her with his hip, and softly said, "Very sneaky, Doctor. You going to claim this as a happy coincidence?"

She kept watching the proceedings and replied in kind. "Not in the slightest, Agent Gunther. I have spies documenting your every move."

The body, stiffened by time and low temperature, was awkwardly removed like a life-sized mannequin and placed onto the tarp. Beverly stepped closer, but let her local investigator actually disrobe the remains and study them, section by section, alongside one of the search techs. Sammie Martens, befitting her driven personality, eavesdropped on their comments, asking questions as they went.

By the time the body had been almost stripped nude, Joe asked Beverly, "We were thinking a blow to the head. You agree?"

Reflective of her scientific approach, she responded cautiously, "I agree that's what we can see, and it appears to be a fracture, but who knows what's going on inside? The autopsy will tell us more in a few hours, and I'll rush the toxicology. I overheard someone saying you'd found child pornography among the contents of the car?"

"Unfortunately," he admitted.

"There's barely any blood in the trunk," Lester Spinney announced generally, having joined them unobtrusively ten minutes earlier. The only member of Joe's small unit not dating back to the

Brattleboro Police Department days the rest of them had in common, Lester was an ex–state trooper, once a member of their Bureau of Criminal Investigation. Lofty, alarmingly skinny, and with a disarming manner, he was Joe's dependable Everyman—steady, constant, hardworking. He was a family man with a son in law enforcement, a daughter in college, and a wife who worked as a nurse.

"Anything else?" Joe asked from the other side of the tarp.

Spinney's lanky body was half-consumed by the trunk. He was holding a flashlight. "Not visibly," he reported in a muffled voice.

Jim Collins appeared and motioned to one of his folks to ease Lester out of the way—a telling sign of the continual if subtle competition between agencies.

Joe spoke to Beverly again. "The theory is that the car was abandoned here after crossing over from New Hampshire, where it was stolen a week ago. Now it looks like the body was dumped, too, having been killed elsewhere and transported here. That sound reasonable?"

She agreed. "Based on the wound and the little blood Lester just mentioned, yes." She raised her voice slightly so her own investigator could hear. "Ted, you've ruled out as best you can that the damage to the temple didn't come from a bullet or some other penetrating object?"

Ted looked up quickly over his shoulder. "It looks like more of a crushing blow, spread out and spongy. I can't see an actual hole. Course, there might be one. Hard to tell here and now."

"Still nothing identifying him?" Joe asked Sam.

As she shook her head in response, Jim Collins said, "I wouldn't mind running a little experiment that might help." He held up a zippered back pouch, adding, "This is on loan from a sales rep. It's supposed to lift fingerprints electronically and make 'em readable for comparison with what we've got on file, in state. I have to relay the image through the truck's computer, but it should be quick enough."

"Give it a shot," Joe encouraged him.

"Just like Ducky," someone cracked, referring to the pathologist on the TV show *NCIS*.

By the time Collins returned from completing his test, the body had been tagged and bagged and was being wrestled up the slope for transportation by a local funeral home for an autopsy by Beverly later on.

"Any luck?" Joe asked, meeting him by the roadside.

Collins pointed at the black body bag on the gurney, trundling toward the hearse. "Joe Gunther? Meet Don Kalfus."

Everyone within earshot looked at him.

"Really?" Joe replied. "You got a hit?"

"Complete with photo printout." The CSST leader handed over a recognizable printout of a mug shot, lifted off the truck's onboard computer. "A native son with a rap sheet featuring burglaries and car thefts in both New Hampshire and Vermont. Looks like he has family in Brattleboro. Perfect fit."

"Any sex crimes?" Willy asked.

"Not known to us. Don't know what might be lurking beyond a records search. The phone we looked at wasn't registered to him, not that that means much."

"Who does it belong to?" Lester asked.

"Lisa Rowell, Keene address."

"A woman?"

"Unless it's like a boy named Sue," a voice said from beyond the light.

Female child porn peddlers were known to account for only 2 percent of the offending population.

"I'd bet Lisa's being screwed by her boyfriend," Willy cracked. "In more ways than one."

"We'll find out soon enough," Joe told him, "after we disturb a few people tonight to get our paperwork rolling."

"Hot damn," Willy reacted.

Joe took advantage of this commingling of senior people, including his own squad, to address them all. "Without wanting to sound dramatic, I'd like everyone to consider this a red ball situation. Above and beyond the unexplained presence of Mr. Kalfus in Mr. Shaw's purportedly stolen Mercedes, we've got Lisa Rowell's phone with what appear to be recent photos of at least one child being exploited. I don't have to tell you how important it is that we draw a line under that last item as fast as we can. Willy and Jim both mentioned invoking ICAC and Homeland Security's TFO program so we can maintain control of all parts of this mess, regardless of what state border might lie in the way. I think that's a great idea and worth making a few people grumpy to make it happen."

He glanced at Collins to ask, "Did you get any information on the car owner beyond his name?"

Collins opened a file he was holding and produced another photo, this one from the New Hampshire DMV website. "I did a criminal check, but no luck aside from an old DUI and a couple of speeding tickets. He might just be a victim, pure and simple."

A snort from Willy reflected what he thought of that phrase. As a combat vet, a retired sniper, a recovering alcoholic, and a survivor of personal violence, he considered his skepticism of all things human hard-earned and richly deserved.

Perhaps cued by the reaction, Joe turned to him and requested, "Could you call Ron Klecszewski and tell him about the late Don Kalfus? What with their past warrants, Brattleboro PD obviously has a dog in this fight. Ask him if we could use their sally port so Jim and his folks can finish processing the inside of Shaw's car in more comfort, along with a corner of their office we can use for the rest of the night."

"Déjà vu all over again," Willy said, extracting his phone and stepping away. Ron Klecszewski was the lieutenant heading the department's detective squad—the same position and office that Joe used to have when Ron, Willy, and Sam were cutting their teeth in younger days.

"Does that work for you, Jim?" Joe asked his colleague. "Moving the car to Bratt to finish your examination?"

"And download its infotainment system," Collins replied. "If it's rigged the way I think it is, that'll tell us everywhere the car's been since leaving Shaw's dooryard, along with everything its driver did— from where he went, when he did it, how many times he opened and closed his doors, and what calls he might've made using the car's Wi-Fi uplink. You name it. For that matter, in case he doesn't have receipts, we should be able to figure out where and when he gassed up so you can find those stations and get video footage."

"I heard the Mercedes's GPS wasn't working, which is why it took a passing motorist to call this in."

Collins was puzzled. "It worked a few minutes ago. I activated it to check. Whoever tried the day it vanished probably hit a glitch and gave up. Wouldn't be the first time."

"Okay," Joe said, moving on. He caught Lester's attention and suggested, "We need a bunch more background on these names, not to mention whatever new ones crop up after processing the other smartphones. You might as well start with fusion background checks, but get hold of NESPIN, too. They've created a pawnshop database, which might be perfect for finding out where Kalfus was hawking his ill-gotten wares."

NESPIN was the New England State Police Information

Network, serving Connecticut, Maine, Massachusetts, New Hampshire, Rhode Island, and Vermont.

"Got it," Lester replied.

"Sam," Joe continued, "could you coordinate all this with everybody here and make sure no one's left hanging or in doubt about what to do? I'll call the AG's office and get Tausha Greenblott to disturb her Homeland Security counterpart at home so we can get the thumbs-up for a task force. She can do the same to the Vermont ICAC commander and get him to alert his New Hampshire equivalent that we'll be showing up."

He asked Collins, "What was the name of the ICAC guy you mentioned?"

"Fred Houston. He's badged out of the Cheshire County Sheriff's Office but is plugged into everybody and anybody across the state. Say what you will about New Hampshire, their ICAC setup is sharp and really well coordinated."

Joe nodded once. "Okay. That's it. We all know more or less what to do. Any questions, Sam's your go-to person for the night. Sorry about the midnight oil. I hope you all drink coffee and that you got a good night's sleep twenty-four hours ago, 'cause it ain't gonna happen tonight."

Joe took Beverly's elbow as he saw her split away to walk to her car, on the edge of what had become a ground fog of light, colorful and pulsing like a fanciful castoff of a Christmas long past.

"I sense a groggy workday in your future," she said, slipping her arm around his waist as they entered the calming darkness.

"I don't guess you'll be getting much sleep, either," he replied. "Not if you're going to open up Mr. Kalfus in the morning."

"Oh, I read between the lines," she said, leaning against the fender and unzipping her coveralls. "Even if you didn't give me marching orders."

"I would love to know if there's more to find," he admitted. "He sounds like a serious player, whether the porn is his or not."

She opened her car door and sat down to remove the rest of her Tyvek suit. He took advantage to admire her coming into better view.

"You'll be going to New Hampshire, from what it sounds," she commented, not looking up.

"If we reach the right people in the right order for permission," he agreed. "With what Jim found on that computer, and the fact that Kalfus clearly hasn't been dead long, we need to move fast."

"Why not call in their state police?"

"We could, but they work differently than we Vermonters do. Here, a cop has jurisdiction border-to-border. Over there, the only true equivalent is the federal route Willy brought up. You still have to bow and scrape to be polite, but you can go anywhere you want, complete with subpoena and warrant powers. It's pretty slick."

"And you get to keep the case," she added with a slightly raised eyebrow.

He bent down to kiss her. "Takes a bloodhound to love a bloodhound," he said.

"It certainly doesn't hurt," she agreed.

CHAPTER TWO

Brattleboro Police Department was under twenty miles away from Rockingham, in Vermont's southeastern corner. Gone were the deputies, the road troopers, the fire and EMS crews, and even the wrecker, which had deposited its cargo in an enclosed holding area off the PD's sally port. What remained was a pared-down, tightly focused group, working toward solving a puzzle containing many more questions than answers.

Among the state's earliest settlements, Brattleboro was named after a Brit who never set eyes on it. Location always played in its favor. Once the beneficiary of being on the edge of the Connecticut River, the region's watery turnpike to points south before paved roads, it still has New Hampshire and Massachusetts within striking distance and is, centuries later, the only town in Vermont with three exits off of Interstate 91.

Modern times have reduced these advantages. Brattleboro remains the first bite of Vermont that any northbound, high-speed visitor consumes of the state. But in truth, the rest of Vermont has essentially left it behind, and most tourists are inclined to travel beyond those first off-ramps. Burlington, 150 miles away, in the state's opposite corner, and on Lake Champlain, is far bigger; Killington, Stratton, and Stowe have the ski slopes; even Waterbury has Ben and Jerry's. Brattleboro, for its lingering cachet of having been a harbor in the countercultural sixties, remains a town of some twelve thousand people often wondering how to stay viable.

That said, it is a hub community with a well-sized, full-service police force, including new facilities and elbow room, which Joe Gunther's four-desk, single-room office downtown did not.

Leaving the crime search team outside to process Lemuel Shaw's stolen car, Joe and his unit repaired to the PD's detective bureau and the hospitality and resources of their erstwhile partner, Lieutenant Detective Ron Klecszewski, who had conjured up pizza and doughnuts alongside the requisite bottomless urn of coffee.

Now, many long, intense hours later, most of it spent online and working the phones, they had transformed a conventional response team into an officially sanctioned task force, including the aforementioned New Hampshire deputy sheriff from Cheshire County named Fred Houston. He'd arrived in the night driving a cruiser loaded with $100,000 worth of ICAC equipment designed to get into and drain the contents of any smartphones, tablets, and computers. A quiet, bespectacled man in his forties, with thinning hair and a disarming smile, Houston had been given an office to himself to spread out a bank of open laptops and mysterious black boxes, into which he methodically downloaded the contents of the electronics found in the Mercedes.

Joe had spearheaded the creation of this newly configured unit, enacting his stated plan to gather all appropriate blessings. Thankfully, everyone contacted knew one another, were used to emergency upheavals, comforted by Joe's reliability and by his squad members' having already been awarded Homeland Security TFO federal certifications.

Interestingly to Joe—and he hoped telling of Houston's character—the New Hampshire ICAC officer had not waited for the ink to dry on all this protocol. Upon first being told of the mere likelihood of an alliance being born, he'd headed to Vermont with his gear. He was not a man given to scrutinizing bureaucratic fine print when a child's life might be in jeopardy. It turned out, according to Collins, that Fred Houston had been chasing child sex traffickers for over twenty years, replacing—as had Joe and the entire VBI—the standard turf and agency parochialism with a true sense of mission. But not zealotry—both ICAC and VBI acted as support organizations, offering manpower and expertise to all law enforcement organizations in need. Neither tolerated grandstanding by their personnel.

The sun had risen by the time Joe appeared in Houston's borrowed doorway and leaned against the jamb. "I don't know if you heard," he informed his new partner, "but we've been blessed by Vermont's Homeland RAC, who's supposedly calling his New Hampshire counterpart as we speak."

RAC was resident agent in charge, who in this case represented Homeland Security Investigations for the state.

"That's good," Houston replied, leaning back in his chair and stretching his arms above his head. "'Cause we definitely have something to move on here. I usually make two-pronged attacks in these situations. The first to unlock everything and get an idea of what I've got. The second to completely drain them so we can see what they contain—photos, contacts, texts—deleted and not, not to mention access any archives in the cloud. Also, geo-locations, visited internet sites, time stamps. That part takes longer, as you can guess. And I'm doing the infotainment system off the car, too, along with its black box—to see what it tells us, especially after Lemuel Shaw reported the Mercedes stolen. By the way, I heard you were asking about why the car went missing for so long. I called around and discovered that after one attempt, the powers that be gave up, figuring the GPS was busted. Human error, once again."

Joe took that in stride. "What about the phone Jim found, belonging to Lisa Rowell?"

Houston nodded patiently. "That's our first stop."

He sat forward, adjusted his glasses, and slid a printout across his desk for Joe. "That's the address listed to the phone. Keene, New Hampshire. Judging from the pictures Jim found at the scene, I'd say they were home builds, all involving the same underage girl. They are recent and they *have* been distributed, for money, according to parallel messaging I also captured."

"Is she alone in all of them?" Joe asked carefully, not sure he wanted to hear the answer.

"Yes. Right now, I have nothing to suggest anything beyond posing. But someone else is clearly holding the camera, and the victim is not happy, suggesting she's under duress. That wouldn't alter the legal violation, but in my experience, it suggests the possibility of other forms of abuse."

Joe folded the sheet of paper and put it in his pocket. "You don't have to tell me twice."

Film noir's demand for rain-slick, midnight settings notwithstanding, the crack of dawn tends to be a good time to stage police raids. Barring the odd pre-commuter dog walker or earplugged jogger, the streets are empty, the likelihood of unexpected foot traffic reduced, and most people with illegal appetites are sleeping in.

Keene, New Hampshire, some eighteen miles east of Brattleboro, is twice its size. Again named after an absentee Brit, it's a college town, an ex-railroad junction, a nineteenth-century manufacturing magnet, a tourist crossroads, and Brattleboro's primary threat to economic survival. It even has a regional airport next door. With its stores, movies, restaurants, and no sales tax, it's a formidable and chronic source of concern to its rival's politicians, merchants, and Chamber of Commerce.

It also has some demographics to help keep its police department busy. Not only does a quarter of its population consist of college students, but its being the largest urban area in the county attracts a number of people predisposed to prey on their fellow creatures. Although generally touting modest crimes stats, Keene can be an active place for select nefarious activities.

Joe was therefore not accompanied by amateurs as final details were worked out by an entry and search team, discreetly deployed around a multifamily residential building southeast of downtown.

This was where Fred Houston had pinpointed so-called Lisa Rowell's location, even though no one from Keene had ever heard of her; nor had a detailed records search revealed her existence.

While not unprecedented, the experience of entering a potentially volatile situation with complete strangers was never comforting for Gunther. It wasn't a question of competence. He had every reason to believe he was among highly trained and experienced professionals. But as within any tribal-style group—a team that ate together, played together, and were exposed to danger regularly—there existed an additional layer of trust. And Joe, for all the advantages of his new TFO role, was acutely aware of his outsider status. For the first time in recent years, he knew what it was like to be the stranger at the party.

As he stood at that apartment door, he was aware that if things went south, he'd only have relative strangers tending to him.

In the pre-op discussion prior to the hit, they had all settled on two things beyond a standard entry scenario: They would begin with a simple knock on the door, there being no indicators to suggest physical violence in the offing, and Joe would take the lead.

In contrast to Keene's relatively open flatlands, the countryside around Gilsum, only eight miles north, consisted of trees, craggy granite ledges, and the Ashuelot River, tumbling on its way through the largely wild tangle.

That sense of enclosure was dramatically offset by the house Lester Spinney and Sammie Martens paused to admire from the foot of a long and winding driveway. Constructed of logs, it could not have been associated with the word *cabin*. It was also situated in the middle of a large, carefully and expensively clear-cut field, now decorously covered with a slowly yielding mantle of snow. The driveway—hardtop, unsurprisingly—was immaculately plowed and probably heated from beneath.

This was the expansive home of Lemuel Shaw, owner of the Mercedes for which Willy had such low regard.

"We don't often get to visit places like this," Lester commented, accelerating up the incline.

Sam was less impressed. On the drive over, she'd been distracted and impatient. Sleep deprivation was one factor. She knew that. But being headstrong and proud, she'd put that on the bottom of the list. This was hardly her first all-nighter, after all. More problematic was Emma, her daughter, whom she'd barely seen in the last twenty-four hours. She'd just been able to race home before setting off on this excursion, kiss her, wish her a good day, and leave her in what was becoming the perpetual care of their almost live-in babysitter, Louise, an ex-cop herself.

Louise was great. Motherly, patient, always available, cheap, and a dyed-in-the-wool friend.

But she wasn't Sam—or Willy, for that matter, who Sam knew was also frustrated by the disparate demands of work and parenthood.

They had a routine approaching normalcy, not unlike Lester and Sue's when their kids were younger. Les worked days, Sue pulled nights, and the kids usually had at least one parent to push them around and make them miserable. Sam and Willy weren't quite in the same boat, both working days. But their schedules under Joe were also not overly regimented, and they worked hard to make sure one of them was at home when it counted. Plus they had only the one kid and Louise, to boot. So why the hell did Sam keep feeling she was letting Emma down? Her daughter wasn't complaining, her teachers weren't reporting problems. There was nothing on the radar.

And yet, it lingered.

Sleeplessness and missing Emma weren't the only things grinding at her. There was Joe, alone in Keene with a bunch of hotshots for company who didn't know his style or habits under fire. He was just the older wannabe who'd parachuted out of the blue to get them to kick open a door. What kind of backup were they going to be if something went haywire?

And finally, there was Willy, who'd pulled the short straw to notify Don Kalfus's next of kin—or whoever opened the door—not only to tell them Don had been found dead in a trunk with his head bashed in, but—oh, by the way—what was the latest crooked thing he'd been up to that had gotten him killed? And sorry for your loss.

"You okay?" Lester asked as if on cue, the car rolling to a stop at the top of the hill.

She pushed open the door as if escaping from a burning building. "Yeah. Stuff on my mind."

Lester peacefully eased his frame out of the car. He knew her well, knew many of the demons hounding her—all the way back to a rough childhood—and was of a forgiving nature anyhow. In his book, Sammie Martens was entitled to a bad day now and then. For one thing, no way Les could imagine having Willy Kunkle as a mate, even if he did admire the man's results.

The building before them, large from a distance, proved immense up close and was tricked out with sufficient wrought iron appendages to satisfy a castle—knockers, hinges, lanterns, and rings large enough to suspend carcasses. Lester couldn't resist commenting, "Looks like somebody made out at the medieval accessories fire sale. Watch out for arrows and moats."

He'd barely pushed the bell before the large wooden door swung open to reveal not a knight but a bearded fat man in an Orvis shirt and high-end blue jeans. Lester was torn between visions of an urban Falstaff and an imitation Hemingway.

"Saw you drive up," the man said. "I'm Lemuel Shaw. I help you?"

"We're cops," Sam said, taking an instant dislike to him. "We need to talk."

Willy Kunkle, at least, was neither among strangers nor wandering onto a theatrical set. He and Ron Klecszewski were on South Main Street, in Brattleboro, heading for the home of Don Kalfus's next of kin.

For Ron, this was a rare and enjoyable reunion, if not an opportunity to catch up. Not for Willy. Indeed, over the years that Ron and he had worked together before VBI's creation and Willy's departure, they had never once had what could be called a "chat."

Nevertheless, they had run cases, interrogated suspects, exchanged a laugh or two, traveled across town a few thousand times, shared meals at the office, and cursed the legal system for messing up their neatly wrapped-up cases. And Ron had been subjected to Willy's unceasingly caustic opinions, judgments, and dismissive one-liners, to the point where Ron's wife had once asked him if the satisfaction of shooting the guy might not be worth the penalty.

While occasionally agreeing that she might've been onto something, Ron had never seen his colleague in that light.

In part due to Klecszewski's own generous nature, he had understood, as he knew Joe Gunther did, that Willy Kunkle's was a special case. There were people, Ron had rationalized, who like Japan's famous living national treasures, had qualities or abilities that deserved special recognition, or in Willy's case, at least limited and continual absolution.

Because, as cranky, outspoken, and thin-skinned as he could be, Willy's saving grace in a self-made ocean of misery, PTSD, old alcoholic memories, war-born nightmares, and underlying anger was his white-knuckled grip on a reborn life as a righteous man. As others in his place had claimed God as their savior, Willy had fought off his devils secularly and dedicated himself to Sammie, their child, his partners, and the truth as he knew it.

He could still be hard to bear. But as far as Ron was concerned, Willy's inner fire was a real and rare pleasure to witness.

For him, hanging out with the man was a treat.

"How's Emma doing?" he now asked.

Willy was driving, as usual. He scowled, keeping his eyes on the road. "Really? Why not cut to the chase and ask why Sam hasn't chucked me out yet?"

"I gave up wondering about that years ago."

"You insulting my beloved?"

Ron shook his head. "Right. You would go there. What can I say? I'm happy she hasn't. Best thing that ever happened to you."

Willy didn't respond for a long count, either taking the comment to heart or simply reverting to silence for cover.

"You are so touchy-feely," he finally growled. "No wonder you never left this beat."

"I like it here."

As Ron had expected, so much for chatting.

Willy pulled over to the side of the street, killed the engine, did a final perimeter check, and opened the door, saying, "Emma's fine. Learning the alphabet at preschool."

Ron chuckled and joined him, standing in the road.

South Main is not one of Brattleboro's ritzier neighborhoods, as the patrol division of the PD could attest. Assaults, domestics, drug deals, and complaints in general were regular trade. But as with most things in this town and Vermont generally, the volume and intensity were not something to impress any big-city cop. Blessedly, the Green Mountain State remained among the three lowest rankers of the FBI's crime statistics, alongside New Hampshire and Maine. Sin City, this was not.

Nevertheless, since they say size isn't everything, Ron had never considered his beat as a walk in the park. Overdoses had gone through the roof, fentanyl was the new baby powder when it came to adulterating heroin, and those three interstate exits, right on the Massachusetts border, had helped turn the town's official slogan of Gateway to Vermont into what many officers saw as a doormat.

The house Ron and Willy were facing, therefore, was no prize on any Realtor's list, but had appeared more than once in the police blotter. It was an unloved and uncared-for example of late-nineteenth-century industrial housing, partly rotting, in dire need of paint, with crooked windows covered in plastic, a sagging ridgeline, and a front porch demanding caution when crossed.

Used to such settings, both men negotiated it without comment or trouble.

The door opened a minute after Ron pressed the bell, following an audible tread and a string of muffled complaints. Revealed eventually was a woman about five and a half feet tall, one hundred pounds, and dressed in a pink top, tight jeans, and a hard face.

Neither of her visitors had said a word before she demanded, "What the hell? He doesn't live here. Hasn't for years. Why the fuck do you people always come looking for him here?"

Joe glanced at the Keene detective beside him, who nodded that he was ready. Each was standing off-center of the door to 3-A, in case someone shot through it from inside. Armed backup was just out of sight down the stairwell, with support troops positioned discreetly outside. The building dated back to the 1940s. It was dark, abused, poorly ventilated, overheated, and transparently running low on longevity.

There are various approaches for a visit involving a child's imminent welfare, each hinging on the perceived level of threat. In this instance, Joe had opted for a heavily supported "knock-and-talk" over the assault rifles and door rams right behind him.

As rationale, he was banking on a computer check that had revealed this apartment to be rented by Trevor Buttner, who had a record of assault, domestic disturbance, and several DUIs, but no weapons charges. The name Lisa Rowell wasn't associated with any of the six apartments in the building, reinforcing their guess that it was a clumsy ruse.

Joe rapped on the door.

Not surprisingly to any of them, nothing happened. In part, that was good news. No dog.

He knocked again, louder.

They heard quiet footsteps approaching and a tentative child's voice ask, "Who is it?"

Instinctively, Joe crouched to answer softly, his mouth near the doorknob, "It's the police. Can you let us in?"

A metallic snap and the door swung back to reveal a skinny young girl, dressed for school, a piece of toast in her hand.

Joe bit back his true emotional response. This was the same awkward child he'd seen naked on Lisa Rowell's phone.

Hypervigilant about what might surprise them next, he asked, "Did we interrupt breakfast? Sorry about that."

"It's okay. What do you want?"

"My name's Joe. We'd like to talk to a grown-up. Is there one at home?"

"Sure, but they're asleep."

"It is early. What's your name?"

"Angie Neal."

"It's nice to meet you, Angie. Could you do me a big favor?"

"Sure."

"Tell me who the grown-ups are."

"There's my mom and Trevor." Joe noticed a slight downturn in Angie's voice as she mentioned Buttner.

"Anybody else?"

"My sister, Pammy. She's little. You don't want to talk to her."

"I think you're right. Maybe your mom. What's her name?"

"Melissa."

"Melissa what?"

"Monfet."

"How about anyone named Lisa Rowell?"

She looked at him blankly. "Who?"

"Okay. And you're sure they're asleep?"

"Sure."

"Couple of more questions, and then we're done. Where's Pammy's bedroom? Or does she sleep with the grown-ups?"

"She sleeps with me. At the end." Angie gestured down the dark hallway.

"And your mom's bedroom? Where's that?"

She pointed again. "On the right. There."

"One last question, Angie, and this one is a little strange: Are there any guns in the house that you know about?"

She shook her head silently, her wide eyes taking them in.

Joe, still crouched, glanced up at his colleague and raised his eyebrows. The question was intuitive. With Joe's recognition of Angie as the victim, exigent circumstances had come into play.

Joe's assigned partner nodded wordlessly and reached out his hand.

"Angie?" Joe began, easing the girl toward the outside hall. "I want you to go with this policeman right now, while we go in to meet the rest of the family."

"You like doughnuts?" the Keene officer asked, escorting her toward the others out of sight. "I think we've got some in the car."

Joe waited until he returned. "So far, so lucky," he said. "You set?"

The man nodded, pulling out his sidearm but keeping it low by his leg.

Joe and he moved to the master bedroom door, quietly followed by several others, one of whom continued down the hall to make sure the other child was where Angie had claimed.

Upon getting a thumbs-up, Joe seized the doorknob and pushed.

"You want some coffee?" Lemuel Shaw asked. "Just made it. It's good stuff, if I do say so myself. It sure as hell costs enough."

The two cops were already seated at an antique trestle table in a kitchen well suited for a cruise ship.

"I wouldn't say no," Lester accepted, taking the lead after assessing Sam's dark mood. "It's quite the place you got here."

"Thanks." Shaw kept his back turned as he tended to an over-built machine whose noises promised an ostentatious cup of coffee, if not a good one.

"I know it looks like a McMansion some downriver yuppie would build to piss off the locals, but I was born in this county. Left as a young man, made my nut in the big city, and then dropped that shit as soon as I could to come back home. This house is my way of flipping the finger to everyone who says no local cracker has a chance in this world."

He joined them at the table carrying a tray with three cups. "You don't fuck it up with cream or sugar, do you?"

Nice way of asking, Sam thought sourly, resigned to drinking whatever this was straight.

"Nope," Lester said cheerfully. "Black's great."

Shaw nodded approvingly and settled down. "Good. What I expected from cops. So, you found my car, huh? I wasn't expecting that. Will I be getting it back, or did the son of a bitch total it, too?"

"He didn't total it, no," Lester continued, "but it'll be a while before you see it again. We're hanging on to it as evidence."

Shaw made a face. "Great. Use a high-end car for a bank robbery or whatever. These guys are such geniuses."

"There was a dead body in the trunk," Sam said shortly, taking a sip of the coffee for its medicinal effects only.

Willy really was rubbing off on her, Lester thought, addressing Shaw's startled expression with, "That's actually why we're here, Mr. Shaw. We need to ask you for details about the theft of your car."

"Damn," the older man said, his steaming mug ignored before him. He then contemplated the expansive view through the window before adding, "I don't know what to say. It was parked outside one night and gone the next morning, just like I reported."

"You live here alone?"

"No. Well, my wife and I do. The kids come by when they can, but they both live out of state, have jobs and families. You know how it is. We built the place so they could visit and have room to run, but it rarely happens. Still, you always hope, right?"

Les reeled him in. "I noticed you have a garage. Don't you use it for the Mercedes?"

"Usually, yeah. But not that night. That's always the way, isn't it? The one time you let your guard down. But it's not like I'm living in the bad part of town. I mean, we hardly see anybody around here, much less some guy with a crowbar, or whatever he used. And like I did with you, I usually can tell when somebody's coming up the drive. That got me thinking about when it was stolen, in fact. I wondered if the thief walked all the way up—probably had a buddy at the bottom in another car. They either saw the Mercedes from there, driving by, or maybe in Keene and followed me or Lucy home and waited. She'd been grocery shopping that day, and I'd been down there, too. Had to buy more wood glue for a project I'm working on."

"You even curious about how a dead man ended up in your trunk?" Sam asked, appreciating how the coffee had sharpened her concentration.

"Of course," Shaw reacted, taking a sip himself. "But I wouldn't know, would I?" he asked afterward.

Sam didn't reply, leaving Lester to ask, "When were you last aware of your car being parked out front?"

Shaw glanced at the ceiling. "Oh, I don't know. You can see the parking area through this window here. I suppose it was sometime after Lucy tidied up after dinner."

"After it was dark, then?"

"Well, it's lit up out there. I mean, from the lights out the windows. It's all in the report. You ought to give that a look."

"We will," Sam said pointedly, having already done so.

"Did your wife notice anything that night?" Les asked. "Where is she, by the way?"

"She's having a nap. Sorry."

"This early in the morning?"

Shaw grinned. "You got me. Truthfully, she's sleeping in." He gestured with his hand, as if holding a glass. "She got a little carried away last night with the vino. It sounds bad when somebody's still in the sack at this hour—to me it does, at least. Sorry for the smoke screen."

Sam had produced a sheet of paper from her pocket and smoothed it out before her. She fixed their host with a stare and asked, "Why're you lying to us, Mr. Shaw?"

He frowned. "I beg your pardon?"

Lester matched his partner's tone. "What about finding a dead body in your car did you not understand?"

"What're you accusing me of?"

"Right now?" Sam countered. "Just lying. I want to know why." She tapped the sheet with her fingertip. "This is a readout from your car's computer system. Amazingly nosy, as it turns out. Keeps track of everything. How many times you hit the brakes, what speeds you drove at, opening and closing doors, where you went, and when. Are you getting the picture?"

Lemuel Shaw didn't respond, rooted in place.

"Your car didn't come back here the night it was stolen," Sam stated. "It was still in Keene."

"How many cars do you own?" Lester asked.

"Three." The man's voice was barely audible.

Sammie resumed. "And which one did your wife use to drive to Swanzey to pick you up?"

"The Jeep."

"We cross-checked the Mercedes's GPS with that date and approximate time," she explained, "based on what you told the officers who came to take your statement." She paused and added, "'Cause we did read the report. We know exactly where you were parked for a couple of hours that night, and we have a good guess what you were up to. You wanna put it in your own words? Or would you like us to just place you under arrest?"

It was a specious threat. What he'd done so far wasn't legal, but hardly deserving of twenty years at hard labor.

Still, it worked, as planned. Shaw hung his head. "I went to a strip club."

"Go on," Les urged him.

"Not much to add. I watched the girls do their thing, had too much to drink, and when I went back outside, the car was missing."

"And your wife?"

"You were right. I called her. She was pissed, but this wasn't the first time. I cooked up the story I told you and the other cops, and she went along so people wouldn't find out."

Lester placed Don Kalfus's photo on the table, facing Shaw. "You know this man?"

He leaned forward and studied the image carefully before asking, "Should I? Was he there?"

"We're asking you."

Shaw looked baffled. "I don't remember him if he was." His expression suddenly transformed with shock. "Oh my God," he said. "Is that the man you're talking about? Who was killed?"

Sam ignored him. "What did you do with your car keys when you got to the club?"

"Put 'em in my pocket, like always."

"It's still cold out," Lester said. "Pants pocket or coat?"

Shaw became crestfallen. "Coat. And I hung it by the door. Anybody could've reached in and taken them."

"In your made-up story, you told police you left them in the ignition, since you live way out here in the boonies. You sure you didn't do the same at the club?"

"No," he replied softly, head hung once more.

Disappointingly, Joe did not find what young Angie had described. As the master bedroom door swung back, they didn't get to see two adults fast asleep in bed, as hoped, but rather a mostly naked tattooed woman, her back propped up against the headboard, a cigarette in her mouth, staring directly at him.

Her reaction was stamped by long practice. Without hesitation or thought, she screamed out, *"Trevor, cops!"* as she simultaneously rolled out of the bed and made a tackling run directly at Joe.

He impressed himself by instinctively pirouetting on one foot, catching the side of her downthrust head with his forearm, and redirecting her past him, right into the wall beyond.

"Go, go, go," ordered the next man in, heading for the open bathroom door, while another dropped onto the moaning woman to cuff her hands behind her back.

The next few minutes dissolved into a chaotic jumble of shouts, radio commands, and bodies in rapid motion. The bathroom door slammed shut, a disorganized and frustrating series of methods— none as seamless as those on prime time—were used to break it open, but only in time to see a hairy-backed, shirtless male disappearing through the window.

From the bedroom, Joe saw him hit the icy roof outside, instantly lose his footing, and roll like a tree trunk until he'd vanished over the edge.

"You got him?" came the reasonable next question over the radio.

"What's left of him."

CHAPTER THREE

For the time being, it was just the two of them, Joe and Fred Houston, in the sudden quiet of the empty Buttner apartment. Trevor had been carted off to repair a broken pelvis and some ribs; Melissa Monfet was being treated for a neck complaint after her close encounter with the wall; the baby had been scooped up by social services; and poor Angie Neal, this storm's central attraction, was for the moment being cared for before the inevitable interview when she'd be asked to describe events she wouldn't outdistance for the rest of her life.

Joe had witnessed such highly structured interviews before, of sexually exploited and/or abused children, and been caught by the metaphor of each victim becoming traumatically transformed into conjoined twins, one destined to lug around the corpse of the other until death. Not the gift a child should expect from supposedly caring adults.

Houston had been searching the apartment with a tablet in hand and now sidled up to Joe, showing him the earlier view of Angie posing, self-conscious and nude. "Look at the background. I found where this was shot."

Joe looked past the thin girl. There was a curtained window, what appeared to be a bedroom wall, papered in faded flowers, and the corner of a piece of furniture.

"This way," Fred urged him, heading to where the baby and Angie had shared a room.

He paused inside the door and held up the screen photo as a reference, comparing it to the room's actual setting. Both men could appreciate how the window, wall, rug, and what turned out to be a fragment of the crib matched perfectly.

"That's gotta help down the line," Joe agreed.

"It's not all," Fred offered. "In his rush to make like Batman, Buttner left behind a laptop—another smoking gun. We'll be able to make his life miserable for the foreseeable future, and probably some of his cyber playmates. And Lisa Rowell? His online avatar. Guess he thought he'd get more mileage as a woman."

"What was he doing with the images?"

"Selling them for bitcoin or some other cryptocurrency. It's definitely a trafficking case. You did good putting this in place, me and the FTO angle. This is solid work."

The subject of this praise didn't respond.

Houston pressed him. "You don't agree?"

Joe waved his hand apologetically. "No, no. I do. Absolutely. Thank you, Fred. I was just thinking that this was the easy one—the unlocked phone, the straight connection between perpetrator and subject. My questions are, one: What about the other electronics we grabbed? What're they going to show us? And, two: Who killed Don Kalfus?"

"You think this douchebag did him in?"

"We have to ask the question." Joe held up his own smartphone. "I've been getting texts from Jim Collins, updating me on what the

crime techs are still finding. The assumption we started with, that Kalfus stole the car and used it for a multiday grab-and-run spree, seems
to be paying off. His prints are everywhere—including on Buttner's
cell. And the local agencies we've asked for help are coming across
with video footage from gas stations and convenience stores showing
him filling up and/or buying things to eat. And there's a growing list
of burglary reports matching when and where he was in any particular neighborhood, in New Hampshire and Vermont, both."

"So?" Houston asked. "That's good, right?"

"In and of itself, sure, but none of it addresses the elephant in
the room. Who killed him? And why was he put in the trunk?"

Joe indicated their surroundings. "For instance, Fred, what about
this place says to you, 'Burgle me'? This is low-income housing with
lots of neighbors who don't work and who watch their neighbors
come and go as if it were a soap opera. Nobody in his right mind
would break in here and steal a single cell phone."

"They knew each other?" Fred suggested.

"Kalfus and the flying Trevor Buttner," Joe agreed. "I think
so, too."

The late Don Kalfus's mother, Cheri Pratt, didn't mess with the traditional grieving process. She cut the line, went straight to rage,
and stayed there.

"You fuckin' people," she snarled at the two cops before her.
"You bust my ass, year after year, about Donny doin' this and Donny
doin' that, never once helpin' me set him straight. And now here
you are, at long last, givin' me shit about how 'sorry for your loss'
you are when what you really want to do is screw him over again.
What? For old times' sake? No. 'Cause clearly he's to blame for his
own death. That is rich."

With that, she left the open doorway and disappeared into the gloom behind her.

Ron smiled at Willy, bowed slightly, and gestured invitingly to him to follow her. "Please," he said. "I insist. I am but your humble backup here."

Willy took the lead, saying, "Fine, but if she hurts me, I want you to shoot her."

The house's interior spoke to a tornado's aftermath, except that the roof was intact and the windows still in place. It was not a hoarding environment, where the contents reveal the owner's genuine attachment to things. Instead, it was sloppier, more careless. Surveying the debris-covered surfaces before them, from furniture to counters to floor, the two men saw evidence of things simply dropped after use. Pizza boxes, canned goods, toys, grocery bags, clothing, two rusty bicycles, trash cans, old food wrappers, kitty litter scattered like rock salt, and countless glasses, plates, abandoned pots and pans—soiled and crusty—piled everywhere. The whole was a gloomy museum of stacked artifacts, arranged to challenge the visitor's access, at the risk of causing catastrophic results. Quaintly, Willy had heard this kind of setting described as Diogenes syndrome. Truly everything, he'd thought at the time, now had a diagnosis.

It didn't smell terribly—either that or they'd been numbed by excessive exposure to such places.

The house was dark. Despite the time of day, all the curtains were drawn, which seemed a permanent state. Willy therefore led the way toward a light in the back, to the kitchen, it turned out— not that it looked any different from the room they'd just left.

Cheri Pratt was sitting at a piled-high table in the room's center, her hands around a stained, half-empty mug of some dark liquid, her eyes straight ahead and her expression grim. Jarring with her environment, her own appearance seemed almost athletic. In a disconnect Willy had seen time and again, her body was lean, accentuated by spangled jeans and the colorful close-fitting top, while her angular features and sinewy hands were lined and worn, as if belonging to someone twenty years beyond her own mid-forties—the results not of exercise and a healthy diet, but of poor nutrition, cigarettes, presumably DNA, and a nervous disposition.

There being nowhere else to sit, Willy leaned gingerly against the rusty refrigerator, while Ron stayed in the doorway.

"Still here?" she asked in a low voice, reaching for smokes and a lighter.

"I know you think it's too little, too late," Willy began. "But we'd like to find out who killed your boy."

"Why?" she countered. "Not sure I do. Won't change nothin'."

"'Cause I doubt he deserved it," Willy told her. "The way I see it, most of us end up doing what we do for reasons we can't even figure out. I didn't grow up wanting to be a cop. I doubt you saw yourself sitting here when you were little. Shit happens. You turn right instead of left. You go to bed with the wrong person. You accept a joyride when you shouldn't. Next thing Donny knew, he was climbing through windows and ripping people off. Why? I don't know. He liked the thrill. It's what he did; who he ended up being."

Cheri lit her cigarette and drew on it. "Yeah," she said, the word catching a ride on a plume of expelled smoke.

"We checked his record," Willy went on. "He wasn't a violent guy. Did a little weed, drank too much, hung out with just the right people to get him into trouble. But he never fought, never carried a gun or knife that I know about. He just liked what belonged to other people. Am I right?"

"Yeah," she repeated.

"So what got him killed?"

She broke off her blank stare to look at him. "That's *your* job."

"Help me do it, then. Tell me a little about him."

"He was a good boy, under all the shit."

"What shit?"

She shrugged a narrow shoulder. "Oh, the show-off stuff. Pretendin' he was cool. What he was like with his friends."

"He was different at home? Here?"

"He would bring me gifts he thought I'd like."

"What kinds of things?"

"A lamp, maybe. A real nice tray I could use in front of the TV. A coat that didn't fit. You know . . ."

"When was the last time you saw him?" Willy asked.

"I don't know. A couple of weeks ago?"

"How did he seem?"

The shrug again. "Normal. He'd landed a part-time job as a bouncer someplace. Nothin' steady, but he thought it was funny. It was, too. He didn't look like no bouncer."

Willy couldn't argue with that. "Where?"

"Keene, someplace. I don't know where."

Ron spoke again. "He talk about any big haul in the planning?"

"Not to me," she stressed. "We weren't partners. What d'you think? I helped him with this? I *told* him it would get him killed someday." She angrily crushed her cigarette into the tabletop before flicking it to the ground, where it vanished amid the undergrowth.

Willy kept at her. "Speaking of partners, who were his friends?"

"He kept them away from here."

"How 'bout a girlfriend? He have one of those?"

"Robin Whiteman," Cheri said. "They been together a few months, I guess."

"What's she like?"

"Wouldn't know. Never met her. Like I said."

Sammie checked her vibrating cell as she and Lester followed Lemuel Shaw down a hallway wide enough for an airport terminal. "From Joe," she apprised her partner. "They located the owner of that unlocked iPhone in Keene."

"Joe okay?" Lester asked.

"Apparently. The other guy's in the hospital. Did a flyer out the window."

"Ouch. How's Willy doing on his end?"

Sammie let out a snort. "Willy? Send me an update? Do you *know* the man?"

At last, the three of them reached the end of the corridor and a pair of carved double doors. Shaw stood to one side and announced, "My lady's chambers. I'll let you have the honors, as requested." He turned the knob, pushed the door open, and retreated whence they'd come. "You know where to find me," he added, not looking back.

"Not without a map," Lester said under his breath.

"We just walk in?" Sam challenged Shaw from a distance.

He kept speaking straight ahead. "Trust me. It's how she likes to hold court."

The room they entered was high-ceilinged, thickly carpeted, and completely done up in gold and white. Chandelier, furniture, pillows, wall hangings, even the cat, were one color or the other. The only standouts were the view out the wall-to-wall, floor-to-ceiling windows, displaying a thirty-mile stretch of woods, fields, and mountains, and the face of the woman clad in white, who was propped up like a royal bauble on a pile of pillows at the head of an enormous king-sized bed. Of the two, the view was the more naturally accessorized.

"Sorry to barge in," Lester began.

"Not at all," the woman interrupted. "I'm Lucy Shaw. You look like you're from the police."

"Yes, ma'am," Sam said.

"Lucy, please. Call me Lucy. I'm old and in denial. Sit and make yourselves comfortable. I hope Lem offered you coffee."

Lester reassured her. "He did."

He and Sam sat uncomfortably on a white love seat placed beside the bed, apparently positioned for petitioners awaiting an audience.

"I hope you're here because you found our car," she said.

"We did," Les began as Sam followed with, "Which is good news–bad news, I'm afraid."

"Oh?"

Sam kept going. "Just so our cards are all faceup on the table, from the get-go, you should know that your husband admitted to lying about how the car was stolen."

Lucy Shaw's features tightened minutely. "Ah," she said, prompting Lester to admire her self-restraint.

He could also tell that his partner had regained her equilibrium since their arrival, allowing him to slip into observer mode as Sam stayed on her line of questioning.

"For our part," she said, "we need to tell you that when the car was found in Vermont, it had a bunch of stolen property in it, along with a dead body in the trunk."

Lester was looking closely, but the reaction this caused was instant horror, accompanied by appropriate body language.

"*What?*" Lucy asked, sitting bolt upright. "A dead body? That's terrible. Oh my goodness. What happened? Oh no. You're saying he was killed."

She paused long enough to look from one of them to the other, wide-eyed, before stammering, "You can't be . . . You can't imagine . . . That we had something to do with it."

"You did lie to the police," Sam stated plainly.

Again, the tiny shifting of expression, this time to something a bit more aggressive. "Well, yes, but that was embarrassment. Neither one of us wanted Lemuel's appetite to get out. I've read the police blotter. Those things are public record. It was a white lie. What harm would it cause?"

She hesitated, as if for a response, but shortly followed with, "Even now. You say a man was found dead. How's that our fault? The car was stolen days ago. We don't know where it's been or what's been done with it. I even thought it might be at the bottom of a lake somewhere. That's what people do who steal things, isn't it? Sell them or throw them away?"

"Not this time," Sam answered dryly. She pulled out Don Kalfus's mug shot and laid it on Lucy's covers, oriented toward her. "Have you ever seen this man before?"

The older woman didn't touch it, craning forward to take it in as she might a tarantula in a cage. "No. He's the one?"

"Tell us about the night your husband called you."

"About the Mercedes?" Lucy sat back as Sam removed the offending photograph. "What's to tell? The phone rang, he told me what had happened, and I drove down in the Jeep to pick him up. We filed the theft with the insurance company and the police the next day."

"You weren't surprised?"

"I wasn't happy, if that's what you mean. I know his habits. Men will be men. Usually, he just does what he has to do, and we avoid discussing the matter."

Sam took in the bedroom with a wide sweep. "You no longer sleep together?"

Lucy frowned. "Many people don't. I don't see how that has anything to do with a stolen car."

"We're not here for a car, Mrs. Shaw," Sam corrected her. "This is a murder investigation, in which your vehicle played a crucial role."

Lucy made an effort to back down. "I'm sorry," she said disingenuously.

"How often has Lemuel frequented that particular place?" Sam asked.

Lucy was still struggling with her poise. "It's not like I keep count."

Sam remained silent, her question lingering.

"Now and then," Lucy conceded. "I am no longer an outlet for those impulses, and as far as I know, all he does is drink and watch. Until you two showed up, I thought it was harmless enough, if a little humiliating."

"Going back to the night in question," Sam resumed. "Run it down for us, step by step."

Lucy sighed before beginning. "He called. He was embarrassed. Said he was sorry a dozen times. It wasn't complicated. He said when he stepped outside, the car was gone. That's all there was to it."

"About what time was this?"

"One o'clock in the morning. That was the other problem. He woke me up, which he knows I don't like."

"Did he say anything about having seen or spoken to anyone? Or did he voice any suspicions?"

She shook her head. "No. He was too worried about my reaction. Rightfully so. I was really angry with him. Still am, especially now."

"How 'bout when you arrived there? What time was that?"

"Maybe an hour later. I had to get up and get ready to go."

"And when you got there, did you see anyone?"

"I wasn't looking," she replied primly.

"But you knew where to go."

There was a split second's hesitation before she countered, "The Jeep has GPS, and Lemuel gave me the address."

Over Joe's career, the quaint and local hospitals of old had grown with the elegance and subtlety of a lava flow. From having names like Mary Hitchcock and Alice Peck Day—small institutions catering to rural clusters of communities—they had become huge, amorphous medical complexes consisting of clinics, hospitals, and health centers, the biggest of which was Dartmouth-Hitchcock Health, exuding, to Joe's ear, all the warmth of HAL the computer.

This was no reflection of the medical care offered, fortunately. D-HH, so called, reminiscent of KFC for trendiness, had in its favor the experts and equipment once available only in places like Boston. Trevor Buttner, therefore, for all his foolishness, was being treated beyond expectations at a D-HH satellite in Keene, and better than he would be shortly at the hands of the legal system.

As if in preparation for this very transition, he was casted and immobilized by a traction device on his gurney and handcuffed to its side rail.

"This is so illegal," he complained to Joe and Fred as they entered his room, Joe gesturing to the cop leaning against the wall that now was his chance to take a break.

"You remember being read your rights and signing them?" Joe asked, looking down at him as Fred moved to the bed's other side and quickly positioned a small audio-video recorder on the side table.

"So?"

"Then you won't mind if we record this conversation?"

"I don't give a fuck."

"Then we're good and great in the legal department. Unlike your stepdaughter, you have nothing to complain about."

"The hell I don't. Look at me."

"*You'll* mend," Fred said quietly.

The emphasis concerning his young victim's fate hung in the air.

"Lieutenant Houston and I," Joe told him, "are here for two different reasons." Joe nodded at Fred. "He's the man taking apart your electronics to wrap you up neat and tight for a long-term federal rap for underage sex trafficking."

"That's bullshit," Buttner tried interrupting.

Joe leaned closer to continue. "And it has nothing to do with why I'm here."

He paused long enough for his suspect to absorb that.

"My specialty is homicide."

Buttner's voice climbed a notch. "I didn't kill nobody."

Joe showed him the photo of Kalfus they were all now carrying around. "You know who this is?"

The image was given a long scrutiny. Too much by half. "Never seen him."

Joe displayed his best paternal expression. "Trevor, I understand you've had experience with being questioned by the police. Is that fair to say?"

Buttner let slip a crooked grin, revealing the teeth of a seventy-year-old. "I've had a few conversations with you guys."

"Good. Just what I figured. Then you know that most of the

time, we ask questions we already know the answers to. Why do you think we do that?"

Buttner scowled. "This a trick?" he asked as Fred Houston snorted softly without comment. "How the fuck do I know?"

"It's our way of finding out if you're telling the truth. 'Cause if you are, then we and the prosecutor, and later the judge and jury, will see that you're really working to make amends."

"Versus being caught out as a lying sack of shit," Fred added in a friendly aside.

"Okay."

"So," Joe went on, wiggling the picture he was still holding in the air. "Do you really want to tell us you don't know who this is?"

"Yeah. I mean no. I don't know him."

Joe looked disappointed, straightening and pushing his lips out sadly. "You do realize the apartment building you live in has closed-circuit TV? That's part of it being low-income housing. To protect people like you from undesirable elements."

Buttner kept his mouth shut.

Joe revealed a second print he'd secured from the housing authority. "This is another picture of the same gentleman. Do you recognize the front door he's entering? See the number on the wall?"

Buttner swallowed hard. "There are other apartments in my building."

"We've interviewed Melissa and Angie," Fred cautioned him, which was partially true.

It proved to be enough.

"Okay," Buttner said. "So what if I know him?"

"By what name, Trevor?" Joe pressed him.

"Don Kalfus."

Joe smiled broadly. "There you go. Nice. Now, how and why do you know him?"

They could both see the effort Buttner was putting into getting this right. It was like watching a kid tying his shoes for the first time.

"You know. You meet people. Like in the neighborhood. Doin' stuff."

"And what stuff does Mr. Kalfus do?"

"I don't know. This and that."

Joe's face turned serious. "Careful, Trevor. Let's not start lying again. You have a lot at stake."

"And you can believe us," Fred added, "that you won't be throwing Don under the bus."

That did the trick. "He's a thief," Buttner said shortly.

"Interesting," Joe challenged him. "If I asked you what you did, would you say a pervert?"

"Fuck you."

Joe chuckled. "Of course you wouldn't. That would be outrageous. It's not all you do, after all."

Buttner's brows knitted with concentration, not following. "No."

"But by accusing Don of being a thief, it implies he stole from you, personally. What was that, Trevor? What did he steal?"

It was clearly becoming too complicated for Buttner to keep straight in his head. "Nothin'. Just some junk. Pissed me off. That's why I said that."

"Was it this?" Joe held up another photograph, of Trevor's smartphone.

"No."

"Because we found it in his possession," Joe continued. "In fact, it led us directly to you. It even had your fingerprints on it, along with some contents I bet you wish we hadn't found."

Buttner had apparently reached a mental corner he couldn't escape. He lay before them, stumped into silence.

Joe eased him out of it. "We've pieced most of this together, Trevor, like I told you. We tapped into the computer of the car Don was using, you know we got the CCTV footage from your apartment building, we downloaded everything from your phone, from dirty pictures to texts to emails to phone logs to geo-locations, contacts lists, and more. The whole kit and caboodle, including the last time you used the thing yourself. We probably know better than you when it was Don saw that phone at your place and thought it might make a good piece of leverage against you in the future. What had you done, Trevor? Had you shown him one of those pictures? We also know the shots of Angie were brand new on the market. You'd just put them up for sale. Did you brag to him about that?"

"You're full of shit," Buttner said halfheartedly.

"You must've been wicked pissed when you noticed it missing, after he left. What did you do about that?"

"Don't know what you're talking about."

"Did you reach out to everyone you know in common, trying to find him? You had to've been kicking yourself that you had no pass code on that thing. But it never leaves your side, right? And you had it registered to the make-believe Lisa Rowell. Why worry about it?"

Buttner's lips were pressed tightly together.

Joe leaned in again, so the two of them were inches apart. "Trevor, do you remember how I described my job when we met a few minutes ago?"

Buttner tried to avoid looking at him.

"Tell the man," Fred urged him softly, supportively.

"A homicide cop?"

Joe stayed where he was. "That's correct. Can you figure out whose murder I want to talk about?"

The flicker of an eye, quickly blinked away. "Kalfus's?"

"That's good." Joe straightened once more. "And right now, guess who's looking like a good fit for his murder?"

Buttner's face reddened as he spoke, but his words were tightly restrained. "I had nothin' to do with that."

"So you knew he was dead?"

"I didn't say that. It's not what I meant."

Joe nodded thoughtfully. "Then you'll have to convince me. You're gonna have to tell me who you reached out to after you saw the phone was missing, everything you did to find Don, everybody you contacted, the works. That's your job, Trevor. Here and now. Just like a courtroom lawyer. You have to convince the jury—that's me—that you didn't kill Don Kalfus. My charging you with murder depends on it. You got that?"

"I told you. I didn't do it."

"Convince me."

New England weather is hard on parking lots. Concrete and asphalt are good if you have deep pockets, including enough to pay the taxes, which increase as a result of the improvement. Parking on grass and dirt ends up how you'd expect it to, especially come mud season. That leaves sure-pack, a slurry of dust and crushed rock that gets harder with time and use, might not look that good, and does need to be maintained, but—most importantly—is commonly not labeled as a finished surface by town listers. This is relevant not only in pragmatic rural New England, but if you run a business where your clientele isn't fussy about appearances.

Like a bar labeled "Nude Girls!"

To that point, as Lester observed, taking in the forlorn-looking structure before them as he got out of the car, "Strip clubs in daylight. You'd think God or somebody would have an invisibility cloak he could drop on 'em till dark."

Sammie cocked her head at him. "Seriously? Where do you come up with things like that?"

He pointed to the building, low, painted in peeling black, hung with a couple of extinguished, pale neon signs, barely readable in the sunlight. "Come on. Ya gotta admit. That's sad."

Sam's feminist instincts were stirred. "What's sad is not its lack of architectural flair. You know that."

"Absolutely," he said affably. "You think anyone's in? It's still kind of early."

Sam's disgust heightened. "You bet. Either counting money or scraping stains off the floors."

"Okaaaay." He drew out the word, following her to the door. "By the way," he added, "did you notice what Lemuel Shaw didn't?"

"What?" she asked, her hand on the knob.

"There's no 911 number on the building. How many patrons of this establishment do you think have its legal address memorized?"

She got his meaning. "And what do you bet Lucy Shaw doesn't have this place preloaded on her GPS? Mr. and Mrs. Shaw are being less than candid. There's a surprise."

With that, she twisted the knob and pulled the door open.

What greeted them was a stench of such complexity and depth as to be symphonic in scope. In an almost dizzying combination, there were odors representing everything from stale beer, old sweat, cheap perfume, cigarettes, and even urine, to name a sampling.

"Far out," Lester murmured, his head almost light.

Sam appeared to take no notice.

The place had no windows, as expected, but its darkness

approached black hole status in the far corners. One dim and distant light in this odorous fog barely revealed what looked like a ghostly painting of a distant bar with a dance floor beyond, floating against an all-absorbing black velvet background.

"We're not open," came a voice in response to the door slamming shut.

"Police," Sam announced clearly, although there was no one to be seen.

At that, a shadow dressed in black jeans and T-shirt loomed vaguely into view, belonging to a paunchy man in a beard carrying a dish towel in his hand.

"I don't care," he said. "We're closed. Come back in six hours."

The man drew near, spread out his arms, and placed his free hand on Sam's upper arm. "Sorry. You have to leave."

Sam stiffened. Without saying a word, she went from staring at him to looking at his hand, still touching her arm. Lester stepped to one side and positioned himself to react.

The man, suddenly aware of his trespass, seemed equally unsure about what to do next.

Sam asked in a frighteningly calm voice, "Are you sure you want to do that?"

The hand vanished as if singed. "Sorry," he said. "Habit. I wasn't thinking."

Lester moved things along, in part to head off a possible pistol-whipping. "We're officers assigned to a federal task force. Spinney and Martens. What's your name, sir?"

"Federal . . . ?" their host stammered. "Reynolds. Al Reynolds. I'm the manager. Sorry for the misunderstanding."

Sam was still glaring at him.

"We're hoping you can help us with something," Lester went on. "It happened about a week ago?"

Reynolds stepped back, deflated by Sam's heat. He bowed slightly. "Sure. Whatever. I mean, I'll try."

"You got an office?" Lester asked.

That brought a bemused look. "I got a closet with a safe in it and boxes of napkins and swizzle sticks. I usually do business at the bar. That okay?"

"Lead the way."

The lighted oasis grew in size as they wended their way through a shoal of scattered tables and chairs. Once there, Reynolds found his safety berth behind the bar, an arm's length from Sam, while the two cops perched themselves on stools. Sam wiped hers first with a paper napkin.

"Mr. Reynolds," she said at last.

"Yes, ma'am."

She didn't bother correcting him. "Are you here during operating hours?"

"Yes. Every night and most days. We keep staff to a minimum, so I'm here all the time. What's the problem?"

"We'll get to that." She opened her iPhone to the photos app. While she was pulling up a shot of Lemuel Shaw, Lester asked, "Then, you were here a week ago when a man complained that his car was stolen?"

Reynolds rolled his eyes. "Oh, shit. I wondered when that was gonna come back to bite me. Yeah, I was."

Sam turned her phone around to face him. "Is that the owner of the car?"

"Yep. Lemuel Shaw. A real flamer, if that's okay to say. I got permission from my boss to ban him from the place. Not a huge loss. Hardly a big spender."

"Run it down from the top," Lester asked him. "Beginning with when you were first aware he was here."

"Not much to tell," Reynolds addressed Les, shooting the occasional nervous glance at Sam. "He was parked over in the far corner. He came in about once a month, staked out a table as usual, bought a couple of beers, and disappeared. He's been doing the same thing for about a year. We get a lot of old-timers like that. Harmless. That night, I don't know what got into him. I thought later he'd either hit the bottle at home, or he'd had a fight with his old lady, but he was wired. I finally had our bouncer show him out. That's when he came back saying his car had been stolen."

"And the shit truly hit the fan?" Lester asked.

"Not really. It was like a bucket of cold water. I guess it was 'cause he knew he was screwed good and proper now. He came in, meek and mild, and said what had happened. He'd called his wife and wanted to wait for her inside, where it was warm. But he'd burned that bridge with me. I told him to piss off. That was the last I saw of him."

"Hold it," Sam finally said. "You're leaving something out. Caspar Milquetoast comes in once a month to watch your girls wiggle their butts, and then one night, out of the blue, he turns into a raging asshole and gets thrown out? On the same night his car gets stolen?"

The manager looked at her as if she'd taken flight. "Caspar who?"

Lester had been similarly impressed, but at least understood the reference. "Mr. Meek and Mild," he filled in.

"It might not've been all him," Reynolds conceded.

Every time, Lester thought. They always leave something out.

"Don't hold back now," Sam recommended.

"Something happened between the bouncer and him. I don't know what. One second, everything's fine and the girls're doin' their thing, next I know, the two of them are getting into it."

"The bouncer and Shaw?" Lester asked incredulously. "He's an old man."

Reynolds pursed his lips, embarrassed. "You're thinkin' bouncer as in *Monday Night RAW* or somethin'. This guy was not that."

Sam picked up on the past tense. "Was? What happened to him?"

"He quit. That same night."

Sam slapped the bar testily. "Goddamn it. Spit it out. All of it."

The manager put on a beleaguered expression. "I'm sorry, okay? This is not Vegas, and we're not made of money. The bouncer's an obligation, but we go through 'em like M&Ms. I've had some turn over so quick, they never even got paid. College kids, old rummies, crippled bikers, who the hell knows? They come and go, they do the job or they don't. Most of the time, it don't matter. Worst that happens is a horny drunk gets escorted out with a free drink voucher, or a bunch of kids get stopped at the door. Hell, these guys get paid so little, some of 'em sweep the floor and clean up after for extra cash."

"Okay, okay," Lester soothed him. "You saying the old guy took a swing at whoever this was?"

"Nah. I woulda called you guys for that," Reynolds conceded. "I think my guy got embarrassed. He tripped and hurt his arm or something. I don't know. It wasn't Shaw's fault. I mean, they tussled slightly, but the whole thing was stupid. The bouncer just walked out, like a girl at a party—I thought just to cool off."

"So it wasn't the bouncer who threw him out?"

"No. I backed his action 'cause Shaw was being a butthead and needed to go, but *I* threw him out. Course, I also thought my guy was still outside. It was then that Shaw came back in and said his car was missing."

Sam was almost open-mouthed by now. "The bouncer stole the car?"

Reynolds protested theatrically. "How do I know? Maybe."

Lester slid in with, "What was the guy's name, Al?"

"Don . . . Something . . . Johnson?"

There was silence at the bar for a slow count. Lester reached into his coat and produced the mug shot of Don Kalfus, laying it flat between them. "Him?"

"Yup. That's Don." Al rubbed his forehead. "And it was Thompson. I remember now. Am I in trouble?"

"Not compared to some," Les reassured him.

CHAPTER FOUR

Joe Gunther was no dinosaur, but he did like some things run old-school, among them staff meetings. He practiced occasional on-screen briefings and had worked his way to texting on the device that had replaced his old flip phone, but to him, nothing beat a face-to-face encounter.

As a result, and to no one's objection, he called the unit together on the second floor of Brattleboro's municipal center, in the small office they occupied despite official urgings that they "co-locate" with the state police. The latter had a brand-new barracks in Westminster, up the interstate a couple of exits, with room enough for extra tenants. But while the VBI had been chartered as supportive and self-effacing, this particular branch of it stayed stubbornly autonomous. The three people Joe had selected to join him in the state's southeast corner had a strong independent streak uniting them, among other things.

He waited until everyone had settled down at their desks before beginning. "This won't last long. You are tired, hungry, and I know you want to go home for some well-earned downtime. We've been going for almost twenty-two hours, mostly because we had to get a child out of harm's way and determine that Don Kalfus's death was not an ongoing public threat. Are there any arguments that we haven't addressed both hurdles?"

No one answered, which he'd expected.

"Okay. Great. You've been fairly good about maintaining the virtual log of this case as we went—"

"You say the nicest things," Willy interrupted.

Everyone laughed as Joe shot back, "I said *fairly* good. That excludes you and makes this meeting all the more necessary."

"I take it back," Willy said, faking a wounded expression. "That hurt."

None of them expected otherwise. In truth, Willy was known for submitting immaculate paperwork, but in his own time.

"As I was saying," Joe resumed, "we've done well enough cross-communicating, so I'm not asking for anything drawn out and detailed, but what's our status quo?"

"The least I can do is start off," Willy volunteered. "Ron and I went by Cheri Pratt's in Bratt—she's Kalfus's mom—to break the news. We didn't give her details, but she knew what he did for a living. He brought her souvenirs now and then, like a tray or clothes. She mentioned a bouncer gig in Keene, which I guess is what Les and Sam dug up over there, and she gave us Don's girlfriend, Robin Whiteman. I haven't put eyeballs on Whiteman yet, but I ran her through the database and got only moving violations and a single citation for underage drinking a few years ago. Course, that might mean we just never caught her."

"But so far," Joe summed up, "Mom supported the image of Don's being a low-level, uncomplicated thief. Any mention of confederates?"

"Only Whiteman, who may or may not be one. But I figure she'll at least tell us more than Cheri did."

"So we're not yet ruling out that he was working with someone and they had a falling-out," Joe said.

"We are not," Willy confirmed.

"Sam and Les?" Joe asked. "You confirmed the bouncer job, yes?"

"Correct," Sam answered. "It lasted under two weeks, and he used a bogus last name. The strip club owner said both were typical for the job."

"Did the manager give any more detail about that fight between Shaw and Don you reported?"

"We pushed him harder at the end," Lester told them. "But he swore he was too far away to hear what happened. Whatever it was, it was bad enough to cause Don to walk out, stealing Shaw's keys from his coat pocket on the way, and drive away with a new ride."

Joe offered a Socratic challenge. "What're the implications there?"

"How did Don get to work?" Willy asked, used to the boss's style. "If he'd had a car, he would've been forced to leave it behind in the lot."

"Did he know Shaw from before, or just see him arrive?" Sam asked in turn. "I wondered about that at the time, but the manager seemed clueless about everything. He didn't even report his suspicion that Don stole the car to the local cops."

"Shaw might've paid the manager to keep quiet out of embarrassment," Willy suggested. "Shaw certainly lied about how it got stolen. Don caused the fight so he could fake being pissed off and leaving. He was a thief, after all, and the car was high end."

"That's some sophisticated thinking," Lester commented doubtfully. "But to your point about Shaw being dodgy, he did play dumb when we showed him Don's picture."

"There's something else," Sam stated. "Something about him and Lucy, his wife. Les and I definitely got weird vibes from them."

"She also lied about the stolen car," Lester filled in, "and we think she did it again when she said she used her GPS to find him on the night she picked him up. There's no street number on the club, and on our way out, I checked the Jeep's GPS. It doesn't list strip joints, and she didn't enter an address. I can see her wanting to save face in the first lie. But the second one? My inner alarm bell tells me she's doing something she's not owning up to."

"To that same point," Sam said, "she did seem genuinely surprised when we told her a dead body had been found in her husband's trunk."

"Leading you both to think what?" Joe asked them.

"Every case leaves you with questions you don't need answered in the end," Sam replied. "Could be he knew about Kalfus and she didn't; could be she's a great actor. Given that we've barely started tracing the loot from Shaw's car, though—some of which might tell us who killed Don—I'm happy to leave both Shaws on the shelf for the time being. We know where to find them if something more solid comes up."

"You good with that?" Joe asked Lester.

"Works for me."

"How's Angie Neal doing?" Willy asked, almost out of thin air.

The source of the question was as telling to Joe as its subject. The arrival of Emma in Willy's and Sam's lives had been unlikely, unexpected, and—just perhaps—lifesaving for them both. Thus, Willy's interest in a young child he'd never met made better sense than his gruff exterior suggested.

"Fred Houston's more the expert than I am," Joe answered him. "But he told me she's remarkably tough under a sweet and generous surface and that it's serving her well. I also gather that despite his other disgusting appetites, Trevor Buttner may not have touched her sexually, at least yet. It's looking like we caught him early in his grooming ritual. He has a history of finding women like Melissa Monfet, with kids Angie's age, to feed his habit."

"Is Fred happy to take this one?" Willy asked. "At least the trafficking part of it?"

"He is tied into a well-oiled enforcement network over there," Joe confirmed. "I'm not going to compete with that. Plus, whatever he does with Buttner for that crime doesn't damage our murder case. It's clear Buttner knew Kalfus and had a reason to want to harm him, so adding a homicide charge is still possible. That makes the task force model as solid as ever for our purposes."

"Not to mention," Sam added, "that we need to link Kalfus to other people who may've wanted him dead. Is Fred still working on the other devices we found?"

"Yes. He's quite the whirling dervish, which is why I'm thinking this is the best time for us all to catch some sleep. A few hours from now, he'll have more to chase down, along with what we've already got going."

That was it, without drumroll or high fives. As Joe watched the three of them file out the door, shrugging on their coats against the outside cold, he could imagine Sam heading for a serious snuggle session with her daughter, with Willy in close support, and Lester driving north to Springfield in time to catch Sue before she left for the hospital. It was a comforting feeling, Joe's knowing their support systems.

This had never just been an investigative squad for him. In the purest sense—the one invoking choice over fate—these people were kin. He'd selected them, nurtured them, and in return been supported by them with more purpose and intensity than he'd seen among most blood relations, where family ties were either taken for

granted or frankly abused, as seemed to be the case with Melissa
Monfet and young Angie.

On the other hand, that now left Joe alone in the quiet office,
where the very stillness was a reminder of his separate status within
the group. Older, a childless widower, with decades on the job, he
had reached a place in life at once vaunted and privately precarious.
He was a statesman in his profession, a secular rabbi whose words
were valued for their insight. But his wisdom had been earned by
accepting that such a reputation could be fragile.

Joe's father had been a taciturn, hardscrabble farmer, holding
his own for a wife and two sons and dying young but debt-free. Of
the few pieces of advice he'd ever given his eldest, the one that had
stuck was the hard-to-hear adage that success usually lagged behind
failure as a teacher.

Keeping that close to heart had kept Joe honest and ethically
hardy, and receptive to the costs of hubris and human blunder.

Every case, every time, he experienced a moment as he was
now—sleep deprived and challenged for answers—when he wondered what would finally be his: the just deserts of righteous toil, or
an empty-handedness earned from too much self-confidence.

It was a tightrope walker's dilemma.

Willy Kunkle was not comfortable with introspection. His excess
of emotional scar tissue saw to that. The same instinct that drove
others to seek shelter in a storm was precisely what kept him outdoors and fighting the elements. As he saw it, action kept him safe,
not soul-searching, and the unexpected harbor represented by Sam
and Emma meant less that he should stay home enjoying their company, and more that he should fight for its preservation and welfare
by keeping hard at work.

And so it was that after escorting Sam home and tucking her

and Emma into bed together—following a family meal of laughter and play and a half-hour nap—he was back in night-shrouded Brattleboro, in search of Robin Whiteman, the late Don Kalfus's girlfriend.

The Department of Motor Vehicles was always an early stop to locating someone's address, right after the police databases, which were called Spillman and Valcour, and variously favored by agencies across the state. The problem with all these resources was that their accuracy depended on people living for more than a few months in one place, which often proved challenging among those of interest to the police.

But not in Robin Whiteman's case. Despite her twenty-three years, she was still living at home with her parents, in a trailer park on Brattleboro's western edge.

Here Willy was staked out in his nondescript car, parked in the shadows of a large tree roughly one hundred feet away from her residence.

The trailer park had been a fixture for decades, and no one seriously referred to any of its homes as being mobile anymore. A few still had tires tucked behind the hay bale skirts designed to stave off the cold air. But that was only because the owners hadn't bothered to remove them when cinder blocks had usurped their usefulness. Otherwise, these fading, sometimes sagging metal boxes had become as natural to the locale as the trees growing up among them.

Trailer parks were endemic to Vermont, as to most other rural locations across the nation. Dismissed by casual observers as harbors for the down-and-out, a huge number rivaled their stick-built suburban counterparts for tidiness and pride, including the presence of gardens and flower beds, playgrounds, and swimming pools, and often being serviced by either paved roads or well-maintained dirt equivalents.

Not this one, however. Where Robin Whiteman's family had put down roots, the streets were little better than forest trails, rutted and gnarly with roots and rocks. There was no lighting aside from what spilled from nearby windows, and any notion of a community center or clubhouse was laughable. This was a neighborhood on the fringes.

It was also not given to the quotidian habits of a block of homes like Willy's, where school and employment dictated schedules. Here, people came and went almost haphazardly, either not having jobs or because their work was less defined, buffeted by unpredictability.

It wasn't crucial that Willy interview Robin Whiteman apart from her parents, one of whom he could see crossing before the trailer's kitchen window, but it was his preference. With that in mind, he was hoping either they or she might leave, allowing him to follow her or be rid of them for the brief time he needed. If he saw her at all.

No sooner contemplated than he did just that. With a bang of the trailer's flimsy front door, a silhouette appeared at the top of the metal steps, and Willy recognized Robin Whiteman, dressed in a Taco Bell uniform.

"My lucky night," he said to himself, watching her cross to a ramshackle car, fire it up, and begin bumping her way toward the distant highway.

He fell in behind her as she led him across town to where the local miracle mile peters out near the northernmost interstate exit. There, he came to a stop beside her parked car at the rear of the employee parking lot.

"Robin Whiteman?" he asked as they separately stepped from their vehicles.

"Who're you?" she asked nervously, eyeing the intimidating combination of his sharp features and lopsided appearance.

He opened his coat to display his badge. "When does your shift start?"

"Five minutes. What do you want?"

"You know what I want. The grapevine's been alive since it happened. How long did you think it would be before you met one of us?"

She looked crestfallen. "I didn't think it would be here. Now."

"I had to find you first."

"I'm sorry."

He responded to what sounded like genuine loss in her voice. "Why? It wasn't your responsibility to chase us down. Unless you know why Don got killed."

Her eyes and mouth opened in shock. "What? Me? I don't. It doesn't make sense. He wasn't that kind of guy."

"What kind?"

"A crook. You know. A bad guy. He was never violent to anybody."

"How long did you know him?"

Her foot scraped on the asphalt. "A few months. He was nice."

"You know what he did for a living?"

She hesitated before admitting, "Sure."

"He used to give his mom presents now and then, from his adventures. He do that for you, too?"

Her embarrassment hung between them. "A little."

"Like what?"

"This." She held up her hand and displayed a modest ring, sporting what looked like a fake diamond. "I have to give it back?"

Willy liked that. He smiled before saying, "I should say yes, but why don't you hang on to it for a while. I'll let you know down the line."

It was a good move. Her expression softened. "Really?"

He didn't answer, letting the gesture sink in.

"What happened?" she then asked, her voice almost childlike.

"We're thinking he pissed off the wrong person. Did he tell you anything about what he had planned this past week?"

She shook her head. "He was happy. Feeling good."

"Did you see the new car?"

She smiled. "He was real pleased with that. Took me for a ride. Made me nervous. I thought we'd get pulled over."

"Here in Vermont?"

"Yeah. Up Route 5, to Windsor and back."

Smart, Willy thought. Avoid the interstate. "Was there stuff in the back?"

"Some. Yeah."

"He talk about where he got it or what he was gonna do with it?"

"Not where he got it, but he said he had a fence waiting for some of it."

"When was this?"

"Maybe three, four days ago?" She glanced at her plastic watch. "I gotta go."

"I know. Did he mention any names, or did you ever see him with anyone he might've worked with?"

"I got no clue." Her body language was ramping up, her feet shifting, preparing to move.

Willy stalled her emotionally, reaching out and barely touching her sleeve. "Robin. Somebody killed him. Help me find out why."

She placed the fingertips of one hand against her temple, her eyes welling up. "I'm so sorry. We didn't talk about all that. It was just kind of funny. Not something that could get you killed."

"Anybody, Robin. A name. A place. Something."

"Corey Browne," she said, stepping back as if she'd dropped something hot. "He was one of Don's friends. Seemed to know what he was doing. I didn't like him. He was scary."

"You gotta go, Robin," Willy encouraged her. "I appreciate your help. We'll talk later, but don't worry about this. Nobody knows we met. You just take care of yourself, okay?"

She looked frail and exposed, wiping her eyes with the back of her hand. "Okay," she half sobbed.

"Go, go," he urged her. "Get to work. Focus on your job. It'll help. Trust me."

He watched her go, waving as she looked back over her shoulder.

"Corey Browne, you piece of shit," he said to himself. "This, I look forward to."

Brattleboro's Overnight Inn was a landmark of sorts, its pool once available to local families, as well as guests, and its selection of conference rooms serving everyone from the Lions to the Chamber of Commerce to the Rotary Club. Telling anyone to meet you at the Overnight was a well-known bit of currency.

Over time, along with a succession of owners less and less committed to the facility's upkeep, the same reference either drew a blank from newcomers or a rueful look from old-timers. The Overnight, with the sad and erosive progression of dementia, had slowly slipped from its apex to ending up on the state's list of forgotten motels, now designated as low-income, Section 8 housing.

In principle, Willy was supportive of the program and empathetic toward many of its users. In practice, he readily acknowledged how tough it was to make such a notion successful. Putting a large, disparate population of disadvantaged, poor, sometimes disoriented, troubled, and even haunted people under one large roof, run by a threadbare staff, was at best a challenge and at worst akin to sharing a voyage on an old and leaky ship.

Willy had gone straight from leaving Robin Whiteman to visit one of these landlocked travelers. Corey Browne wasn't an actual resident. He made it his business to come and go from their midst, sowing as much quiet destruction as he could without being caught. Like a virus introduced into an ICU, Browne was a lethal if inconspicuous presence.

Willy, reasonably enough, was also a familiar sight to some of the Overnight's denizens, but where one might expect a drug dealer like Browne to be embraced and a cop to be shunned, Willy had never suffered that fate. His manner and appearance aside, he was known for being evenhanded and honest, and even generous when it came to balancing infractions against the law. It was understood to this slice of society that Kunkle valued justice above all and would only rarely use an arrest to get his way, and then usually with good reason.

Thus, he entered the Overnight nodding familiarly to the young man at the desk, who didn't challenge him, and began wandering the long, dimly lit corridors in search of familiar faces who might tell him of Corey Browne's whereabouts.

Because that was one thing of which he was almost certain: Browne was also prowling these hallways, a hyena circling weakened prey.

"Hey, Detective Kunkle. Long time no see."

Willy paused outside an ajar room door. Unlike during the Overnight's previous life, many of the rooms were now left open to passersby, enhancing the place's transition from anonymous nightly refuge to long-term communal neighborhood.

Willy leaned against the doorjamb, taking in a short, thick-waisted woman whose smile offset the hard times etched on her face. She was standing before the TV set, a remote in her hand.

"Hey there, Jen. How you been?"

She put aside the remote and began teasing a hank of bottle-blond hair in need of a touchup, her ringed fingers lingering by her cheek and revealing an elaborate sleeve tattoo. "Been good. You know, holding it together."

"And Derek? He's gotta be in his twenties by now."

The smile widened. "He drives a truck for Point-to-Point Hauling, thanks to you."

"Good for him," he said. "*He* deserves the credit there, Jen. I just got out of the way. You know, boys'll be boys. He knew what was what. You must be proud."

"You know it," she replied, coming to the door and standing close. He could smell the breath mint struggling against the alcohol. "What're you doin' wandering around? You on the job?"

"Looking to chat with Corey Browne. You seen him?"

She frowned. "Here? Now and then. I try to avoid him."

"He got anyone special in tow right now? Somebody he likes to hang with?"

"Margie Sullivan's his latest. Me and some of the others warned her not to cozy up, but you know how it is. You dangle a little candy in front of some women, they can't say no. And he's got the candy."

"What's he selling nowadays?" Willy asked.

"Some shit called Killer-Diller. I heard it lives up to its name."

Willy had heard the same. Heroin/fentanyl mixtures were commonplace by now, most of them sold in packets stamped with catchy names. Willy had given up questioning why anyone would inject, ingest, or inhale something that sometimes literally had a skull and bones stamped on it. On the other hand, as a recovering alcoholic, he wasn't one to stand in judgment.

"Where's Margie hang her hat?" he asked instead.

"Room 373. Upstairs." Jen pointed with her thumb.

More hallway, a set of stairs, the elevator being unreliable. The carpeting had faded and become stained, the wallpaper torn and defaced. Here and there, plaster had broken away, leaving divots and scars unlikely to be repaired. It all reinforced the impermanence of such places, along with that of their inhabitants.

Willy reached Room 373's firmly closed door and knocked.

"Who is it?" came the response moments later.

"Police," he acknowledged, knowing the woman behind the voice could see him through the peephole.

"What d'you want?"

"Open up, Margie. You're not in trouble, at least not with me."

After a pause, the voice said, "Hang on," and the lock snapped open.

It didn't matter. Almost ferally aware of his surroundings at all times, Willy sensed before he saw a figure appear down the hall, a small bag in his hand.

He and Corey Browne took each other in for a slow count of three before Browne pivoted on his heel and ran as Willy shouted his name.

"Goddamn it," Willy spat out, giving chase.

Willy was unexpectedly fast, given his disability and age. Fortunately for him, Browne was as athletic as your average substance-abusing drug dealer. Nevertheless, the one had the distance on the other and vanished down the stairwell as Willy was still pounding along the corridor.

The staircase proved a blessing. Running clockwise as it descended, it offered the cop its inner-right handrail as an anchor, which Willy seized as he went like a one-armed ape swinging off a branch. He made good yardage on the way down, the walls reverberating with the heavy footfalls of both men.

Browne still outdistanced him on the first floor, if barely, further impeded by the number of people hanging around outside their rooms.

"Police!" Willy yelled out. "I want that man."

It was too much to expect. It was commonly said that the bigger a group, the less likely aid will be forthcoming, and indeed, most of these onlookers merely stared in surprised silence as the two sprinters went by. At least, Willy thought, no one bothered to trip him instead—always an option with this audience.

But all was not lost. As Browne entered the old motel's vast lobby, now a place to commingle socially, with tables and seating, one of the Overnight's residents responded probably less to Willy's shouting and more to his own personal feelings about Corey Browne. Rising gracefully from his straight-backed chair, this older man completed the gesture by grasping the chair by its wooden crest rail and swung it sideways like a garbage can lid, sending it directly across Browne's pathway and toppling him like a bowling pin.

Willy gave the old-timer a grateful grin as he leaped over the same obstacle and landed with one knee in Browne's back, his muscular right hand on the nape of Browne's neck. He shoved Corey's face into the dirty carpeting, noticing a concealed pistol tucked into his waistband. "Gotcha, you son of a bitch," he panted. "And packing, to boot. Time to catch up."

Even Willy couldn't deny he was feeling the lack of sleep, leaning against the wall on the viewing side of the one-way mirror, gazing at Corey Browne sitting at the small room's bolted-down steel table, one wrist handcuffed to the wall beside him.

Willy let out a slow breath. His preference would have been to leave this turkey where he was for what was left of the night and catch some shut-eye, curled up next to his small family.

But that choice was past. He'd opted to stake out Robin Whiteman's place when he had, and now it was up to him to see this through.

He straightened, squared his shoulders, and entered the room.

Browne glared at him as he closed the door behind him. "'Bout fucking time. I have rights, you know?"

"I do," Willy countered pleasantly. "I read 'em to you." He crossed to the other side of the small table and sat down.

"What you did was totally illegal. It was entrapment and a violation of my civil rights, and profiling, too."

"Let's talk about Don Kalfus," Willy started as if Corey hadn't uttered a word.

Browne blinked once. "What?"

"How do you know him?"

Browne proved amenable. "Kalfus?" he asked, his string of objections forgotten. "Around. You know. Just one of those guys."

Willy was gaining confidence that Corey hadn't heard of Don's death. "Friend of yours?"

"Not particularly."

"When did you last see him?"

A small bulb lit up Corey's brain. "Why you wanna know?"

"He's part of a case we're running. You ever have any dealings with him?"

"What's it to you?"

Here it comes, Willy thought, suppressing another sigh. He placed his elbow on the table and cupped his chin in his hand. "I think I ought to tell you something," he said. "Just between us."

"I don't have to help you just 'cause," Corey said.

"That's true," Willy agreed. "But keep in mind that all I wanted to do in the first place was have a conversation. Instead, you're now chained to the wall facing a federal weapons charge, a parole violation, and a drug rap, among other things, all because you made like a rabbit. You might want to consider who's got the upper hand here."

Corey considered that before asking, "We talking about a deal?"

Willy scratched his forehead. "Do you know what I do nowadays?'

"I heard you moved up. Not with the PD anymore."

"Correct. I only chase things like homicides. In fact, right now, I'm working as a Fed, with all the powers and penalties that suggests."

Corey was mocking. "Oooh. Way cool. That how you impress the girls?"

"What's cool is how federal jail time differs from what you're used to in Vermont."

Browne's eyes narrowed. "What're you sayin'? I haven't done nothin' against the Feds."

"That's not how it works, Corey. If it suits me, they get involved. You don't get a vote. Unless . . . ," he added as an afterthought.

That worked. "What d'you mean?"

"Not to sound like a broken record, but tell me about Don Kalfus."

"A broken what?"

"Just tell me."

As Willy had hoped, Corey finally recognized the offer being tendered, although no deal had been articulated.

"Sure. What the fuck. What d'ya wanna know?"

"What're your dealings with him?"

"He's a go-to guy. You need somethin' like a car or a computer, maybe a gun. Hell, damn near anything, come to think of it. He even has things you don't know you want."

"Give me an example."

Corey leaned forward, his wrist still dangling from the wall. "Well, since this is just between you and me, I've sold pills and shit now and then, right?"

"Okay."

"Well, that's how it worked. Guys like me need a supply. Normally, that's a pipeline from New York or Holyoke or someplace, but those get interrupted sometimes. I ask people like Don to keep an eye open for rainy-day situations—for Oxys or shit like that. Other times, he'll reach out and let me know he has something and would I be interested?"

"And you pay him?"

"Sure. Drugs aren't his thing, but he keeps his eyes open, and he's real good, you know? He never sticks it to you. Reasonable rates."

"A one-stop shopping outlet for stolen property," Willy suggested.

Corey laughed. "Yeah. That's good."

"And he does this a lot?"

"Busy enough, yeah."

"He has a lot of product."

Corey had to think about that. "Sure. I guess. Not so much pills—those were just if he happened to find 'em around. Why d'you care?"

"It means more customers than just you. Other fences. Does he have a storage spot? A barn or someone's garage?"

"How would I know?"

"You might. He has a girlfriend, doesn't he?"

"Robin? Yeah. Nice kid, but clueless. His mom knew what's what. She's an old-school broad. Probably taught him what he knows."

Willy made a note of that. So much for poor, innocent Cheri.

"Speaking of that," he continued, "how does he operate? Does he plan ahead? Do research?"

Browne was by now enjoying himself, either forgetful of what lay ahead for him or a fatalist at heart, which is what Willy suspected. "Why're you askin' all this shit? Who cares about Kalfus?"

Willy sidestepped. "All you guys make waves. It's up to us to sort through them. Tell me who he might've pissed off. Any deals you know about that went south?"

"He's a thief," Browne protested. "He doesn't leave people feeling *happy*. I don't know. I mean, I sorta called him a doofus before, but he's good at what he does. He's a busy man. Always workin'."

Willy allowed for a reflective pause, which Browne filled seconds later. "But people get their nose outta joint. And they talk too fuckin' much. That's probably how you got me. Yap, yap, yap. And the phones don't help. Everybody's on those damned things. So, sure, he probably gets jammed up now and then."

"By?"

"Darren Bader's one I can think of. He had a hard-on for Don for a while. You wanna hear bad things about Don, Bader's your man, 'cept for his being full of crap."

"But there was bad blood between them?"

"Not from Don. Darren's the one who got worked up, claiming Don was the reason for his last vacation at government expense, if you get my meaning."

"He thought Don squealed on him?"

"Don sold him a car, and he got nailed by a state trooper, driving it around. Couldn't've been his own damn fault, right? So he blamed Don. Typical. But it *was* his fault. Everybody knew it."

"And Darren was one of Don's fences?"

"Yep. They went back to it after he got out, too. That's the way it is. Bygones become bygones. Money talks."

"You think Darren might've borne a grudge?"

"Against Don? Probably, knowing him. He's never blamed himself for anything in his life."

"Bad enough to want to harm Don?"

Browne gave that a moment's thought. "Darren? Could be. Nobody else, but I could see Darren doin' that. The man's an asshole. I'm surprised you don't know him."

But of course, Willy did, and now, even if he doubted Corey Browne's reliability, he had to check out Darren Bader.

CHAPTER FIVE

Joe began the next day in Keene, New Hampshire, in the basement of the Cheshire County Sheriff's Office. There, Fred Houston had a long, narrow, windowless office packed with computers and expensive-looking black boxes, all of which appeared to be interconnected via a tangle of thick and colorful high-speed cables.

"Welcome to the skunk works," Fred greeted him as he entered, having been escorted there by a uniformed officer.

Joe chose an upholstered stool to sit on, not wishing to be in the way or disrupt any device whose function he didn't understand. "I hope you got at least a couple of hours' sleep," he said.

Fred was moving between his two opposing counters, checking screens as he went. "Oh, I never need much. I'm doing fine. You?"

"Sure," Joe replied, moving on. "Have your electronic gremlins been hard at work?"

"Hard at work and productive," Fred confirmed, indicating a neatly arranged row of the variously colored and sized smartphones from the stolen Mercedes. "I concentrated on them, since they're what most people use these days, and as usual, they've each been a piñata of human misbehavior."

"A piñata?" Joe asked, amused by the reference.

"That's how I see it. A hot car, a bunch of these, *and* a dead body. Each one with a story, each demanding an explanation. It's a piñata to me."

Joe nodded. "I like it. Did you find more like our new friend, Trevor Buttner?" he asked, young Angie Neal's face still lodged in his memory.

"Thankfully, no," Fred replied, adding, "He's entered the bowels of the federal system for trafficking, by the way, which'll make him that much easier to find if and when you dig up more linking him to the late Don Kalfus."

"We're not there yet," Joe replied. "I would still like to know what the two of them had in common, though. Yet another odd loose end."

Fred settled onto a stool himself to continue speaking. "Well, to answer your first question, the phones run the gamut from the boring to the actionable. Among the former is a banker who's cheating on his wife with a teller, and a minor blackmail scheme featuring a car salesman who's pressuring his manager for better perks before he squeals to the dealership's owner. I have no clue what that means yet, but it doesn't sound like anything for us. I did enjoy it since it didn't seem to have anything to do with porn. I'm tiring of seeing pictures of children's privates."

He reached behind him and picked up a couple of the phones, still talking. He held up the first. "Slightly more interesting is a part-time teacher who's playing middleman between his students and a pill dealer. Very low end, and I already forwarded it to the state police."

He moved to the second one. "Here, we're back to porn, but this time, it's got hair on it. Adult, in other words. Creative—I'll give them that—but of no interest to law enforcement."

He replaced both phones, adding, "I will never understand the interest in filming yourself having sex. Of all the footage I've seen, not once have I seen a body deserving public viewing. We are an amazingly saggy and unattractive species."

Joe was wondering what it was like to live with this man. He did sport a wedding ring. Not that anything he'd revealed so far was particularly appalling. Vermont's and New Hampshire's images as chaste retreats for pacific nature lovers notwithstanding, such behavior was no more atypical here than anywhere else.

"So, nothing beyond the Buttner phone to go on?" Joe asked.

Houston turned back to face him, another unit in hand. "I didn't say that," he replied. "Check this out."

He handed over an old and battered flip phone, which Joe opened gingerly. "What's this? It's like the first one I ever owned."

"It is, and dead as the proverbial doornail when I got it. What's the name Scooter Nelson do for you?"

Joe stared at him. "A lot. Why?"

Fred looked pleased. "I thought it might. It wasn't easy getting it up and running again, not to mention the prehistoric software, but long story short, that's his. It's clean of prints and DNA, but the contents confirm its ownership."

Joe turned the flip phone over in his hand, thinking back. Scooter Nelson was a case dating back years. Scooter had been the preteen child of a prominent and well-heeled local couple—she an attorney, he a physician—who'd simply vanished one day, never to be seen again.

The squad, assisted by the Brattleboro PD and Ron Klecszewski, had run itself ragged trying to find the slightest clue. They'd scrutinized the family, Scooter's school, any and all friends. They'd scoured the internet, hoping to pick up some mention, either by him, if he'd run away, or about him, if he'd been kidnapped. They'd run ads, circulated his details nationwide, contacted the various missing children organizations, and even posted flyers. His parents had contributed financially and with unflagging effort, even pulling strings to get on late-night Boston TV to appeal for help.

All for naught. The Nelsons were not to get their Scooter back.

That had stuck in Gunther's craw forever after.

Joe gazed at the phone in his hand as he might at a cherished talisman. "What's it got on it?" he asked.

"That's the bad news, I'm afraid," Fred conceded. "Outside of it being his, its logs and texts told me squat. Typical teen text stuff—'Yo, dude, whatcha doin?' crap. You know the style. But there's nothing like, 'Oh my God, here comes John Smith about to kidnap me,' complete with a quick selfie. It's a historical artifact, more likely to add to your frustration than not."

Joe was taking this in, studying the phone as if it might suddenly speak, and recalling Fred's reflection about a piñata earlier. "It's way more than that," he finally said.

"What're you going to do with it?" Fred asked.

Joe gave him a sad smile. "Right now, it's my first lead in a presumed homicide, or at least a missing person's case."

He held it up, adding, "I'll have my team go through it, but I'm thinking its real value will be in answering: Where the hell did Don Kalfus steal it from?"

Winchester, New Hampshire, is known for its beautiful Victorian-era library, a couple of picturesque covered bridges, an annual pickle festival, and for being a hard-luck, down-at-the-heels, minor industrial throwback that few outsiders can find on a map. In Willy Kunkle's world of places harboring people who targeted others for money, drugs, sex, or pent-up frustration, Winchester was an unfortunate standout.

This is why Willy was here now, in a rainstorm that appeared at odds with the ruined snow on the ground. It was cold, dark, and miserable, despite being midmorning. He'd grabbed another few moments of sleep and then headed off on his own, invoking his temporary federal reach and ignoring his unit's protocol about informing anyone where he was or what he was doing.

This was archetypal Willy, reflective of his solitary nature.

His goal was Darren Bader, whom Corey Browne had probably mentioned to get Willy off his back. Nevertheless, Willy had no doubts that Bader and Browne, among many like them, had trafficked in stolen goods with the ambitious, hardworking, and now late Don Kalfus. That alone was enough to justify at least a short conversation.

The timing of this visit was calculated. Men of Bader's social stratum are not morning people, and Willy wanted to find him at home, operating below par. Not, if memory served, that Bader was an overachiever in any department.

Browne had said Bader lived in the hills west of the Monadnock Speedway, another of Winchester's landmarks, but Willy was impressed by just how remote that proved to be. His department-issued SUV was handling the forest road ahead of it but was being tested when at last a small, patchwork, plywood-walled cabin came into view.

Willy stopped the car, rolled down the window, and waited for a full two minutes, honoring the common phenomenon of an unseen guard dog being off the leash. Still following backwoods protocol, he emerged from the vehicle in full view of the cabin's windows and stood facing the building with his good hand holding his coat open to reveal his badge, despite the pouring rain.

Only then did he approach, slowly and deliberately, as if a rifle was trained on him.

That was a possibility, given the man he hoped to visit, the overall setting, and the circumstances behind Willy's visit.

Willy knew Darren Bader from PD days, when the daily cycle was more likely to involve burglaries and domestics than murders. Vermont's citizens did not kill one another with the regularity of a Detroit or a Los Angeles. Before the advent of the VBI and its specialized charter, Willy and his municipal squad dealt with whatever illegalities occurred. That usually meant lowlifes like Darren, who, for all his nasty habits, craven appetite, and amoral outlook, was no stone-cold killer, despite an occasionally nasty temper.

But it never hurt to be careful, and times had changed. All it seemed to take recently was the lightest pressure on an emotional trigger.

Rain now dripping off his forehead and nose, Willy deliberately climbed the two spongy steps to the door and stood long enough to peer through the grimy glass. It was a one-room building, and he could see a clothed body stretched out on the bed.

He knocked on the glass, ready to dive for cover if he didn't like what he saw.

But there was nothing to see. The body didn't move.

"Great," he said to himself, and knocked louder.

Still seeing no effect, he risked breaking the glass and tapped again with the butt of his gun.

Still nothing.

Irritation yielding to curiosity, he holstered the gun and tried the doorknob. The door opened.

Willy slipped inside, closing the door behind him. Standing with his back against the wall, he took in his surroundings. It was surprisingly warm, thanks to a small woodstove he hadn't noticed, and it smelled as he expected it would, which was better than raw sewage, if reminiscent of it.

It was filthy, ramshackle, dark, and cluttered with a decorative flair not dissimilar from what Ron and he had enjoyed at Cheri Pratt's.

Satisfied at last that they were alone and no booby traps were evident, he crossed over to the body and studied it, avoiding the two plastic jugs partially filled with urine.

It was Darren Bader, and, comforting enough, he was breathing. Also, as Willy appreciated, he wasn't yet peeing straight into the mattress. That had to be a good sign.

The thin pallet being stretched out upon the wood floor, Willy reached out with his foot and nudged Bader on the shoulder. Hard. Leaving a shoe print.

There was a catch in the man's breathing, but otherwise nothing. Willy repeated the gesture with more force and stood back, in case the reaction put those jugs at risk of spilling.

Bader flinched, groaned, shook his head, and responded, "What the fuck?"

His eyes opened, and he took in Willy standing over him. He blinked in amazement. "Kunkle?" he said thickly. "What the hell?"

"Wake up, Darren," Willy told him. "Time for a talk."

Like a water buffalo extracting himself from a mud bath, Bader struggled to work his arms and legs, until finally achieving a half-sitting position.

"What the fuck?"

"You said that already."

Bader rubbed his face. "What're you doing here?"

"I told you."

"You can't just walk into a man's house."

"Exigent circumstances. I was hoping you were dead."

"I'm not. Go away."

"Too late. I'm saving your life. You were in the middle of an alcoholic overdose."

Bader shifted again and found the rough wall with his back. "The hell I was."

Satisfied, Willy wiped his own face with his sleeve and sat in the room's only chair, located beside a rickety card table.

"I love what you've done with the place. You're clearly putting your ill-gotten gains to good use."

"You just come by to give me shit?"

Willy tilted his head. "Maybe a little. I need to know something, too."

"What?"

"What do you know about Don Kalfus?"

Bader looked incredulous. "Jesus, Kunkle. Why don't you ask him yourself? You are so weird."

"I've heard that," Willy agreed. "Kalfus is dead, and some people think you might be involved."

At last properly stimulated, Bader sat up completely, his mouth open in protest. "Oh, no you don't. I know shit about that. I done some business with Kalfus, that's all. I never killed nobody in my life, and I sure as hell never killed him. I didn't even know he was dead. You *know* that, Kunkle. Why're you giving me crap?"

"You're low-hanging fruit, Darren. I bring you in, I can get on with my day. It's up to you to prove me wrong."

"*What?* You can't do that."

"Convince me."

"Damn. That's not fair."

"When did you last see Kalfus? Give me what you got."

As Willy had hoped, Bader needed no more persuasion.

"Okay. I seen him maybe a month ago."

"Why?"

"Just a deal. Nothin' new. He had somethin'. I said I'd take it off him for a cut."

"What was it?"

"I tell you, you lock me up. I'm not stupid."

Willy slid off the chair and squatted down to adjust their sight lines, making things slightly friendlier. "This is a conversation, Darren. I'm here to talk only. I'm working for the Feds now. If I busted you, they'd throw you right back. They have minimum requirements, like with fishing limits. You're too small. So talk."

"It was a car. I know people he doesn't. He found an easy steal on one of his shopping trips. That's what he called 'em. So he comes to me, I get rid of it, and I give him a finder's fee. It's dumb. He could make more peddling it himself, but he doesn't want to."

"Wasn't it a car deal with him that got you put behind bars?" Willy asked. "I heard you were steamed about that, and now you tell me you're doing the same thing all over again. You know what that makes you, right?"

"Up yours."

"You weren't still pissed at him?"

"I was the one who got caught at the wheel."

"You blamed him anyhow."

"I got over it. I had to blame *somebody*."

Willy was impressed by the self-analysis. "Okay," he said. "You two work together often?"

"Now and then. Lotta cars out there. Lotta rich people with nice rides."

Willy figured anyone with a used Yugo would strike Darren as rich. That made for a large marketplace. "Don sounds pretty offbeat," Willy commented. "Tell me about him. We never met."

"I could never figure him out," Darren admitted.

"In what way?"

"Like not doing dope. Everybody does a little. But not him. What's that about?"

"What did he do with his money, if he didn't blow it like the rest of you?"

Bader chuckled, looking baffled. "He had a checking account. Can you believe that? He saved it, like he was gonna buy a house or some crazy shit. He ran around, ripping people off, so he could end up just like them, protecting his stuff behind a locked door, worrying about mortgage payments and car repairs and insurance. It was nuts. He totally didn't get it."

Yeah, Willy thought, glancing around. *As against living in clover.*

"You're implying he worked with a bunch of people like you," he said. "You handled cars, probably somebody else took jewelry, computers, silverware. Is that right?"

"Sure."

"You know some of these people?"

Darren tried looking crafty. "Everybody knows somebody, Kunkle, just like you know me. It's all based on money changing hands."

Willy stood back up, his expression grim. "Right. And I know cops, like on the Winchester police force. The Feds may not want you, Darren, but one phone call from me will bring down guys who'd love a bite out of you. My sworn statement will get them a search warrant to tear this dump apart and bust you for whatever they find. You really want to play cute?"

Bader's silence was eloquent enough.

"So," Willy continued. "Here's my question: Of the fences Don worked with, who do you think might've been pissed at him, or twitchy, crazy, or nasty enough to kill him?"

Darren didn't seem put out by Willy's stance. In their world, such exchanges were coin of the realm. "I could maybe come up with a couple. I gotta give it some thought."

Willy decided he'd had enough. "I think I changed my mind. I'm gonna take you to the PD after all." He made to grab hold of the man.

Bader pressed against the wall. "Whoa, whoa. What the hell?"

Willy paused, his face closer, looming above. "You just admitted it, Darren: You were pissed at Kalfus. You blamed him for getting locked up. You wanted to get even, and now he's dead."

Darren recalculated. "Don't get your shorts in a twist," he urged, holding up both hands. "I *was* pissed. I told you that. I was wrong. We did a deal later, and it went great. No bad feelings. Bygones and all that shit. We were cool."

"Who killed him, then?"

Credibly or not, Bader chose to suddenly cooperate. "I did hear a rumor."

Willy relaxed and resumed his seat. "What?"

"I didn't know Kalfus was dead till you told me. Honest. But a couple of days ago, maybe three, I heard somebody was looking for him."

"Tell me more."

"That's sorta it. Grapevine had it Don had overstepped. Poked the wrong bear."

Willy sneered at him. "The man was beaten to death, Darren. Of *course* he poked the wrong bear. That's why I'm here. You need to give me somewhere else to go, or I'm not leaving. And it had better be accurate, or I'll be back with company."

It was an empty threat, but Willy was counting on past experience to inform Darren's thinking. He'd spent half his life in jail. He was resigned to authorities doing what they chose with him.

"He spent most of his time in New Hampshire," he began.

"I don't know why. He didn't ignore Vermont, but his mom lives there, and his girlfriend. Maybe he wanted distance between them and what he did. Plus, there're more rich people living here, 'cause we're near Boston and the coast."

"I'm not a tourist, Darren. Get to it."

"I am, I am. Don liked the southern part, where all the people live. And he liked to unload what he found in Vermont. That was just him being old-fashioned, like the cops couldn't cross state lines or something. In a way, he's right. It does make it harder on you guys to build a case, so maybe he was right."

He read Willy's expression and spoke a little faster. "Anyhow, to get to it, what I heard had somethin' to do with this general neck of the woods. You know, Hinsdale, Keene, Claremont area. The border towns. Scuttlebutt was that this somebody—and I swear to God I don't know who—was lookin' to straighten things out with Don. Which I guess he did."

"Any idea what Don had done? Was it something he stole or something he saw?"

Bader reflected a moment, which was the first time Willy had ever seen the expression on him.

"I never thought of that. I don't know."

"This is cool," Lester said half to himself, his eyes on his computer screen.

"What?" Sam asked from her desk, four feet away in the tiny VBI office.

"It's from Fred Houston. He sent us the map download from Don Kalfus's stolen car. I've never seen one of these before." He twirled his monitor around so she could see the screen. Against a blue road map background was a tangled, self-interweaving, utterly confusing yellow ribbon.

"Looks like spaghetti," she observed. "Can't make head or tail of it."

"Well, we know where it ended up," Lester stated, "and from what we've figured so far, the part we're interested in begins at the strip club, where Don became the proud new owner. It's hard to read. I'll give you that. But I bet it'll get easier if we retrace it in real time."

Sam saw the wisdom in that. "He had the damn thing for almost a week and clearly covered hell's half acre in it."

Lester didn't argue, adding, "Filling it with stolen goods, one of which may have gotten him killed."

She gave him a long, appraising look. "Okay. Might turn out to be an interesting trip."

Diagonally across the state, in the basement of the University of Vermont Medical Center, Dr. Beverly Hillstrom positioned her camera, equipped with an LED halo light, and carefully squeezed off a couple of shots.

She was in the morgue of the OCME, shorthand for Office of the Chief Medical Examiner, finishing up Don Kalfus's autopsy. Despite her comments to Joe at the scene, she hadn't been able to get to this as quickly as she'd anticipated. Returning to the office, she'd found two other procedures in line.

But she was nearing the end with young Mr. Kalfus now, just shy of peeling down his face and scalp in order to open his skull. The head was the last part to examine in her process, the rest of him speaking of her thoroughness so far. He was unzipped like a grisly duffel bag, his organs removed, awaiting her doing the same to this sole remnant of his intact anatomy.

But not quite yet. First, she wanted to carefully document the injury to his temple that Sammie had first noticed when pretending not to disturb the body.

It was visibly an impact wound, and Hillstrom's experience made her confident it had involved something blunt and heavy, probably wielded at high speed. Beyond that, she couldn't tell yet.

She put down the heavy camera and placed a magnifier headset over her scrub cap, adjusting it before her eyes. Carefully, working with a dental probe, she began examining the damage at Don Kalfus's temple.

She took her time, as was her habit. The office, for a state the size of Vermont, was remarkably busy, especially since, from a peak of three in-house pathologists, they were now down to her and one deputy. This despite a recent and apparently permanent surge in numbers. Vermont's population had been aging, drug deaths had taken off, as had fatal resolutions to what had once been fistfights and screaming matches.

Nevertheless, Hillstrom rarely rushed. The world might choose to speed up and risk going off the rails. Beverly, like Joe, she was pleased to admit, took her time and aimed for consistent accuracy. If a few people or events had to wait as a result, so be it.

It was peaceful in the morgue right now, which helped. It had been a hectic morning, following only a few hours of sleep. She'd felt badly about letting Joe down with this procedure, especially after she'd been so confident she'd get on it upon reaching Burlington.

But here she was at last and feeling much better. Not only was she comforted as always by her environment, a facility for which she had fought long and hard, years ago, featuring all the accoutrements of an A-level forensics lab, but right now, she thought she might have found something to lift Joe's spirits a little.

Reaching for a long pair of tweezers and working them alongside the probe, she carefully extracted an approximately four-centimeter sliver of blood-soaked wood.

"Look at you," she said, holding it up. "Won't it be nice to find where you came from?"

"Things are warming up," Joe told the assembled squad that afternoon, the rain still beating against the window. "Last meeting, Fred was unpacking the phones, and we knew next to nothing about Don Kalfus. From what you've been filing, it looks like we're making progress. Fred used the image of a piñata to describe how this case fell open at our feet." He held up his prime exemplar of that, explaining, "So, it should come as no surprise that something else has fallen out of nowhere."

"That a flip phone?" Lester asked.

"It is. More than that, it's Scooter Nelson's."

"You're kidding," Willy said, in an unusual show of surprise.

"Does it still work?" Sammie asked. She had been particularly devoted to the case at the time. The mother's death by overdose shortly thereafter and Mr. Nelson's permanent departure from the region in an alcoholic stupor hadn't helped. All of them were used to the shambles left in humanity's wake, but this case had left its mark, in large part because of its lack of a conclusion.

"It does," Joe answered her, sitting on the edge of his desk, facing them. "It doesn't have much to offer, according to Fred, but I'll leave it to you three to sniff out something more. He was just looking for anything obvious."

"And you want to know where it's been all this time," Willy suggested.

Joe agreed. "Exactly. When that young man vanished, it was as if he'd been grabbed by a flying saucer. No witnesses, no evidence, nothing left behind. I'm sure you all remember. Well, most of you do. But we took his life apart—friends, family, teachers, schoolmates, you name it. Nothing came up. He was there one minute, gone the next."

He pointed at the phone. "And now this."

"Was it charged when Fred checked it out?" Lester asked.

"Good question," Joe replied. "No, it was not. And its software was way out of date. I have no idea what Fred did to get it running, but it functions."

"You think it may be a souvenir?" Sam ventured.

Joe nodded. "Could be."

"Les and I," she continued, "were thinking of retracing Don's travels using the downloaded GPS map from the car's navigation system. Try to trace not only the places he hit but whoever he might've sold things to along the way."

"He was like an old-fashioned peddler," Willy threw in. "From what I got from Corey Browne and Darren Bader, he often stole and sold as he went, depending on the route and who he knew."

"Good idea. That's what I got from Trevor Buttner, too," Joe confirmed. "Buttner even said he was never sure whenever he saw Don whether he was there to sell, steal, or shoot the shit. He described the kid as a bit of a klepto. Couldn't resist anything small, shiny, and lying in plain view."

"Is that Trevor's explanation about how his porno phone ended up with Don?" Lester asked.

"It is," Joe answered. "Supposedly, during booking at the hospital, he claimed that a watch, some drugs, and a little money went missing after Trevor hit the can to take a leak."

"Hang on," Willy protested. "If Don had stolen from me before, I'd never let him in again, and I'd kick his ass next time I saw him."

Joe pushed back. "I asked him about that," he said. "He claimed they were friends and Don had sold him a thing or two in the past, and he'd never stolen from him before. This was a first."

Willy wasn't buying it. "We're being told Don had a network.

How do you maintain that if you steal from your friends? I think Trevor's covering something up."

"Could be Trevor wasn't his buddy," Sam suggested, "Melissa Monfet was. If Don came by to see her and Trevor only found out about it later, wouldn't he try to save face? He strikes me as a macho type."

"Did Trevor say he got a lead on where Don went next, after he'd left their apartment?" Lester asked.

"No," Joe said. "His story is that he called around and got nowhere."

"Maybe because everybody thinks Trevor's an asshole," Willy suggested, "and wouldn't tell him. That might support Sam's idea."

Joe asked directly, "You saying Melissa and Don were an item?"

"Not necessarily," Sam said. "Just that Trevor wasn't the reason Don was there. It would explain why Don felt free to grab some of Trevor's stuff as he headed out: he didn't care about Trevor."

"Okay," Joe agreed. "Sounds good as a theory." He looked at Willy. "You met Robin Whiteman. Did she say anything about Don cheating on her?"

"I didn't have the chance to ask," Willy explained. "But I will when I talk to her again."

Joe scratched his neck thoughtfully. "Good. This has *all* been good. We've definitely identified a few paths to explore. Willy, go for that longer conversation with Whiteman. Sam and Lester? I like your idea of retracing Don's last journey. And if you're right about Melissa being the reason Don was at that apartment, it becomes an additional reason Trevor Buttner had an axe to grind. I'd like to put Trevor in the frame for killing Don if that's where he belongs, so maybe a chat with Melissa will help."

"What about Scooter?" Sam asked.

"That's on your plate, too," Joe told her. "Don Kalfus grabbed that phone from somewhere. Let's hope you and Les get lucky and find out where."

"And Shaw meeting Kalfus at the strip club?" Lester asked. "We still leaving that on the back burner?"

"You and Sam're going to pick up Don's trail in that parking lot," Joe replied. "Keep your eyes open for exactly why he might've stolen that particular car. We will be shining more light on Mr. and Mrs. Shaw, but when we do, it would help to have more weighing them down than a marital spat with a couple of unexplained loopholes."

The squad began readying to disperse, when Joe glanced down at his desk and saw a printout from the ME's office.

"One extra piece of news," he spoke over the general rustling. "I heard from Dr. Hillstrom that she found a long sliver of wood in Don Kalfus's head wound. Likely cause of death was single blunt force trauma, as Sammie suspected, but now we have a vague idea of the instrument used."

"Baseball bat?" Willy aired generally. "How quaint. I guess the candlestick was missing."

"Beverly thinks not," Joe answered seriously. "She suggests we look for something like a two-by-four."

CHAPTER SIX

"Hey, hon," Lester greeted his wife, dropping his coat over the back of a chair and settling in beside her on the couch facing the TV. "Looks like I'm gonna be spending quality time with another woman for a few days."

Sue, still in scrubs, kissed him and replied, "Sammie again? When're you two going to make it official?"

Lester laughed. "Probably two minutes before Willy cuts my throat with a KA-BAR."

She muted the sound on the local news. "What're you two up to?"

"It's very cool, actually," he replied. "We got a printout of a stolen car's GPS, and we're going to follow everywhere the guy went before somebody knocked him off."

She made a face. "Delightful. You do the funnest things."

"I know, right?" he responded, nudging her in the ribs. He then tugged on the top half of her scrubs. "You coming or going? I forget."

"Just back," she said, putting her sneakered feet up on the coffee table. "I covered for somebody today, so I got the night off."

He still had hold of her top and now pulled on it enough to admire what lay underneath. "You're kidding," he said more softly. "We get to spend the whole night together?"

She gently pushed his hand away as he kissed her neck. "Unless you get called out again for another body. Plus, I thought you were seeing another woman."

This time, he slipped his hand up under the top and laid it on her bare stomach. "That's not until tomorrow," he said, adding, "Where's Wendy?"

She left his hand where it was this time and kissed his ear. "She's due back in half an hour, tops, tiger, and I want more of you than that, so hold that thought."

"I will," he chuckled, running his hand higher up. "I promise."

"The wood splinter was a hit," Joe said on the phone. He was lying on the couch at home, an open can of vienna sausages balanced on his chest, competing for Gilbert's attention. The cat was on Gunther's stomach, batting at his hand every time Joe extracted another tempting offer. Their eyes were locked throughout this contest. A second can, of fruit cocktail in heavy syrup, awaited its turn as dessert on the nearby coffee table. This was of no interest to Gilbert.

"You are so romantic," Beverly responded. "So which one opined that it came from a baseball bat?"

His eyes widened. "Do you have my office bugged? How the hell did you know that? It was Willy."

She sounded dismissive. "It had to be someone, but I would have expected better of him. Such a cliché."

"It was a throwaway. We know we're looking for something rougher. You are dealing with the Four Musketeers of homicide, you know."

He could just envision her expression at that. He popped another sausage into his mouth.

"What are you eating?"

"Sorry. You weren't supposed to notice that. Very rude."

"Less the act of eating than the likely ingredients, knowing you," she commented. "A shish kebab of Spam and Velveeta?"

"What a horrible idea," he protested as Gilbert gave up and thrust his paw right into the can, causing Joe to grab hold of it.

"Is the case proceeding well?" she asked, wisely moving on.

"Depends on which part you're asking about," he replied. "That car was as full of separate cases as it was of stolen goods. Thankfully, we're only interested in the juicy ones—your customer, Don Kalfus, being on top of the list. But Scooter Nelson's made an appearance, too, in the form of his missing flip phone from back then."

"He was the preteen who vanished without a trace?" she asked.

"The same. There's nothing on the phone that we've found yet, but the mere fact that it ended up in Don's stolen car is intriguing enough. Sam and Lester are retracing Don's travels to see if they can find out where he stole it from."

"If he stole it," she countered.

"True," he conceded. "That was his job, though."

"It might have been in the car before he came into possession," she suggested.

He was familiar with her scientist's reluctance to presume. "Granted. But that would imply it belonged to Lemuel Shaw, begging the question: Why would he be driving around with a keepsake like that? The car postdates the kid's disappearance by years. Did he hang on to it like other people suspend family crucifixes from their rearview mirrors, moving it every time he bought a new set of wheels? Plus, it was found in the trunk."

"You're asking if human beings are capable of eccentric and in-explicable actions?" she asked.

"Fair enough. We are looking at Lemuel, or both Shaws, for other reasons. Their story about his whereabouts when the car was stolen has holes, as does Mrs. Shaw's role in it. For one thing, we're not sure he and Don Kalfus didn't know each other before-hand."

"This is sounding like a game of six degrees of separation."

Joe put a delicate damper on that idea. "Well, only if that last part is true. We only know they had a fight at the strip club that suggests ancient history. Could be each of them was having a bad day and just lashed out. We're keeping our options open. Between you and me? I think Don was a thief by nature and saw an opportunity to grab Shaw's car. Pure and simple. Let's not forget Shaw reported the loss to police pretty fast, immedi-ately after trying to tidy up his appetite for barely clad female anatomies."

"Poor Mrs. Shaw," Beverly said.

Joe snorted. "Don't go overboard there, either. It sounded like she reminded Lester of a hard-edged Wanda Sykes. Warm, cuddly, and vulnerable she is not."

"Have you ever visited a club like that?" she asked him.

"Only professionally. Not to my taste."

"I have," she confessed.

He laughed hard enough to threaten his dinner and send Gil-bert leaping for a calmer perch. "*Really?*"

"Yes. Rachel's father thought it would be a good idea if we went."

Rachel Reiling was Beverly's daughter, now a reporter living in Brattleboro. Beverly and her husband, a high-powered Burlington attorney, had divorced many years earlier, and while each was loving and attentive to Rachel, neither kept in touch with the other. It had been, in the vernacular, a "civilized" parting of the ways. Joe had heard rumors that Mr. Reiling had always had an eye for women not his wife.

But mention of attending a strip club was a surprise nevertheless. "That must've been awkward," he said, impressed if not surprised by her customary imperturbability.

Ever the analyst, she replied, "It was interesting, less for the floor show than for what made him think such an outing would benefit the marriage."

The next day's weather was an offshoot of the rain twenty-four hours earlier, offering the worst of an early New England spring—foggy, bone-chilling, and sloppy underfoot—combined with winter's deep snow and propensity to turn moisture into ice. As Joe drove out of Vermont and entered New Hampshire to visit Melissa Monfet in Keene, he kept a wary eye for black ice, as he had watched his footing in the parking lot upon setting out. Bing Crosby had never warbled about breaking his neck while dreaming of a white Christmas, telling Joe the old crooner had never experienced a season like this one—if he'd ever visited New England at all.

The old and worn apartment complex where Melissa Monfet lived was all the more depressing as a result, its barracks-like grayness and monotonous, cracked vinyl siding almost blending into the lowering, threatening sky.

He hadn't called ahead. That was rarely a good move, even with the chance that a drop-by visit could result in no answer. For that matter, a forewarned interviewee often guaranteed a wasted trip.

And Melissa's visible disappointment upon opening the door told Joe that the currency of surprise was holding its value.

"Oh," she said bitterly, "it's you," before turning and retreating down the hall.

"Mind if I come in?" he called after her.

"As if I could stop you," she answered, not bothering to look back.

He took that as permission and followed her into the familiar living room, as disheveled as ever. Over time, visiting so many such homes had encouraged Gunther to leave his own every morning neat and tidy, with his bed made and dishes washed. One of many odd by-products of being a societal proctor.

Monfet flopped into a rickety armchair, barely missing a cat, who escaped with inches to spare. "You people put my man in jail and took my kids away, and from what social services and the lawyers're saying, I'm probably looking at jail time myself. What the fuck more do you want?"

"There's a murder to talk about," Joe said conversationally, taking a seat himself.

"A *murder*?" she reacted. "Oh, that's perfect. Of *course* there's a murder. Why didn't I think of that? I'm the cooperative one, after all. The one always doing favors. Why not dump it all on me? Who did I murder, policeman? I want to get his name right for the trial. Don't wanna embarrass anybody, after all. Hell, it might look like you framed me or something, and we wouldn't want that."

Joe waited until she caught her breath. "Don Kalfus," he said.

It stopped her cold. She stared at him, her mouth half-open.

"He was beaten to death and shoved into the trunk of a car," Joe finished.

"Donny?" she echoed softly. "Oh, no."

"When did you last see him?" Joe asked.

"About a week ago."

"Trevor wasn't here?"

"Not at first."

A picture of what must have happened filled Joe's brain. "He came home unexpectedly."

"Yeah."

"He caught you."

Her earlier bluster vanished; she looked suddenly frail and smaller, embraced by the ratty chair. Even the cat returned, perhaps sensing a need to lend comfort.

"Yeah," she repeated, barely audibly.

"You and Donny were an item," Joe suggested.

"He was really nice."

Something Robin Whiteman might agree with, Joe thought. "How long had you known each other that way?"

"Not long. A few months. He was sort of a bar buddy of Trevor's."

"Until that day."

"Yeah."

"What happened?"

She pointed at the couch against the wall. "We were there. He walked in."

"And?"

She looked slightly surprised. "Not much. He was pissed, but it wasn't that big a deal. He pulls the same shit on me all the time. I don't care. I didn't think he'd kill somebody over it."

"You think that's what happened?" Joe asked. "Trevor killed Don for what you and he did together?"

"I didn't till now," she answered vaguely. "Isn't that what you're saying?"

"Take me back," Joe requested. "Trevor walks in and finds you two."

"He yelled, we . . . rearranged ourselves. Then it was like no big whoop. I might as well've been his sister, for all he cared."

"Trevor?"

"Yeah. Said something like, 'If you're doin' her, you might as well have a beer, too,' or somethin'. And he got Donny a beer."

"Did you believe him?"

Melissa was genuinely doubtful. "I didn't know. I woulda been happier if he'd stayed pissed. It made me feel like nothin', you know? The way he was, it was like Donny'd borrowed his car without askin'."

"And Don? How was he?"

"Nervous. I could see it in his eyes. Trevor's a big guy, and he has a short fuse. It's not like they were best pals or nothin'."

Joe was remembering the squad's theory about how this might have gone. "Go on," he urged her. "What happened next?"

"I left. It was too weird. They were starting to tell jokes, talk like it was old times. I went into the bedroom. Next thing I knew, Trevor damned near kicked the door in, lookin' for Donny."

"What do you mean?"

"He'd gone. Donny had. And Trevor was really mad. Said he'd stolen stuff."

"What?"

"His phone? I think that was it. And some money. Trevor always emptied his pockets when he got home. He did it this time. I guess he'd gone to the shitter and Donny'd ripped him off and ran. That's how Trevor made it sound."

"What did Trevor say he was going to do about it?"

Melissa regained a fraction of her old contemptuousness. "Well, he didn't say he was gonna kill him, did he? He stormed out and left me alone. I don't know what he did. Probably saw if he could find Donny and get his things back."

"What then?" Joe asked. "A day or two later? How did Trevor seem?"

"How do I know? I wasn't gonna ask him. He was fine."

"He didn't refer to Donny? Or talk about his missing phone?"

"Nope."

"Did you hear from Don again?"

"Nope."

"Did you try contacting him? Texting him?"

"You're kidding," she shot back. "I got lucky. I wasn't gonna mess with that again."

Because Trevor Buttner was such a catch, Joe thought. He considered asking her about Trevor's relationship with Angie Neal, and perhaps even Melissa's dreams and hopes concerning her daughter's future, but then figured he didn't want to hear what she'd say. He'd let Fred Houston handle that.

He did take one shot into the dark, hoping for a miracle. "Did you ever hear Don talk about someone named Scooter Nelson?"

The answer wasn't unexpected. "Nope."

"You got red, Daddy?"

Willy pulled a red crayon from the box by his side. "Sure do."

He slid it across the kitchen table to his daughter, who was studiously filling in a rainbow arching over the top of several stick children kicking a ball in a field.

Willy was busy with the picture of a weeping willow tree next to a house.

"Thank you, Daddy."

"You're welcome, Emma. That's coming along well. Are you happy with it?"

"I want to give it to Mommy."

"She'll like that. You want something to drink?"

The girl looked up. "Ooh. Yes. Can I have a chocolate milk?"

He rose and crossed to the fridge. "Sure. I'll have it ready wicked fast."

"Wicked fast," she mimicked, getting back to work.

It was late afternoon. He'd given Louise the day off, picked Emma up from preschool, and would do a shift change with Sam when she got back from her day trip with Les. That's when Willy was planning to leave for his more detailed conversation with Robin Whiteman.

It was one of the perks of working for VBI and under Joe Gunther that he could rearrange his schedule on the fly. He conceded that the agency got far more out of him than he was contracted to deliver, but he appreciated the flexibility and trust imparted in the exchange.

He needed it more nowadays, he realized. Never before had he seen time off work as more than the edge of a black hole. From childhood on, lack of mission equaled loss of control. Then, decades ago, just before self-destruction, he'd traded the NYPD for the Brattleboro PD, the city for the country, alcohol for abstinence, and a failed marriage for uninterrupted work. It had not been graceful. He knew how he'd come across—at best irascible, judgmental, and sarcastic.

But then had come that crippling bullet, and Sam, and finally Emma.

He gazed at the child as he mixed her chocolate milk with a spoon, still impressed by the depth of emotion he felt for her. Salvation clearly came in unexpected ways. All that was left now was to tame the panic he kept deep within that he'd lose it all through some blindingly stupid false move. People asked him why he didn't replace the arm with something robotic, or just have it amputated to lessen the hassle. *Not likely*, he'd thought. *I earned that arm. It reminds me of my frailty.*

Lester emerged from the car and stretched his arms above his head, making him look to Sammie as if he were standing on stilts.

"My God," he said, "Kalfus sure did love to drive. He shoulda been a cop."

Sam didn't argue. Tracing Shaw's stolen Mercedes was turning out to be as bad as the tangled, knotted, indecipherable GPS print-out had promised. Kalfus had seemingly explored every road available across southwestern New Hampshire, stopping at everything from gas stations to substantial private homes far off the beaten path. At some of these addresses, the two cops had found his victims; at others, they'd been met with blank stares, probably because the people had been in residence at the time. Kalfus might have planned some of his heists, but Sam and Lester were discovering that he'd been equally open to the luck of the draw.

She got to work filling the tank from the pump while Lester entered the station to talk with the manager. As agreed, they were proceeding methodically, hitting each stop in sequence. There had been some discussion about matching Kalfus's timetable as well, but the man had apparently rarely slept, presumably catnapping in the car to better hide his activities, but also, Sam imagined, so as not to be picked up during busy traffic hours driving a stolen car. As a result, she and Les had chosen largely daylight hours for their multi-day expedition.

Not to mention that each had families to see at night.

Lester came out only fifteen minutes later, holding a thumb drive aloft for her to see. "Believe it or not," he announced as he got in and slammed the door shut, "the little bastard only stopped

for gas this time. No schmoozing, no groceries, no beer or cigarettes."

Sam was studying the map printout, calculating their next leg.
"It looks like he was on a mission this time."

Lester leaned toward her to read the document. "Really?"

Kalfus had not been given to long stretches, any more than he'd
been fond of busy roads. But now, it was clear that from where they
were presently—a little west of Manchester—they were to drive a
long way to somewhere north of Keene.

"Back there again?" Lester complained. "What did he have
against the coast? Or somewhere scenic? This guy was a total work-
aholic."

Sam recalled the text message they'd received earlier from Joe.
"He did drop by to see Melissa Monfet. That didn't sound like
work."

"Okay. Point taken. One exception."

They hadn't reached their own stopping point for the day yet.
It looked like that would come after the trip they were about to
take.

As they headed off, Lester ruminated, "I know why we're tracking him this way, and I'm not sorry, but the difference between his
timeline and ours does kind of throw me off."

"We can match that if we ever think it's crucial, somehow," Sam
said. "But much as I enjoy your company, I don't want to use your
shoulder as a pillow."

It took them almost two hours to cover what should have been a
sixty-mile trip, again because the GPS directed them down every
country lane and virtual cow path it could find.

Nevertheless, by the time they'd arrived, the reward proved
worth the effort.

"Wow," Lester said as Sam pulled off the road and killed the engine, a quarter mile from their goal, which they could see through the windshield, high above them on the hill. "It's just like they say: déjà vu all over again."

"I didn't see this happening," Sam agreed.

They were looking at the ostentatious near castle of Lemuel and Lucy Shaw.

"Does this go back to the fight Don and Shaw had at the club?" Lester asked.

"Could be. Nothing we've found so far connects Kalfus in any way to Shaw before that night. Am I right about that?" Sam asked.

"Not according to any fusion reports or database we've read," he replied.

"So, out of the blue, in the middle of a shopping spree that brings him damn near to Manchester, he suddenly takes off and heads for the house of the man he stole the car from? Why?"

Deep in thought, Lester didn't respond.

Sammie pressed on. "Did we find anything in that vehicle belonging to Shaw? I mean, beside the usual junk everybody carries around like flashlights, pens, and coffee mugs?"

"Not that we know of," Les answered carefully. "Why?"

"Because it implies that while he stole the fancy car, he didn't drive straight to the rich guy's house to steal even more. It's what I would've done."

"Because he and Shaw were in cahoots?" Les ventured.

"Then why steal the car in the first place?"

"To embarrass him?"

"Lucy already knew about his appetite."

"Kalfus may not have known that."

Sam shook her head, still wondering. "What do you remember about being in that house?" She gestured toward the log mansion.

Lester considered that carefully, knowing what she was asking. "Depends," he eventually answered. "In her bedroom, there were a ton of baubles that would fit in your pocket. But where we met with hubby? Everything looked too big or was mounted to the wall. It also looked more like an office building than a home. Of course, we only saw a small part of the house."

"We didn't find much jewelry in the car, did we?"

"A piece or two."

"That's interesting, isn't it?" she asked. "I'd assume jewelry would be a natural, given some of the houses we've visited. Plus, the owners we interviewed told us their jewelry went missing."

"Meaning Kalfus unloaded them first thing," Lester filled in.

There was a silence as they each weighed their thoughts.

"That leaves another question: If something was stolen from here," Sam asked, "why not report the loss, especially if you've already called in the car theft?"

This time, when Willy bounced his way along the rutted lane toward the Whitemans' trailer, it was earlier, with a remnant of daylight still staining the sky through the scraggly canopy of old and neglected pine trees.

His intention had been to ask Robin to join him in the front seat of his car, where he often conducted interviews privately but in plain sight. But as soon as he'd rapped on the tinny aluminum door and Robin opened up, she announced, "My folks are out. You might as well come in."

Given the trailer park's worn appearance and this particular trailer's bedraggled looks, Willy's expectations of its interior were low. He was not anticipating making himself comfortable within it, nor even accepting any standard offer of coffee.

He stood pleasantly corrected. The place was not new, nor was it ritzy. Nothing could have made it those. But it was clean, fresh smelling, neat, bright, and homey.

He looked around admiringly. "Nice place," he commented.

"Thanks," Robin said. "My folks can't afford to fix up the outside, but they work hard at this. Coffee?"

Willy sat in the built-in alcove by the door, amused by his own prejudice. "It shows. Thanks. I think I will. How're you holding up?"

"I'm still a little numb. The way Don acted when I was with him, being in danger just didn't seem like part of it. He made it look like fun."

He noticed as she was preparing the coffee that her finger no longer sported the ring Kalfus had given her.

"You knew he was stealing from people."

"I know," she conceded. "And I know that's not right. It's why I didn't go with him the one time he invited me. I told him it was wrong. But he kept telling me he was careful, that he only stole from rich people who had insurance and that they took advantage of being robbed to trade up. You know, get a better watch or computer or whatever. He made it sound like a service, almost."

And you swallowed that because it served you, too, Willy thought, who didn't take the bait.

"Last time we talked, Robin," he said instead, "you admitted the ring he gave you was probably stolen." He noticed her closing her hand as if trying to hide what he'd already seen. "That being the case," he went on, "and boys being boys and liking to brag, I'm betting he told you about his adventures now and then. Am I right?"

"Sometimes," she answered vaguely.

"In fact, you told me about Corey Browne, who you obviously met, since you thought he was scary."

She poured him a mug of coffee from the machine and gestured with it, asking, "You want anything in it?"

He extended his hand. "No, that's good. Thanks."

She poured herself a mug but stayed at the counter. He indicated the bench opposite him at the breakfast table insert. "Sit, Robin. Make yourself comfortable."

She did as instructed, although comfortable was not a part of it.

"I'm going to take a flier here," he said, "and suggest you haven't been totally straight with me."

She flared up with a weak show of protest. "I answered your questions."

"More or less," he agreed. "But I seriously doubt you missed out on joining him for at least one escapade."

She stared down at her untouched cup, resting on the polished tabletop. "Maybe."

"Where to?"

"Stratton. You know: All those mansions they got next to the slopes."

"How did you do it? Just driving around till you found a place, or was it more targeted?"

She spoke barely above a whisper. "He knew where he was going."

"Tell me about it."

"It was big. Real fancy. We weren't there too long. Under an hour."

Willy sampled his coffee. "No, Robin. Break it down. You know what I want to hear. Step by step." He raised the mug. "Good coffee, by the way."

She half smiled, caught off guard, and perhaps starting to

believe his benevolent tone. "Thanks. He had a key. No, wait. He knew where it was. He got it out of one of those fake rocks, near the door."

"He explain that?"

"Yeah. Said one of the cleaning crew was a friend of his."

"So you got in," Willy suggested.

"Yeah, but there was an alarm. That made me nervous, but Don just typed in the code and that was it."

"Okay, keep going."

"That's all. He collected what he wanted, and we left."

"Just like that. In and out. Five minutes."

She hesitated.

"I didn't think so," Willy said. "Like I said, he wanted to show off. Details, Robin."

"He gave me a tour," she admitted.

"He'd been there before?"

"No. We were exploring. It was like visiting a museum or something. They had everything—pool table, big fireplace, a sauna, even a racquetball court. At least that's what Don said it was. I never seen one. They had a telescope, too, in one of the bedrooms. He said they probably checked out their neighbors with it, since it wasn't aimed at the sky. We played with that for a while. He was right. You could see some of the other places really well."

Willy read between the lines and suggested, "One of the bedrooms, huh? I'm guessing one thing led to another?"

Her face reddened. "Maybe. I guess."

He let it be. "And after you were done, he got to business. How did he go about collecting what he wanted? Had you brought a bag along?"

"Yes. A big backpack."

"Did he know where to go? Seem to know what he was after?"

She was shaking her head. "He was talking as we went, telling me why he was taking some things and not others. It was all about moving the product. That's how he said it. You didn't want anything too fancy or too big. You wanted regular, high-end stuff. Watches, laptops, jewelry that wasn't antique or have inscriptions. He looked really closely at that to make sure."

"What else?"

"Money, for sure. I couldn't believe how much was in drawers and closets. A couple of guns, a camera, two clocks, and some glass things he called Steuben or something, off a bookshelf. We found some drugs. And medicine," she added as an afterthought. "He looked at that carefully, too. Said some of it had good street value." Her voice trailed off. "I don't know. Junk like that. I got sort of bored and ended up watching TV till he was done. That's all I remember, but he almost filled the bag."

"And afterward?"

"We left. He set the alarm, locked the door, and that was it."

"Except for unloading the goods. Is that how you met Corey?"

"Yeah. He wasn't happy Don brought me along. They had a fight about that."

"A real fight?"

"No. I mean an argument."

"Did Don unload everything?"

"About half of it. He told me he had different people who fenced different things. That was why he collected the way he did, picking and choosing. That's what he said."

"Did you meet other fences?"

"It didn't go well with Corey, so that was it."

"Any more shopping sprees at other people's houses?" Willy asked, purposefully keeping his tone light.

"No. Like I said, I got kinda bored. And I didn't want to get caught, 'specially for not doin' nothin'."

Willy moved on. "Did Don make a lot of money?"

"I suppose."

"This is all he did for income?"

"No. He did other things. He said it helped him check people out, but I did wonder if it had something to do with not having enough money. He used to complain that the fences never paid him enough and that moving to California or someplace would probably be better for him."

"What sorts of jobs did he take on?"

"He was a cabbie for a while. He delivered packages. What do they call it? A courier. He was one of those. He was a bouncer."

"Where did he do that?"

"Keene. Some strip club."

"Tell me about that."

"Nothing to tell. It was on the edge of town. That was recent. I just dropped him off. I never went in. That's not my thing."

"Why didn't he drive himself?"

"No car," she answered simply.

Willy wasn't expecting that. "He only drove cars he stole?"

"I suppose. He didn't seem to have one. I was happy the bouncer job fell through, 'cause I didn't want to drive him way out there every night."

"What happened?"

"Another fight. That's how he got the fancy car you asked about. The one he drove up to Windsor and back. He said he got into a fight with one of the old guys who drink one beer all night and sit in the back and ogle the girls, and so he stole the geezer's wheels. That's how he put it. Got his keys right out of the man's coat pocket. Don was laughing his head off about that."

"Wasn't he worried the owner would report him?"

"I wondered that, too. Don said he used a fake ID. The owner didn't really know who he was."

"Did Kalfus know this older man—the car owner?"

"Not that he told me."

Willy leaned back, sipped again from his coffee, and checked his watch. He rose then and explained, "I have to make a quick phone call outside. You good for a few minutes more? I don't have much left to ask, but while I'm doing this, try to remember whatever else Don told you about the strip club fight, okay?"

"Sure."

He stepped out into the cold night air and crossed to his car. Getting in, he pulled out his phone and turned on the dome light, which he rarely did.

This was a special situation.

"Hello?" Sammie said after the third ring.

"Hey," he replied. "She still up?"

Sam laughed. "What the hell's going on? She said you were going to read to her. I told her you were working, but she wouldn't believe me. Really dug in her heels."

"Yeah. Sorry I'm a little late. You in her room?"

"Yup. I was trying to replace you, not too successfully."

"Put it on speaker."

He did the same with his cell, pulled over a copy of *Goodnight Moon* from his passenger seat, and asked, "You hear me, sweetheart?"

"I hear you, Daddy. Mommy didn't believe me," Emma said.

"I was going to surprise you both. You ready?"

Sam said, "We are."

"You all tucked in, Emma?"

"I am, Daddy."

"Okay. Here goes. *In the great green room,*" he began, "*There was a telephone and a red balloon . . .*"

Ten minutes later, he returned to the trailer to wrap up his interview with Robin Whiteman, content that tonight, at least, he'd done a little more than just chase bad guys.

CHAPTER SEVEN

Lester slid back into Willy's living room armchair, a second piece of pizza balanced on his paper plate. "If this outfit ever adopts parliamentary rule, I vote we hold all our briefings here," he said, setting the plate on his lap and reaching for a half-empty beer bottle.

"Never happen," Willy responded shortly.

They were keeping their voices low for Emma's sake, although they all imagined it would take a small explosion to roust her from her slumber at the far end of the hallway.

This was very pleasant. Joe could only agree. He'd sprung for the meal, which he'd never pass along as a business expense. These were perks he kept off the books.

"That being said," he addressed their hosts, "thank you for letting us invade your home for this."

Willy hoisted his own slice of pie. "You're paying for it."

Sam gave her partner a look before replying, "It's a pleasure, boss. Thanks for being flexible, and the meal. It's nice not to always call on the sitter."

"Good word to start with," Joe picked up. "Flexibility being our operative mode right now. And things seem to be shifting as we speak."

"Just more three-dimensional," Sam countered. "We'd never heard about Don Kalfus before, then we got a picture of a good son and a steady boyfriend, even if he was a crook. Now we're finding he was a little flexible himself in the fidelity department."

"And probably smarter than I'd first guessed," Willy admitted.

"Not so smart now," Lester pointed out.

"Maybe just unlucky," Willy argued. "Think of it. Your whole life is sneaking around, poking your nose where it doesn't belong, stealing from one set of strangers and selling to people who'd just as soon rip you off or trade you for a plea deal. I'd say he did okay for as long as he lasted."

"You like this guy?" Sam asked, surprised.

"I don't *like* him. I just mean he had a certain animal cunning going for him. Which also means," Willy added, "that I don't think his screwing Melissa Monfet is the last rabbit he's gonna pull out of his hat."

"Well," Joe said. "Rabbits are why we're here. I sure wasn't expecting the Shaws to pop up again like they have."

"No," Les agreed, taking another swig. "Us, neither."

"What do you make of it?" Joe asked generally.

"Could be several things," Sam suggested. "Or a combination of them. The obvious one is they had a fight that caused Don to steal Shaw's car, probably out of spite, which then prompted him to burgle the Shaw house later. It was what he did, after all."

"How did he know where Shaw lived?" Lester asked.

"Same reason he took his time before doing it," Willy answered, asking, "What's the one thing every stolen car has on board, regardless of age, rank, or serial number?"

"Its Twenty-Eight," Sam replied, using ten-code to refer to a car's registration.

"Usually kept in the glove compartment," Willy said. "So while Don was rummaging around Shaw's fancy ride, he found the reg and decided on the spur of the moment to find out what other toys the old man had. That would fit."

"How 'bout he drove up there to blackmail Shaw?" Lester proposed.

"Over what?" Willy challenged him. "Shaw had already called his wife to pick him up."

"Did Don know that?" Les came back. "For all he knew, Shaw hired a cab. It's what I woulda done."

Willy chuckled. "To have Sue meet you at the door with a shotgun."

"What about the fight at the club?" Sam asked. "We keep pushing that around. First, it means they knew each other from before, then it was a setup so Don could justify storming off and stealing a stranger's car. Are we missing something there?"

"Probably," Willy muttered. "We usually do." In a louder voice, he added, "Robin told me Don didn't know Shaw before stealing the car."

"I'm not necessarily saying he did," Sam persisted. "All of it—the fight, the car theft, the later trip to Shaw's house—could be connected somehow. It's not that it's smaller than we're thinking; it might be way bigger."

"What do we know about Lemuel Shaw?" Joe asked.

"We did the usual checks," Willy replied. "But we didn't hit up New Hampshire's Information Analysis Center for one of their . . . what do they call their reports? It's got a funny name."

"Products," Lester said.

"Right. And what about NESPIN?"

That was the more extensive New England database that the state police used. "Yes on Kalfus, not yet for Shaw," Lester told them.

"Throw in Lucy Shaw while you're at it," Joe recommended. "I don't want the Shaws becoming a distraction, but they are growing in importance."

"Before we move on," Sam cautioned, "let's not forget that while they reported the car stolen, they did not report any break-in."

"Because it didn't happen?" Lester asked.

"All right," Joe intervened. "Let's put them aside until those backgrounds come back with something meatier. Willy, you mentioned a remeet with Robin."

"Yeah. She's another case of waters running deeper. Turns out, she went joyriding with Don, breaking into a place in Stratton, putting the master bed to good use, and filling a backpack with trophies. Suddenly quite the party girl. She's claiming she didn't know who knocked him off, but she did describe Don as someone with a fuse."

"Does that bring you back to Corey Browne?" Joe asked. "You said he wasn't happy with Don."

Willy made an equivocal gesture with his hand. "Browne told me they kissed and made up, before suggesting I talk to Darren Bader. All these losers are kind of the same that way. Like I reported before, Bader told me about some mysterious somebody who was supposedly looking for Don, whatever that means. Could've been the amazing flying Trevor Buttner; could've been Shaw; could've been pure fiction. Who knows?"

"You don't think either Corey or Darren did him in?" Lester asked.

Willy was unusually candid. "I don't know. As Don becomes more complicated, his potential enemies list grows. Speaking of which, I did ask Robin toward the end if she ever thought he'd cheated on her. She seemed surprised by the idea, and for what it's worth, I believed her." He paused a moment before adding, "And I don't think we should walk away from Cheri Pratt without a second thought, either."

"Oh?"

"Talking about Browne and Bader reminded me that Corey said Cheri probably taught Don everything he knew. His quote was Cheri knew 'what was what.' While we're putting people under microscopes, it wouldn't hurt to include her." He fixed his boss with a look. "What happened between you and Trevor's love goddess, Melissa?"

"Let's start by admitting," Joe replied, "that none of them will be spokespeople for eHarmony anytime soon. That being said, we were right about her canoodling with Don. And Trevor did walk in on them. But according to her, he blew up fast and cooled down faster, to the point where she headed off to bed because the two boys were getting along too well and her feelings got hurt."

"You believe that?"

"Not for a second. Melissa told me Don ripped off Trevor on his way out the door, while Trevor was using the can. Trevor beat feet after him, but that's all she ever heard about it. She never asked, and Trevor never told."

"So he might've whacked him," Lester mused.

"Without taking back the phone?" Willy challenged him. "Unlikely."

"Unless there were complications that got in his way," Les countered. "Like he couldn't find it afterward."

Willy, opinionated but open to this kind of back-and-forth, nodded. "True," he said. "Okay."

"Willy," Joe asked him, "just to switch things up, you want to take Trevor Buttner around the block for another heart-to-heart?"

"Absolutely," Willy agreed.

"Sam and Les," Joe addressed them. "You're still working Don's last walkabout, so to speak. Given what you're finding, I don't want to get in the way of that. In the meantime, I'll swap with Willy and go after Corey Browne."

"What about Cheri Pratt?" Sam asked.

Joe replied, "Willy and I will compare notes after we've finished with Trevor and Corey. One of us will take her on at that point. Her background report might've come in by then, too." He glanced at Kunkle. "Work for you?"

"You know me, boss," Willy answered him. "I am putty in your hands."

The laughter risked waking up Emma at the far end of the house.

In contrast to the rain earlier in the week, it was snowing the next day when Joe pulled up opposite a ramshackle business on Canal Street named Hughie's. A licensed bar, Hughie's was otherwise difficult to describe. It had no outward appeal. The building it occupied had a narrow side door leading to apartments upstairs and a more centralized but completely unmarked entrance in the middle. It was unpainted, poorly maintained, slightly swaybacked, and sported no advertisements revealing its purpose. You either knew about the place or you didn't, and the owner—named Pete and not Hughie, whom nobody had ever met—didn't care.

Surprisingly, Pete was a pleasant, easygoing man, if a large and imposing one. His encounters with police, licensing agents, and the town's board of selectmen had always been cordial and cooperative. No one Joe knew understood the business logic of running an anonymous bar, but its longevity spoke to its word-of-mouth appeal.

Hughie's did in fact cater to a specialized clientele, and where the establishment rarely caught official attention, its customers were a well-known lot to Brattleboro police.

Corey Browne among them.

It was early by most societal standards, being ten o'clock in the morning, but this bar was where Joe had been told to go first to find Corey, and, as he stamped his feet free of the damp snow and closed the door behind him, he could see several patrons already sprinkled about the long, dark, low-ceilinged room. Most of them were alone, all of them silent, and each had a bottle or mug stationed before him. They were all men.

Joe unzipped his coat and shook the snow from his shoulders as he approached the bar running the length of the right wall. The place was very still. There was no music, not even a jukebox, and the TV was on mute. This was a place to drink. Period.

A shambling and bearded behemoth drifted up the bar to greet him, as it turned out, by a title dating many years back. "Lieutenant. Nice to see you. It's been a long time."

Pete held out an enormous meaty hand, which Joe shook as he might grasp a slab of beef. "Pete. Good to see you, too. You been well, I hope?"

"Can't complain. Nobody would listen anyhow."

Joe nodded at the shopworn phrase.

"Can I interest you in anything?" Pete asked. "If I remember, you were a Coke man."

Joe gave him a startled look. "My God. How long ago was that? Twenty years?"

The smile was barely visible under the thick beard. "It pays to remember these things."

Joe couldn't refuse him now. "Okay, I'll take a glass. Sure."

It was readily delivered, upon which, Pete knew to ask, "Now that that's done, why are you really here?"

This was someone used to dealing with a particular slice of civilization.

"Corey Browne," Joe responded, taking a sip of his beverage. "He here?"

Pete pointed with a sausage-sized finger. "Corner booth. You can just see the top of his head. Should I be prepared for anything?"

Joe wrapped a napkin around his frosty glass and made to head for the back of the room. "I hope not. I'm only aiming for a conversation."

"Have a good one, then."

There's a psychology to how and where to sit in a bar like Hughie's. Someone like Willy, despite being a teetotaler, spent considerable time in bars, and always put a wall to his back and his eyes on the door. That usually meant near the bathroom or the kitchen. Others, too preoccupied by their own private miseries to care, settled for a stool, where continual lubrication could be maintained by rapping on the bar. People like Corey—more secretive, less watchful, perhaps as much in need of harbor as alcohol, tended to orient toward corners and relative invisibility. These were folks who saw each day as containing far too many daylight hours.

Joe stopped at the booth and looked down at the man whose face he knew only from a mug shot at the office that morning.

"Corey Browne?" he asked, placing his glass on the table, removing his coat, and sliding onto the bench opposite.

Browne stared at him openmouthed. "Who the fuck're you? I didn't say you could sit down."

"I'm a colleague of Willy Kunkle's," Joe said, using a name that would certainly make more of an impression than his own.

Browne had both hands cupping his beer as if it were a small, nervous pet. "Well, you can leave and tell him to fuck himself when you see him."

"He was telling me about your conversation the other night," Joe began, ignoring the predictable bluster. "I thought we might keep that going."

"You thought wrong."

"The subject," Joe went on, "is still Don Kalfus, and the reason for you to be cooperative remains the legal charges you racked up last time by not thinking before you acted."

"He said those were dropped."

"Actually, he didn't. He just let you go. The charges haven't been filed. Yet. And who knows? They might not be."

Browne gave his beer a thoughtful quarter turn on the tabletop before sighing wearily. "What d'you want now?"

"There's a feeling among my colleagues that you coughed up Darren Bader because you knew more than you wanted to tell, and Darren was a good patsy. But Darren was a dead end, as you knew he'd be."

"That's not my fault. I heard Darren was ticked off at Kalfus. I told Kunkle about it, just like he asked. How was I supposed to know how that would turn out? I'm no mind reader."

"You still know more than you told Kunkle. You and Don did a lot of business together. You said he'd pass along whatever prescription drugs he came across, but it was more than that. I've been asking around about you. You also handled electronics for him, as you do for others—and small antiques, guns, portable and valuable pieces that rich people like to show off. You're a broad-minded fence, Corey. A man for all seasons."

"If you say so."

"The Vermont State Police say so, and the Brattleboro cops, among others."

"Fine."

"So, with that on the table," Joe continued, "let's pick up where

Kunkle left off, but without your tossing around Bader or anyone else to get us out of your hair."

Browne sighed again. "Fine."

"You implied the first time that Don's mom knew what he did for a living, that she might've even played a part or got him started. What was that about?"

Browne smiled. "Cheri? Yeah. She's a piece of work. You ever know her old man? Dave Maccio? Long dead now, but he was a unit. I only heard about him. He was before my time, which is why I thought you might know him. Called himself an antiques dealer, but half the crap he carried was stolen. People don't know that about this part of the woods. They come up here, looking at the cows and trees and shit, buying maple syrup that's probably from Canada—if it's even real—and thinking they're making like bandits at these hole-in-the-wall antique places. Totally clueless that the silver knickknack they just so-called stole for two hundred bucks was ripped off from a little old lady a month before."

He laughed and took a pull from his beer bottle.

"Cheri was a part of that," he explained, "and you know she passed it on to her kid. But he chose the supply side, not the retail end. Sharp, if you ask me. Bigger risks, but better profits."

"Not necessarily," Joe suggested.

Browne was becoming collegial by now. "You mean this?" He held up his bottle. "And the drugs? Yeah, you're right. That's the norm. You pull off a job, you blow it on girls and dope over a single weekend. Bada-bing. End of story." He leaned forward and tapped his temple with his finger. "Not Don Kalfus. He may be dead now, but he was smart."

Joe reserved applause. "Did Cheri work in her son's business?" he asked.

"You ever meet her?" Browne challenged him incredulously. "She might know stuff, but I don't see her playing Ma Barker."

"You think she knows where he kept his overflow? There's rumor of a warehouse or storage shed somewhere."

"I heard that."

"Where?"

"I don't know. Hampton Beach somewhere?"

When Lester was a kid, he'd been told the Inuit had a hundred words for *snow*. He'd imagined that to be an exaggeration, and as an adult, he'd been told fifty was nearer the mark. Being a born New Englander, he did know one thing: the single word, *snow*, didn't cut it.

Right now, for example, as he and Sam were driving through the same snowfall in southern New Hampshire Joe had kicked from his boots in Brattleboro, he was struck by how distinguishable this precipitation was from other forms, and how they all had peculiarities of moisture, density, appearance, and a dozen other characteristics that everyone lumped under the same bland title. Nature was a wonder to him, and programs concerning it his favorite thing to watch on TV, even though he did so alone. His two kids just found it weird, and Sue refused to join him on the basis that every program concluded with some animal eating another.

"You like snow?" he asked Sam.

Living with Willy, she was used to catching fly balls. "Sure, in moderation. This is okay."

She was driving and had the wipers on intermittent only. The snow was free of rain, not coming down hard, and unaccompanied by wind. Given time, it would be just the kind to balance two or three inches high on the twig of every tree, making of their surrounding world in the next morning's sunrise a sparkling, meringue-like opera set.

But not so close to spring. In reality, by morning, all this was forecast to be replaced by rain again, the set doomed before the curtain even rose.

"You already missing it?" she asked him.

"Oh, no. I take it as it comes. I can live without breaking my neck on the ice, but winter or summer, they each have their appeal. I like the warmth and hate the bugs; love the snow and hate to shovel."

He consulted their ever-ready atlas of confusing routes taken, overlaid above the road map, and told her, "Next right."

She glanced at him. "There is no right. You mean coming up?"

"Slow down," he said, squinting. "It's got to be a driveway or a dirt track. Yeah. There."

She checked the rearview mirror and slowed to a crawl. "You sure?"

He gestured with the map. "I'm just the messenger."

Gingerly, she entered an undisturbed, thickly covered track and began creeping along it into a pristine curtain of falling snow.

"I hope to hell there's a turnaround at the end of this."

There was better than that. Emerging like a black-and-white photograph in an old-fashioned developer tray, the ghostly image of an ancient wooden barn took shape.

"This is creepy," she said half to herself. "I'm happy it's not after dark."

"You see any other buildings?" Lester asked, turning around in his seat and checking all windows.

Sam pulled to a stop fifteen feet from the barn's door. It wasn't large, not much beyond an oversized shed. Made of raw wood, a story and a half tall, equally wide and deep, its roof under the snow looked stressed and imperiled.

Both of them left the car without saying a word, their coats unbuttoned so they could reach their weapons if necessary. Moving deliberately, each proceeding down an opposing exterior wall, they checked for footprints, sounds, and any movement.

Having circled the building, they reconvened between the door and the still-running car.

Sam nodded at Les as he approached the door, extracting a flashlight while she watched their perimeter.

The door was seamed with wide cracks, making whatever lay behind it visible. His caution quieting, Lester fit an eye to one of the broader openings, with his light just below it.

"What do you see?" Sam asked.

"A delivery-type van," he reported. "That seems to be it. With Vermont plates."

He returned to the car. Sammie stayed outside, ignoring the snow covering her head and shoulders.

Inside, Lester pulled over the mounted laptop to face him and typed in the numbers he'd memorized from the van. He then leaned over and ran down the window nearest her to say, "Bingo."

"What?"

"It's registered to Cheri Pratt."

"No kidding. Small world. Is this where we put our new federal superpowers to work and get a warrant?"

He chuckled. "Let's say it's where we get to find out how well they work, if at all." He set to work getting hold of Fred Houston.

Trevor Buttner was still in the Keene hospital, having segued from being a victim of gravity-defying antics to the target of a stubborn infection. The sterile setting and Buttner's vulnerability suited Willy Kunkle fine.

He nodded to the deputy outside the door as he displayed his credentials. "He being a good boy?" he asked.

"He's loving the painkillers, from what the nurses tell me, but none of them're loving him. The last one called him a pig."

"There's a stunner," Willy replied, adding, "Still no request for a lawyer?"

"Nope. Don't know why not, but you're good to go."

The mention of painkillers was a good heads-up for Willy, and a potential stumbling block later if Buttner ever ended up in court following a confession. His lawyer could insist that his client was "under the influence," and thus not lucid enough to have spoken at all.

Given Willy's general attitude, this was not a deal breaker. He opened the door, ambled over to the foot of Trevor's bed, and stood looking at him silently.

"Who're you?" Buttner demanded.

Willy revealed the badge clipped to his belt. He took advantage of the gesture to also reach into his pocket, pull out a recorder, place it on the rolling table nearby, and turn it on. "Not someone you ever wanted to meet."

Buttner looked away angrily, growling, "Fucking cops."

"I'm also your best friend right now," Willy told him.

"How do you figure?"

"You remember being read your rights?" Willy asked him.

"So?"

"You want me to answer, you can't say later you wanted a lawyer."

"I didn't," he protested.

"You still don't?"

"Nah. They never done me any good before."

Willy wasn't sure whose fault that might have been. "Then that makes me the one to talk to," he answered, "because if you cooperate with me, you might cut down on whatever federal time you're facing now." He then added his name, Buttner's, and the date and time for the sake of the recorder.

"You a Fed?"

"I am attached to a federal task force and thus endowed with federal authority, yes."

"And you can cut me a deal?"

"I'm not a prosecutor. But I am the guy who talks to them."

"Then you're no fuckin' good to me."

Willy placed his hand on Buttner's foot. Although he did nothing more, the threat to the broken hip farther up was clear.

"Are you free enough of the influence of painkillers and other drugs to think and speak clearly and coherently?"

Buttner's eyes widened. "What the . . . ?" His gaze switched to Willy's hand before he finished in a flat voice, "What d'you want?"

Willy chose the direct approach. "We're thinking of hitting you with the murder of Don Kalfus after all."

"I told the older cop I didn't do that. I never found the son of a bitch after he ripped me off."

"You told the older cop all sorts of things, Trevor, but you left out where you walked in on Don screwing your wife on your living room couch."

Buttner made to protest but apparently thought better of it, shutting his mouth again.

"You going to deny that?" Willy asked.

"I didn't care," he then said. "I cheat on her all the time."

"Good for you. I don't think you like her doing the same thing to you."

"I told you. I don't care."

"Which is why you tore out of the house right after, looking for him? I don't think so."

"I was looking for what he stole."

"And why do you think he did that? Your old buddy?"

"He's an asshole. He's no buddy."

"Why, Trevor?"

"*He's a thief.* That's why."

Willy shook his head and gave Trevor's foot the tiniest nudge, causing him to wince. "I don't believe that. I think he knew he'd need leverage over you, 'cause he knew how pissed off you were, despite all the kidding around. *And* you'd just showed him your footage of Angie."

"You're full of shit."

"You two weren't alone in the apartment, Trevor."

That brought him up short, although Willy had no proof of any private viewing.

"Did you track your own phone?" Willy pressed him. "Find him that way and then knock him off? What did you use, Trevor? Knife? Gun? Your fists?"

Trevor became sullen. "What do I know about tracking? I'm no computer nerd. I put out the word, sure. He fucks my woman, steals my shit. Damn straight I wanna even things up." His eyes narrowed as he emphasized, "But I never found him. Next I knew, you people told me he was dead and you had my phone. I did that, okay? I admit I took those shots of Angie and offered them up, all right? Is that what you wanted? Fine. But I did not kill Don Kalfus. You cannot lay that on me."

Willy considered that, nodded once, gathered up his recorder, and left.

The system worked without a hitch. Lester phoned Fred. Fred, on his behalf, completed the proper federal application online and forwarded it to the Boston-based agent assigned to expedite such matters. In just over an hour, Lester heard back. His warrant to enter the barn and search the vehicle was granted and on file.

Angie Neal's being trafficked by her stepfather, along with the reemergence of Scooter Nelson's case, with interstate implications, had secured the VBI's federal task force legitimacy.

Lester turned his screen toward Sammie so she could see its contents. "Signed, sealed, and delivered," he said.

"Way to go," she responded, getting out of the car to retrieve a pry bar from the back.

No key could have bypassed the padlock faster than she did with her pry bar. She was already pulling the old barn door open as Lester got out of the SUV with his camera.

Their discovery turned out to be an older Ford Econoline—a little rusty, a few minor dents, dark blue in color—the perfect vehicle to at once carry a lot of belongings, while remaining invisible in plain view.

It was unlocked. Disappointingly, it was also empty. But not, they were pleased to find, pristinely so. As they systematically processed it from back to front, at last reaching the console between the two front seats, Lester let out a self-congratulatory grunt as he held up a key, complete with an identifier tag.

"Aha," Sam reacted, looking up from searching under the passenger seat. "That say where it goes?"

Lester studied the tag. "Specifically? No. Generally? You bet.

Ocean Storage Rentals." He handed it to her, adding, "Where that is exactly, I have no clue."

"I think I do," she said, smiling. She showed him her phone, explaining, "Joe just filed his interview with Corey Browne. Given our present location, I'd say we're the closest players to the beautiful Hampton Beach area, where Corey thinks Don kept his stash."

Lester straightened, looking pleased. "I love the seashore in the winter."

"And I'd love to bug Fred Houston for another warrant." She glanced at the key chain again. "Specifically to search unit forty-eight."

CHAPTER EIGHT

It is one of the curiosities of the Vermont / New Hampshire twins phenomenon that, although each looks like the upside-down mirror image of the other on a map, they have so fiercely maintained separate identities as to be products of opposite coasts.

Much of that difference is bunkum, born of pride and parochial competitiveness. Despite their mutual disparagement, both states, nestled along the Connecticut River like two old lovers spooning, had once had remarkably similar outlooks. Only since the 1960s has Vermont become the liberal enclave it's now known to be. Before then, it was an outspoken bastion of rock-ribbed Republicanism.

Modern politics may have fostered the greatest schism, with labels like blue and red, but migration and proximity to urban centers have contributed additional geographical quirks. Vermont's population is largely concentrated just below Montreal, while New Hampshire's citizens cluster in its southeast corner, making of it a virtual suburb of Boston.

It was in response to this last fact that Lester Spinney had admitted to Sam about knowing Hampton Beach. Whenever legions

of Bostonians had an appetite to leave Massachusetts for a few hours
on a summer weekend, away from the lingering prudery of their Pu-
ritan forebears, Hampton Beach had become the customary destination. Lester and many like him had similarly been attracted from
far and wide, although he was one of the few to prefer the place's
austerity in winter over its summertime excesses.

Occupying barely two of New Hampshire's paltry dozen and
a half miles of coastline, the resort town exuded an open-armed,
freewheeling, blue-collar ambience that appealed to denim over
sequins, motorcycles over Ferraris, and beer over champagne.
Hampton Beach, according to Lester's description to Sam—who'd
never been—was summed up as a "redneck vision of paradise."

Cheek-by-jowl along a gentle crescent—consisting of Ocean
Boulevard, the beach, and the open Atlantic—were uncountable
bars, casinos, motels, strip joints, novelty stores, tourist dives, gift
shops, arcades, beach supply vendors, souvenir outlets, yogurt and
T-shirt shops, and multiple food counters offering gyros, fried
dough, pizza, Italian sausage, fudge, ice cream, corn dogs, and sea-
food that—despite the ocean's proximity—had been trucked from
as far away as the burrito ingredients right next door.

At the height of the season, Lester told Sam, eyes gleaming, near
gridlock is a given, parking impossible, noise a continual roar punctuated by muffler-free motorcycles, and crowd control a nightmare
for the local constabulary, who have become over time regional experts on DUIs and overdoses.

"It's sure no place for introverts," he stressed, "except for right
now." With that, he left where Route 101 petered out, turned south
onto Ocean Boulevard, and stopped.

Before them was the flat, gentle curve he'd detailed, with buildings to the right and the beach and ocean to the left. But almost
without exception, the entire stretch was deserted, clad in snow,

and now that the weather had cleared, under an uninterrupted gray dome of high clouds.

"This is why I love this place," he said happily.

Sam looked from the desolate view of boarded storefronts and empty parking areas to him, and back again. "Les," she said. "There's nothing here."

"I know. Isn't it great?"

He put the car back into gear and continued, following Ocean to where it branched to become Ashworth Avenue, a deserted, one-way street paralleling its cousin and heading south. "This is the only way they could make any traffic flow at all," he explained. "By making the whole place a huge, one-way circle. Kids come here in their convertibles or Harleys just to 'scoot the loop' all night long, around and around, up and down, drinking, smoking weed, and screaming their heads off."

Sammie looked ahead, struck by how remarkably Ashworth Ave differed from Ocean. Here, with no view of the water, the gaunt buildings faced each other across a narrow street whose open daylight was smudged by thousands of crisscrossing electrical and telephone wires. The hotels and rooming houses, often peeling and worn, seemed designed for people paid to cater to the better-heeled strollers just one block over. Sam imagined this street, correctly or not, populated by tired shift workers, waitpeople, ice cream scoopers, strippers taking smoke breaks, and hundreds of others waiting to return to the glitz and bustle a hundred yards to the east.

At the bottom, Lester turned around and showed her Ocean Boulevard from the south, as visually different from Ashworth as she'd just been contemplating—open, airy, clean, and graced by the vast spread of water lapping at the wide, now snow-covered beach.

"It's like a movie set without the actors," she commented.

His pleasure was unabated. "Right. Right," he agreed, craning his neck as he drove. "I've never been here during a hurricane, but can you imagine? It's got to be so eerie."

"This is strange enough," she said quietly, pulling her thoughts back to the task at hand. "And Kalfus kept his storage unit here?"

"Not really," Lester admitted. "The warrant says Seabrook. But since you'd never been here, I had to show you Hampton Beach, especially looking like this." He returned them to Ashworth, continued south across the Hampton Bridge, eventually to the 286 intersection, and drove inland a few miles to Route 1 North which turned out to be no more unique to Seabrook than any other stretch of miracle mile anywhere in the United States.

"Now, this," he announced as they progressed through a series of stoplights marking a string of bland shopping plazas, "is the perfect place to have a rental facility. Anonymous, nondescript, and within easy reach of three states."

This time, because of their outsider status, along with the political sensitivities of a number of turf-conscious local police agencies, Les and Sam had requested a state trooper to meet them at Ocean Storage Rentals. As FTOs, they had a loose rein, jurisdictionally, but they knew from experience the benefits of at least a show of political correctness.

In this instance, it turned out to be a meeting of similarly uninterested minds. The trooper, an old-timer, met them at the storage yard entrance, exchanged greetings and information, participated in a unified show of force presenting the facility's owner with the warrant, and casually returned to his cruiser while Sam and Les moved on to investigate unit 48.

There was a pause as Lester fit Kalfus's key into the padlock securing the overhead tambour door. They were seasoned enough cops to know that surprises awaited the unwary, including booby traps, and that merely throwing open a wide portal like this didn't allow for much time to move aside fast if necessary.

Nevertheless, it had to be done. With a quick nod, Les snapped open the lock and wrenched up on the door handle in one smooth move, while Sam rested her hand on her holstered weapon.

The result was blessedly anticlimactic. Like the mouth of a yawning whale, the storage unit opened wide, revealing only darkness, a slight mustiness, and a mundane stacking of ordinary belongings.

"Your guy was a busy boy," said the trooper from behind, having surreptitiously returned like a curious tourist.

Lester turned and cocked an eyebrow, replying, "He won't be the only one. Once we go through it all to see if anything relates to our case, it'll have to be cataloged, identified, and parceled out to whoever reported it stolen in the first place. That's likely to be a ton of fun."

"For somebody else," the man said, laughing. "Thank God I don't get tapped for jobs like that."

Having satisfied his curiosity—and perhaps warned off by Lester's comment—their partner once more faded away.

As Sam located the switch and hit the lights, Les stepped into a small central clearing, surrounded by piles of stolen goods, and did a slow survey, taking it all in.

"It's a little like pawing through a pirate's stolen treasure," he said. "And just like Don grabbed whatever caught his eye, now we have to find the one thing that made somebody kill him."

Sammie joined him amid the booty. "With no clue what it might be."

The Brattleboro Senior Center is located on Main Street in the Gibson-Aiken building, named after two of the most influential political leaders in modern Vermont history. An imposing brick building, it was built in the 1920s as an armory. Indeed, to escape most of its lingering martial severity, the Senior Center had several years ago moved down to the tamer, less militant, low-ceilinged basement.

Joe Gunther was here to catch up with Cheri Pratt, Don Kalfus's mother, who, according to her neighbor, was taking advantage of the affordable senior meals program, despite not yet qualifying as a senior herself.

He followed the sounds and smells of a large lunch in full flower and entered the room he was after, half-filled with diners who were crowding the tables or ambling about getting drinks or chatting. He paused by the door, Willy's description of Cheri in mind, scrutinizing the scene while he paid his entrance fee, which dropped several dollars for those over sixty, until he located her sitting in a far corner—a lean, tough-faced woman who was as "thin as an axe handle," in Willy's words.

Fortunately, she was not only alone, but had a couple of empty chairs beside her. She wasn't the only one. For the many people who were there to socialize, there were just as many simply desiring a cheap meal. They wanted to eat more than to converse.

As he wended his way between tables and people, Joe was unsure what category Cheri fit, since he also saw her waving familiarly to several passersby.

Reaching her table, he stood long enough for her to notice him and finish chewing her mouthful of lasagna.

"Mrs. Pratt?"

The smile he'd seen from across the room was not the restrained version she showed now.

"Who're you?" she asked neutrally, her eyes calculating.

"May I sit?" he replied, indicating the chair beside her.

"Would it matter if I said no?"

He smiled and sat. "No."

"I hope you never do undercover work," she told him. "You have cop stamped all over you."

"I should," he agreed, shrugging his coat off onto the chair back behind him. "I've been at it long enough. The lasagna good?"

"I think so," she said. "I don't go for fancy."

"No," he said. "Me, neither."

"You here about Donny?" she asked, breaking off a piece of roll and putting it in her mouth. "You're obviously not interested in lunch."

"Yes. We're trying to discover as much about him as possible so we can find out what happened."

"Or if a guy like him is worth the trouble?"

"Ouch," he reacted. "What makes you say that?"

"Experience. What's your name?"

"Joe."

"Well, Joe, I told all this to the guy with the floppy arm. Talk to him."

"I have. Things have developed since you two met."

Her tone became cautious. "Okay."

"You and Don have grown in our estimation, Cheri. When we started looking at this, we thought he was a minor player and you were just the grieving mother. But there's more going on here, isn't there?"

"If you say so."

Across the room, a reedy chorus of "Happy Birthday" floated into the air, accompanied by a sudden blossoming of four balloons and a single sparkler stuck into a cupcake.

"Don't misunderstand," Joe said as they watched the distant festivity. "Your skepticism notwithstanding, we're applying the same resources to your boy as we do to every homicide. But in that process, we look at everyone very carefully, including the victims."

"Here we go," she said barely audibly.

"It helps us better understand, sometimes, why it was they were killed. In your and Don's case, Cheri, you two appear to have more to tell than we'd first thought."

"Meaning what?"

"We pulled your backgrounds. We know you did time for burglary in the past, you've been a person of interest in more than one of Don's escapades, we even found your van parked in that barn in New Hampshire."

Cheri remained silent, but her eyes had slipped off the birthday and were now studying the center of the table. She ignored a man who walked by saying, "Hey there, Cheri."

Joe moved slightly closer to speak confidentially. "We found the storage locker in Seabrook. We're going through it now."

"Don't know what you're talking about."

"Well, that's the beauty here, isn't it?" he said. "I wouldn't care if you copped to having filled that unit single-handedly, without Don even knowing about it. I'm not here for that. My interest is in who killed him. I need you as an ally, Cheri, not someone who thinks I'm setting her up for a fall."

At last, she turned her head to look him in the eyes. "You being straight?"

"As an arrow. You've got connections. Ask around about me. Joe Gunther's my full name. Back in the day, I ran the detective squad for the PD here. Find out if I'm true to my word. We can talk later once you've checked me out. I hate to lose the time, but I need you on board. If that's what it takes, so be it."

She didn't move for a slow count, studying his face as if deciphering the fine print, before she returned forward and took a sip of her water.

"Okay," she finally said. "What do you want to know?"

"Thank you," he started. "First off, just so all our cards are faceup, you were aware of your son's activities, yes?"

"Yeah."

"We've already interviewed a couple of his fences, but did he have confederates, people who went out with him to commit the burglaries?"

She paused before saying, "I know he took Robin on one."

"Right. To Stratton?"

She straightened a fraction. "You know that?"

Joe shifted in his seat for emphasis. "Cheri, we're doing our best work here. It doesn't matter what he did for a living. We're talking to everybody we can and looking hard. So, other than Robin, was there anyone he worked with?"

She shook her head. "No."

"How 'bout someone he pissed off? He didn't practice a risk-free occupation."

"He had fights," she allowed. "Some of the people he dealt with are dirtbags, but I don't see anybody killing him."

"Tell me about Robin. How did they get along?"

That caught her off guard. "Robin?" she asked. "They were good. From what he told me, she's not the sharpest knife in the drawer, but nice, and she didn't give him crap about what he did. I think she just saw it as his job, and not that interesting."

"Did any of Don's victims figure out who he was?"

"Not that I know. He was careful about casing places out, checking security and dogs and all that. He never aimed too high." A hint of pride crept into her voice. "That's what I taught him. Rich people are thinner skinned, have more to lose, bigger egos, and the junk they like is usually too hard to fence. Steal a midrange Bulova or a Seiko, not a Rolex. He paid attention."

"He steal jewelry at all?" Joe asked.

"Sure, but not fancy. Small diamonds at most. Middle-class things—engagement rings, earrings, gold class rings. But be careful about engravings, initials, or inscriptions. I warned him about those. Keep it simple."

Joe fantasized for a split second that he was sitting with a female Fagin, getting a crash course on picking pockets. "We know about his dealings with Corey Browne and Darren Bader," he told her. "There have to have been others."

"Sure," she said. "A bunch of 'em, some legit, some not so much. I mean, if you get the right pawnbroker in the right mood, you can sell him something with a convincing bull story about a dead grandmother or whatever. That was another thing I taught him: don't be greedy. It didn't cost you anything to steal; don't get uppity about the price you ask. People get suspicious."

Her face softened. "And Donny was such a nice boy. He could really sell that to people. Make 'em believe almost anything."

That made Joe think of the same nice boy cheating on Robin with Melissa Monfet. "How about something beyond the stealing?" he suggested. "It might've been a jealous husband or boyfriend. We may be barking up the wrong tree."

She didn't reject the notion outright, confirming a pragmatic nature. "Could've been," she conceded. "I wouldn't know about that."

"Okay. Let's move on. Did he have other warehouses? Seabrook is kind of far away. He have somewhere closer by?"

She reached again for her drink, which was possibly a time killer to invent a lie—a standard, almost uncontrollable bit of body language. It reminded him of when politicians respond, "I'm glad you asked that."

"Nope," she said after swallowing.

Joe made a mental note to ask Willy or Ron if Cheri had a

garage or to see if she visited some nearby hiding place in the next couple of days. He was convinced by now that Cheri's involvement with her son's activities went beyond simple advice. If so, this conversation might stimulate another habitual nervous twitch, which was for a thief under pressure to head for his or her cache to check its security.

Colored conical hats had been passed out across the room to the birthday crowd, and a trolley appeared bearing a few gifts and more cupcakes.

Joe rose and leaned forward to speak. "Thank you, Cheri. You've been a big help. No guarantees. You know that already. But we'll do our best to find out who did this."

"Sure," she said, not looking up at him.

Back in Seabrook, Sam and Lester were discovering how well Don Kalfus had heeded his mother's guidance. They had chosen a systematic approach to analyzing and tracing the contents of the storage unit, succeeding more or less in the first and essentially failing at the second. It was easy to deal with the trove physically—large items went in one corner, electronics in another, guns and tools in a third, and boxes of miscellaneous items, from trophies to knick-knacks to watches and jewelry, completed the divisions. But while many of these had serial numbers or other identifiers, it turned out that much of it was of little use.

Investigators are no less prone to happy fantasy than wishful civilians. In this instance, Sam and Les had hoped to tumble upon the one obvious icon of revenge by one person against another. An example for Lester would have been a weapon connecting its owner to a major unsolved crime—thereby making of Kalfus a marked man for stealing it.

But no such reward appeared. As he and Sam spent hours comparing discoveries to laptop-mounted lists of recently stolen items, the hits were here and there, but nothing above the mundane. The guns were either too old to be registered or simply belonged to law-abiding victims of burglary. The jewelry and watches were bland to the point of anonymity. Computers, tablets, and phones were promising, but slated to be delivered to Fred Houston for more protracted examination.

Nowhere could they find the "aha" item that spoke of something deserving of a homicide.

By the end of it all, discussing this very point—now tired, hungry, and covered in dust—Sammie sat on a box, closed her laptop, and glanced at her colleague.

"Why does somebody kill somebody else?" she asked rhetorically.

"Could be anything," he allowed. "One guy shot another over a parking spot."

Sam indicated the pored-over piles surrounding them. "Meaning all this was for nothing. Our smoking gun could've been that off-the-shelf bowling trophy we found in the first five minutes. What's that leave us with?"

Lester stood up. Smiling down at her, he suggested, "Scooter's old cell phone? I do know one thing," he added.

"And now you're gonna tell me."

"This ain't over yet. Like our comfy friend in the heated cruiser outside, returning this crap is going to fall to someone else. You and me? We're goin' back on the road, finding where else Don Kalfus might've traveled. We got miles to go."

"How's Emma doing?" Joe asked.

"Pretty good, I think," Willy replied. "Kids are a mystery to me. She acts happy, she's doing well in preschool, not torturing animals or setting the house on fire—even with me as a father—but what do I know? Thank God she's got her mother and Louise to keep her on track."

"Don't sell yourself short," Joe counseled. "I've seen you with her. You're doing fine."

"For a borderline psycho, you mean."

Joe barely shook his head. The man was his own worst enemy, he thought.

"Here we go," he said, changing the topic and turning his attention to what was occurring across the darkened street. They both watched Cheri Pratt step out onto her porch, lock the door, and slowly make her way to her car in the driveway. The weather had now opted for a drizzle that landed on the windshield like melted snowflakes—neither fish nor fowl, but still wet and cold.

"You know she could just be going for milk," Willy cautioned.

"Let's hope not," Joe responded, slipping the car into gear.

She wasn't going to the store. Turning south, away from downtown, she led them past Brattleboro's high school on Fairground Road, then onto Route 5 toward the neighboring town of Guilford.

"Chess club?" Willy asked. "Reading group? Monthly Mensa meeting? What d'ya think?"

"Could be." Joe laughed, genuinely curious about Cheri's true destination. He might have arranged this stakeout immediately following his interview with the woman, but he hadn't truly believed she would then act on his question about Don's local storage facility by rendering it a visit. That was just too easy.

But sometimes, it turned out to be true. On the outskirts of the cluster of buildings that constitutes Guilford's town center, Cheri's car veered right, left the pavement, bumped up onto a muddy parking lot, and aimed for the farthest left-hand unit in a neat row of rental boxes, each the size of a large dumpster.

Joe killed his lights and pulled over nearby, discreetly shielded by some brush lining the breakdown lane.

"Feel like a short walk?" he asked his partner.

Closing their doors softly, they approached the rutted parking lot through the misty blanket of falling slush, watching as Cheri left her car, fumbled with a set of keys, and approached the unit's padlocked door, using her headlights to see by. Eventually standing next to her car, their presence washed out by the glare reflecting off the snowdrops, Joe and Willy waited patiently as she opened first one door of the unit, then its mate, fully exposing its contents.

There wasn't that much—perhaps one-third of the Seabrook container. That might have been the reason Don had been heading in this direction with his carload of stolen goods—if he had been.

It was hard deciphering a man's intentions when he was discovered in the trunk of that very same car.

Joe waited until Cheri had entered the unit and was about to open a box, a small flashlight in hand.

"Need some help?" he offered, stepping into view.

Cheri dropped the flashlight. "*Fuck!*" she yelled at them. "What the hell?"

"That's my question, Cheri," Joe told her. "You said you knew nothing about a place like this."

She rallied quickly. "This isn't Don's," she said. "This is mine."

"Really?" Willy stepped up to the threshold and asked, "You mind?" He indicated his interest to enter with a gesture.

"No, no," she said. "I don't care. It's just some old junk."

Joe followed, crossing over to her. He stooped, lifted the box she'd been about to open, and held it up at chest level. "Here you go. Let me help. It's heavy. This'll make it easier to get what you were after."

She looked from him to the box and back again, stuck for an answer. "No, thanks," she finally said.

"It's my pleasure, Cheri," he said, not moving. "Really."

With painful reluctance, she folded back a flap of the box, while Willy, having retrieved her light, used it to reveal the contents.

All three of them studied a jumbled collection of watches, rings, necklaces, bracelets, a silver ashtray, and a heavy lighter.

"Wow," Willy said innocently. "Fancy. I thought you said it was junk."

"It's not mine," she said.

"It isn't?" Joe asked. "That's not what you just said."

"I don't know where it came from."

"You used a key to get in, Cheri," Willy reminded her. "How did it get here?"

"I don't know."

"Well," Joe concluded, "if it's not yours, you think it belonged to Don?"

"Maybe."

"You think he might've stolen it?"

"Could be."

"Huh," Joe persisted. "What do you think we should do with it? It's not yours; it might be stolen. Kind of awkward, right?"

She pushed the box against his chest. "Take it."

"We can give you a receipt for it."

She seemed to understand the peril in that. "No," she said. "No receipt. It's not mine."

Willy flashed the light around the unit's corrugated walls. "What about the rest of it? Does any of it belong to you?"

Cheri took a step backward. "No. It's all Don's. I don't know anything about any of it."

Joe placed the box on top of a nearby stack and gave her a severe look. "Cheri," he said sternly, "we all know what just happened here. You can wash your hands of it for the time being, but we got an eye on you. We'll be talking again. You got that?"

"I can go?" she asked.

"Not far," Willy told her. "Don't leave town."

Joe held out his hand. "And give me the key."

She quickly released the key from the ring it was attached to and offered it, virtually in the same motion as she turned on her heel and headed back to her car.

Both men watched as she backed around and returned to the road. Joe at that point produced a light of his own and shone it down onto the box again, echoing questioningly, "Don't leave town?"

Willy laughed. "Always wanted to say that."

He squatted down and pulled out the heavy silver ashtray. "This is old-fashioned. Who the hell gives these to anybody anymore?"

"It have an inscription?" Joe asked. "I thought I saw something."

Willy flipped it over and revealed the following to the flashlight's halo:

TO LUCY

TRADITION SAYS THIS SHOULD BE CRYSTAL

BUT YOU'LL ALWAYS DESERVE SILVER IN MY EYES

HAPPY 15TH ANNIVERSARY

LEMUEL

"Well, well," Joe said. "Seems like we just fell over another connection between the Shaws and Don Kalfus."

CHAPTER NINE

Much is made about the cooperation and networking among law enforcement agencies, as when Jim Collins had suggested Fred Houston to grease the wheels of the VBI's investigation.

But as in most such situations, the truth often boiled down to not only who you knew, but in how they were approached, the nature of the request, the tone of voice used, and who else might be hovering just out of sight, in support or opposition.

That's where Joe had several advantages. He was a veteran operator, well known and liked, he kept his ego in check, was quick to praise others, and always worked to avoid credit when it might better serve someone else.

He wanted to make an impression on Lemuel Shaw, beyond knocking on his door and confronting him with the growing inconsistencies between what the cops kept finding and his and Lucy's avowed tale of innocence.

For that, Joe needed a show of force. From New Hampshire law enforcement. He began with Fred Houston.

As Joe had partially explained to Beverly earlier, New Hampshire law enforcement territories were clearly set out and observed. Municipalities tended to their own, sheriffs operated within their counties, even the state police had restrictions on where they could go and what powers they had. Pragmatism had been applied to smooth out obvious rough spots. Formal agreements, signed memoranda, verbal understandings had been reached here and there, allowing one agency to function inside the realm of another. But the process was tricky and often relied on the personalities and instincts of individual leaders, some of whom were political, progressive, provincial, or pigheaded.

Fred, by grace of his ICAC skills, the charity of his boss, and his own accommodating manner, was one of the few officers in the state whom everyone knew, welcomed, and valued. The fact that he was as generous to most as he'd been to Joe—encouraging a homicide investigation to piggyback a child abuse case—meant that by association, Joe was on the side of the angels, even before his own reputation was added to the mix. Sometimes, it did boil down to whom you knew.

So it was that a small but impressively representative cluster of troopers, deputies, and Joe's fellow federal task force officers rolled up the hill to Lemuel Shaw's front door, prepared for a serious conversation, even if they didn't have enough probable cause at this stage to enact a search of his house.

What they got instead was an athletic man in his early twenties, opening the door with a look of astonishment.

"Can I help you?" he asked reasonably enough, scanning the array of uniforms.

"We're here for Lemuel and Lucy Shaw," Joe told him.

"They're not here," the man stammered.

"Who're you?" Joe asked.

"Seamus Kyle. I work for Mr. Shaw. What's happening?"

"You have any identity papers? A driver's license?" one of Joe's colleagues asked.

Kyle was startled. "What? No. I don't drive."

"Where are they, Mr. Kyle?" Joe asked as the other cop snapped a picture of Seamus, using his phone.

The younger man shook his head in wonder. "I don't know what to tell you. He's in Claremont, upstate. That's where she is. At least, I guess he's there by now. He was in Boston when I called him."

"Why?"

"That's what I mean," Kyle said. "Lucy Shaw died this morning. They're at the funeral home."

Not every death gets an autopsy, not even ones nobody saw coming. Often, an apparently natural death will earn a glance from a medico-legal investigator, whose report is then forwarded to the state's chief medical examiner. But usually, that report—given the time and money invested in the investigator's training—is taken at face value and accepted in lieu of the body itself. Only rarely does the boss reverse a recommended course. Such is the level of trust granted to the field-based "eyes and ears" of the office.

In other words, there is wiggle room concerning the necessity for a pathological examination. And without one, the next steps are death certificate and disposal, both of which can be and often are quickly facilitated. This, Joe keenly wanted to head off.

He did not waste time grilling Seamus Kyle at the Shaw residence. Instead, he told Willy to drive and began working his phone as they traveled at speed up to Lebanon.

Echoing the process he'd employed to assemble the team he'd just abandoned, Joe chose not to call the funeral home they were rapidly approaching, but rather Beverly Hillstrom in Burlington.

"Hey there," she greeted him upon picking up. "This is unusual. To what do I owe the pleasure?"

"Business, I'm afraid," Joe said. "I need to ask a big favor."

She didn't hesitate. They both knew how rarely he did this. "Absolutely. What is it?"

"A woman named Lucy Shaw died this morning at her home in Gilsum, New Hampshire, supposedly of natural causes. She was on meds for high blood pressure and diabetes, according to the housekeeper."

"Okay . . . ," Beverly said.

"I'm hoping you still have enough pull with the OCME over here to get an autopsy ordered on her."

"You think she was murdered?"

"I don't know. I have no reason to think so right now, but she is tangentially involved in the homicide I'm working. She's the stolen car owner's wife."

"Right, right. I remember the name." Her voiced changed slightly, as it did when she entered professional mode. "Let me start working on this," she said. "We certainly don't want the funeral home acting prematurely. I'll call my counterpart, delay the issuance of the death certificate, and offer my services for free. That can only help. I can do the procedure in Lebanon if everyone's amenable. I'll call you back."

Joe gave her Lucy's date of birth along with the funeral home's name and hung up.

"Ah," Willy commented. "The beauty of knowing people in the right line of work."

The Dartmouth-Hitchcock Medical Center in Lebanon, New Hampshire, is a colossus—towering, hulking, gleaming, and imposing. Surrounded by trees and hills as if buried in the countryside, it looks like a transplanted castle whose architect had enjoyed one *Star Wars* movie too many.

It is arguably the biggest hospital complex in northern New England, with satellites all over the region, like the offshoot housing Trevor Buttner in Keene.

It was also where Beverly Hillstrom was employed part-time by Dartmouth Medical School.

By the time Joe and Willy found their way through the inner workings of the place to the large and busy pathology department where the medical examiner's office conducted autopsies on an as-needed basis, the remains of Lucy Shaw had been delivered from the funeral home where she'd been awaiting a death certificate and subsequent cremation.

Beverly, an hour and a half away in Burlington, still had fifteen minutes to go, a time slot put to use when the two cops saw Lemuel Shaw pacing the hallway just outside the pathology department.

"You feel like having a little fun?" Willy asked softly. Shaw hadn't yet spotted them.

"Sure," Joe replied.

Shaw reached the end of the hallway, turned on his heel, and was heading back when he saw them studying him.

"What?" he asked, pegging them as cops by their demeanor. "You here for my wife?"

Joe nodded. "Yes, sir. We are."

The man's rage came off him like radiant heat. "What the fuck for? She died of natural causes. She took medicine. She had a doctor. He'd warned her to be careful. What do you people *want*, anyway?"

Joe indicated a cluster of upholstered chairs by a distant, windowed alcove. "Why don't we sit over there?" he suggested.

"I don't want to *sit*," Shaw fumed. "I want an explanation for why you're about to cut her open like a Christmas turkey."

"Sit anyhow," Willy said in a flat tone, all the more menacing as a result.

Shaw studied him for the first time, recognizing something about him that deserved watching and merited care—like the aura given off by a natural predator.

He stalked over to the alcove and sat rigidly. "There. Happy?"

Willy settled down comfortably opposite him as Joe sat with his back to the window. "Delirious," Willy said.

"You've got an attitude," Shaw grumbled.

"I've heard that."

He shifted his attention back to Gunther. "You gonna answer my question? Where do you get off taking my wife out of the funeral home? You'd better know I'm considering legal action."

"We're investigating a serious and expanding criminal case," Joe began. "And your name keeps turning up, first as a victim, then as a person of interest, and finally as something murkier. Speaking honestly, Mr. Shaw, we're not quite sure what to make of you in all this."

"But not as an innocent bystander," Willy added.

It was Shaw's choice now to either leap to his feet and bluster as before or take a breath and begin conversing.

He opted for the second, repositioning himself as if ready to spring, and saying between clenched teeth, "My wife just died, you assholes. The woman I loved and shared a life with. And you're operating on her because why? You think I killed her or something?"

"Maybe," Willy said agreeably.

Shaw's mouth fell open.

"Where were you when she died?" Joe asked. "We heard you weren't at home last night."

"I was in Boston."

"Why?"

"None of your goddamned business."

"Really?" Willy asked, almost smiling.

"I was seeing my money guy," Shaw conceded. "Fitch, Mayhew. Call and ask if you don't believe me." He pulled out his wallet, extracted a business card, and threw it down onto the small table in their midst. "Keep it."

"Meeting them at night?" Willy asked, picking it up.

"No, you snarky bastard. But I had dinner with Fitch last night." Shaw clenched his fist. "*Fuck.* What the hell. Now you'll tell me I drove up afterward and killed her in her sleep."

"Did you?"

He collapsed back into his chair, sighing deeply. "Christ almighty. Why bother?" He rallied and sat up again, asking, "Okay, then why? Tell me that? If you really think I killed Lucy, then why? You must have a reason. Money? Good luck. She just spent the damn stuff. That thing at the strip club the other two morons were asking about? Lucy couldn't have cared less about my staring at girls. It wasn't that kind of marriage."

"What kind was it?" Joe asked.

Shaw scowled. "Private. That kind."

"Why didn't you tell us you'd been burgled?" Joe asked as if randomly.

"What're you talking about?"

Willy chuckled.

"The silver ashtray," Joe replied. "Your anniversary gift to Lucy? Number fifteen?"

Shaw pressed his lips together before blurting out, "Don't know what you're talking about."

"We've got it in evidence."

"So what? I haven't seen that thing in years. That's partly what landed her in this place." He waved his hand. "She used to smoke."

"So you bought her an ashtray instead of NicoDerm patches?" Willy asked. "Feelin' and the love."

Joe gave the man that much. He didn't fly off his chair in a homicidal rage.

"We tracked Don Kalfus when he was driving your car," he explained, "right up to your front door, *after* he'd stolen it at the strip club. He was clearly casing your place, having found out where you live from the registration."

Shaw was dismissive. "Well, he didn't do it, if that's what he was planning. We didn't have any break-in."

"Then how come the ashtray and matching lighter?" Joe asked.

Shaw spread his hands. "How the hell am I supposed to know? Lucy probably pawned them. She did finally quit. She didn't need them anymore. Maybe they gave her bad memories. Maybe she wanted the money and didn't want to admit it. I have no idea. That's your job. Instead of slicing her up, you should be finding that out."

Joe's phone vibrated in his pocket. He removed it to see that Beverly had arrived. He nodded to Willy and stood up.

"Mr. Shaw, consider yourself under a microscope. As you're discovering, it's an increasingly less private world we live in, and right now, we've barely begun opening the book on you. I recommend you get ahead of this and start being honest with us."

Shaw sneered at them both. "That would do me a lot of good, wouldn't it, considering how you've railroaded me so far?"

"Interesting answer," Willy reflected. "It implies you *haven't* been honest."

Beverly met them behind the secure doors of the pathology lab, already dressed in a pair of scrubs.

"How long you been here?" Joe asked, surprised, stroking her shoulder in greeting.

"You know me," she replied. "Quick-change artist."

"Kids, kids," Willy protested. "Overshare."

Beverly's expression became severer. "Agent Kunkle. Nice to see you, too."

He laughed. "I doubt that, but thanks."

Joe hadn't met Lucy Shaw in life and had therefore missed the white-and-gold-adorned Zsa Zsa Gabor imitation that Sam and Les had encountered. What he got to see now were her naked, pale, overfed remains on the steel autopsy table, blotchy, sagging, and inert, her violently bright finger- and toenails gleaming under the bright lights as if fed by some inner electrical force.

Trained by years of experience, Joe and Willy knew to find an out-of-the-way spot in the room and remain silent and observant. Beverly had her routine, based on algorithms and well-honed habits, designed to keep her focused, methodical, and accurate. She spoke to those assisting her, sometimes commented into a recorder, other times made a notation or a quick sketch. Each time, the progression was almost precisely the same: an inventory, a survey, an external accounting, and then the actual examination, beginning with the classic Y-shaped incision of the torso, and proceeding, step by step, through the organs and major structures until reaching the skull and brain. Throughout, there were collections made of fluids, samples, scrapings, and slices for later histological scrutiny, along with a steady barrage of photographs. It took a long time, especially in a case like this, where the cause of death was presumed but possibly inaccurate and elusive.

Throughout, consistent with his contradictory nature, the often hyperactive Willy Kunkle remained as still as an icon, watching, waiting, and taking everything in.

At the end, as Beverly stepped away from the table, removed her outermost gloves, and realigned her spine with a quick rotation of her shoulders. Joe, who by contrast had been wandering the outer perimeter of the room, leaning against the wall, sitting on the edge of a counter, or even squatting a couple of times to mix things up, broke the quiet and asked, "So, what's the verdict?"

Beverly lowered her mask as all three of them moved to a far corner, allowing the lab assistants to sew the body back together. "You're not going to like it," she warned them. "I don't like it."

"Swell," Willy interpreted. "Undetermined?"

This was the least favorite of the five MODs, or classifiable manners of death. Among "natural," "suicide," "homicide," and "accident," the last, which Willy had aired, was at once the rarest and the most unsatisfying.

Beverly chose not to go there quite yet. "Until the tox results return, it's pending. But I won't argue against your pessimism."

"What did you actually find?" Joe asked.

"Nothing terrifically healthy," she replied. "She had multiple degenerative diseases, most if not all related to lifestyle choices. But none stood out as a primary cause of death. As you know, that doesn't necessarily exclude some other mechanism coming into play. Also, the human system is complex enough to collapse if too many oppositional forces conspire to overwhelm it. In geriatric cases, some pathologists will revert to 'failure to thrive' as a cause, although I prefer not to. It's imprecise and, I think, a little lazy. But I sympathize with the frustration it connotes. It's also academic here. Mrs. Shaw would have had to have been fifty percent older to qualify."

Both men were inured to her high-flying syntax, barely noticing it anymore.

"What about time of death?" Willy risked asking, knowing pathologists dislike the question and blame television for its nonsensical ubiquity.

But Beverly surprised them by answering, "Not terrifically long ago, given lividity, rigor, and algor. All indicate death a few hours ago, versus, let's say, sometime early last night. But as you know, I won't be held to that as an absolute."

"You mentioned some other mechanism coming into play," Joe repeated. "What were you thinking of?"

She resumed removing some of the outer layers of her operating costume, returning to the scrubs in which she'd greeted them. "There are ways to get away with murder. Injections, mechanisms, environmental factors that don't leave a trace or disappear by the time an autopsy is conducted. Joe, you had a case decades ago, I recall, where curare was administered. It wasn't the terminal COD. The person was killed some other way, after being immobilized with the curare, but we didn't find it in the tox screen because we didn't know what to look for."

She gestured vaguely at the body. "She might have something on board we'll never find, because it falls outside the scope of the standard panel of tests."

But Joe knew this woman well and recognized when she was edging toward a finding where her footing was less than absolute.

"Speak to me," he therefore prodded. "What's running around in that analytical brain? You found something that's bugging you."

"I did," she admitted, her cheeks coloring slightly like a schoolgirl's, which flooded his heart with affection. "In and of itself, it establishes nothing, but in the context of this woman's attention to makeup and personal care, it's an anomaly. She ate too much and exercised too little. But her nails, lips, and eye shadow tell me she was self-conscious about appearance—at least to that extent."

Willy finally broke. "Come on, Doc."

She didn't take umbrage. "I found what appears to be a fragment of plastic wrap on the inside of her right index fingernail, with a corresponding blanching of the nail itself, consistent with it having been stressed through a levering or scratching motion."

Both men considered that before Joe responded, "Wrap or a bag?"

"Bag, I think. It was thicker than what 'wrap' implies."

"You think she was suffocated?" Willy asked.

"I do not. Not on the evidence. But she may have been."

Willy pressed on. "A bag was put over her head?"

"Perhaps."

"And she clawed to tear it off."

Beverly didn't answer.

"Wouldn't there be something more? A scratch on her own face, like when people try to get the rope off their neck when they're being strangled? They claw like crazy."

Joe followed a different tack by asking, "How would that work? Could someone do it while she was sleeping?"

"Her blood alcohol content was very high," she told them. "I don't know how heavily she drank on a daily basis. Her liver is that of an alcoholic. But it's conceivable she was in a stupor when this happened, *if* it did."

"So, someone might've gotten her into that state, or she did it on her own beforehand."

"Good luck proving that," Willy muttered.

"There is another possibility," Beverly suggested.

It was rare for her to entertain hypotheticals, so Joe was keen to hear this. "Go on."

"There is sound documentation about the use of inert gases in these instances. The circumstances almost always concern suicides, but I don't know why it couldn't work in a different scenario.

The pathologist would have to be aware of such a mechanism before autopsy. Otherwise, she wouldn't enact the special procedure needed to extract the gas before it dissipated. And even then, after that small time window is closed, there's no longer any evidence to be had."

"Inert gas?" Willy asked. "What's that mean, exactly?"

"It could be nitrous oxide," she ventured. "Laughing gas. Or helium. Even simpler. You can rent a bottle of it at any balloon store for a birthday party. What I'm suggesting is that someone could place a bag loosely over a sleeping person's head or face before introducing the gas into what's now a largely closed environment. I suspect that a heavily inebriated victim might not even notice."

"Except for one feeble scratch at the bag before dying," Joe suggested.

"Correct," she agreed before adding—pure Beverly—"Keep in mind, this is all purely theoretical."

"For you, maybe," Willy said. "But I can work with this."

"You *are* thinking what I am, aren't you?" Willy asked later.

Joe was driving this time, returning to Brattleboro. "About Shaw's alibi?" He weighed his response before continuing, "Instinctively, yes. I think he's dirty. More globally? We have some hurdles to jump before we can put him on the spot, beginning with the fact that we don't have a homicide with Lucy Shaw. We don't even have an undetermined. You know as well as I do that her tox'll come back six weeks from now with no more than booze and some therapeutic levels of prescription meds. If somebody was clever enough to knock her off without leaving evidence, it's unlikely a bolus of arsenic will suddenly show up at the end. Beverly's going to be stuck with a ruling of natural death."

"What're you saying?"

"That what we got is what we got. You and I can *suspect* a killing all we want, but aside from a tiny bit of plastic bag under a fingernail, we have nothing, and Lucy's tox results aren't going to help."

"What about tearing into his alibi?"

"We'll do that, for sure," Joe answered. "But there again, so what? Let's say we find a hole in his timeline, that we establish he could've made it home in time to kill her and get back to Boston to be found and told face-to-face about her death. If we still don't have hard proof of a homicide, we could have him standing by her bedside with a chain saw and still not be able to pin a murder on him."

"It's like the reverse of double jeopardy," Willy grumbled.

"What do you mean?"

"Well, he's wearing belts and suspenders, both. He knocked her off without a trace, *and* he gave himself an airtight alibi."

They drove in silence for a while, enjoying Interstate 91's deserved reputation as being among the nation's most scenic freeways. Between the Connecticut River to their left and the hills and farms opposite, each coming in and out of view as the pavement undulated across the earth like a low-flying helicopter, it was a soothing and inspiring sight. Even the weather was finally cooperating, being neither snowy nor wet, but instead almost balmy and capped with a bright blue sky.

"Let's step back and not look at this in terms of proof and evidence," Joe suggested. "Let's ask *why* he killed her."

They found Sam and Lester back at the office that afternoon, staring at their computer screens, and visibly happy for the opportunity to take a break.

"So the autopsy was a bust?" Lester asked as they entered, Willy having texted the results from the car.

"Yes and no," Joe replied. "There was nothing to say she was murdered, but nothing to say she died of any obvious natural cause, either."

That led Sammie to ask, "Which is another way of saying we're dealing with a clever bad guy in the person of Lemuel Shaw?"

"That's how I see it," Willy confirmed.

Joe sat on the corner of his desk, facing them—his usual perch. "I'm open to disagreement on this, but as I was telling Willy on the way back, challenging the man's alibi is probably what he wants us to do. We will obviously cover the basics and ask Boston PD to interview a couple of people, but I'm thinking we need to sneak up on Mr. Shaw from a direction he doesn't expect."

He nodded at Sam and asked, "I take it from your being here that you've finished retracing Don Kalfus's last journey?"

"I hate to sound like a parrot," she replied, "but we've got to say yes and no, too. We may or may not be done finding storage dumps for his swag, but we still haven't finished checking out every last place he stopped at along his travels. He was out there for almost a week."

"That being said," Lester volunteered, "we're also thinking that finding the ashtray may be our high point, which makes it another piece of circumstantial evidence putting Shaw in the bull's-eye."

Joe was amenable. "No argument from me. Let's just not forget to completely finish Don's trip at some point, assuming it makes sense down the line."

Willy returned to Joe's earlier point. "Is Shaw's motive the direction he won't see us coming from?"

"Which one?" Sam asked. "Why he killed Lucy or why he killed Don? 'Cause that's still unanswered."

"Both in the long run," Joe confirmed. "But for starters, I say Lucy. My instincts tell me that was rushed. Somehow or another,

Lucy suddenly became a liability, meaning she must've known, seen, or done something that would've incriminated him."

"Like knowing he killed Don?" Sam asked.

"Or that she saw him do it," Willy suggested. "Let's not forget she lied about the strip club. The key would be, why now?"

"Which goes to history," Joe said. "Her knowing of his sins had to go far beyond girlie shows. What have we collected on Shaw's background? Did the New Hampshire fusion folks spit out one of their 'products'?"

"They did," Lester reported. "Shaw told Sam and me that he'd quote-unquote made his nut in the big city. Turns out that was Boston. On the face of it, he was a college-trained electrical engineer with a knack for numbers who made a killing at one of Boston's hotshot financial firms. End of story."

"But . . . ?" Willy asked leadingly.

"That's where we're gonna have to dig a little," Lester confirmed. "New Hampshire's Information Analysis Center cranks out what we're used to here in Vermont. Eighty percent of it lists names and addresses and past phone numbers and family members, and so on. Goes on for pages. Where it gets interesting is in the criminal records. He doesn't have any personally, but he pops up in a couple of involvements where he's listed as a person of interest."

"What kind of cases?" Sam asked.

"That's the thing. There are three altogether. A noise complaint, a disturbing-the-peace violation, and a missing child."

"Far out," Willy said.

Everyone in the room immediately thought of Scooter Nelson.

"Okay," Joe said quickly. "Are the three related?"

"Not that I can tell," Lester said, no longer relying on memory and referring to the actual document on his computer. "The dates are far apart."

"Is there anything specific about the last one? Case number? Investigating officer?"

"All of the above," Lester confirmed. "I just sent you an email with the relevant info. It was while he was living in Boston, in the West End."

"Fancy," Willy said.

"I haven't had a chance to dig up the case details, but the implication is that Shaw surfaced in some context or another, enough that he rated mention as a POI, and not just a man-on-the-street interview."

Joe swiveled his own computer screen around so he could see the email Lester had just sent him. "Quite a few years ago," he mused. "Interesting. Before he moved back to New Hampshire and before Scooter vanished. Anyone here know Molly Ryan, from the PD down there?"

It was an unlikely question. Boston alone had twice the number of cops than the entire state of Vermont. But continuing ed trainings were a perennial constant, sending all of them at least around New England and often farther on a regular basis. And while the topics addressed could sometimes be valuable, they often paled against the usefulness of networking.

The question therefore prompted Sammie to ask, "Which district?" reflecting how Boston divided up its turf.

Districts were Boston's version of New York's more famous precincts. Joe checked his screen again before replying, "A-1."

"I was at a conference two years ago with a woman from the A-1," Sam said, turning toward her own computer. "I'll reach out and ask if she knows Molly Ryan."

"She's got to," Lester encouraged her. "Women make up less than twenty percent of that entire department."

Sam made no comment, already typing.

"Les," Joe asked, "I take it the fusion report lists Shaw's kids?"

"It does, and when we were at his home, he said one reason they built that palace was so the kids could spread out when they visited. That being said, in the next breath, he implied it had mostly been a wasted effort, given how rarely they did."

"Makes you wonder if the kids have even seen the place," Willy mused.

"Look into that," Joe urged. "Nothing like a disaffected child to dish the dirt on a parent. And what was the name of that guy who met us at the door?"

"Seamus Kyle."

"Let's get some background on him, too, along with anyone else who crops up. Time to put Lemuel Shaw and his world on center stage."

Sam was at home that night when she heard back via text message from her Boston PD contact. It was straightforward, no-nonsense, and contained only the name, Molly Ryan, and a phone number, followed by, "Call now."

"What d'you wanna know?" was the greeting she received moments later.

"Molly Ryan?" Sam asked.

She could almost hear the eye roll. "You called me."

Sam shifted gears, abandoning her more countrified manners for something more urban. "You been brought up to speed?"

"I know you want to hear about that slimeball Lemuel Shaw."

"Correct. You dealt with him?"

"Not like I wanted to, but yeah. This being taped?"

"No."

"Anyone else on?"

"No."

"Okay. Go."

"We came across mention of him in a missing child case you ran, as a POI. It caught our eye since we're working something similar up here. Did you ever close that?"

"No."

Sam hesitated, before pressing for more. "Did you like him for it?"

"Oh, yeah."

"So, you're telling me he was a suspect."

"I just said that."

Sam smiled at the phone. This woman was beginning to remind her of Willy. "Can you give me the cheap-seats version?"

"Simplicity itself," Ryan said. "Rich kid vanishes on his way home. Parents say he was snatched. We try to rule out that he didn't just beat feet."

"How old?"

"Eleven."

Just a year younger than Scooter. "Isn't that young to be walking around on his own?"

"It's the West End. They don't think like other people."

"And what was your read of the family dynamics? Maybe he was a runaway."

"I wouldn't've split from a deal like that," Ryan said. "Life of luxury, every need met. Plus the parents seemed over-the-top upset."

"You believed them?"

The other woman's silence told what she thought of the question.

Sam moved on. "How did Shaw come into the picture?"

"He lived in the neighborhood, he'd been seen talking to the kid in the past, and his own son—now an adult—said he wouldn't put it past him."

"You're shitting me."

"Nope. We went by the house, a fancy brownstone, and the son was there. Clearly no love lost. We wanted to talk to Shaw himself, but he was out. We got lucky anyhow. The son was leaving for Australia and had just come by to get something. I don't remember what. Anyhow, one thing led to another, we mentioned that a kid had gone missing and we were doing a standard door-to-door. No big deal. We didn't tell him his old man had been seen with the kid. But the son threw him right under the bus. Without a pause. 'No wonder you're here,' he says. 'I would be, too.' We pressed him, but he had nothing. He just hated his dad and was giving him shit."

"It's a big step, telling the cops you think your father's abducting children," Sam reacted as Willy came in from putting Emma to bed. She gestured to him to sit beside her and eavesdrop, stressing he keep silent.

"My money was on child abuse," Ryan explained. "The son, named David, wouldn't spill the beans. He made no bones that he wanted to get as far away from Boston as the planet would let him. He wasn't goin' to tell us anything that would delay that. Plus, it was clear his gripe was ancient history."

"Our background check said there's a daughter, Annabelle," Sam said.

"We got nothing from her. Lives in California, has no contact with the parents, and when we got her on the phone, she all but hung up on us. I've had better talks with a hydrant."

Willy straightened at that, smiling.

"What else made you look at Shaw?" Sammie pressed her, sensing there had to be more.

"We had an eyewitness who claimed to have seen the actual grab, but at the photo lineup, it fell apart. This happened in the afternoon. A weekday. We thought we had Shaw nailed when we couldn't find anyone who'd seen him at work at the same time, but then his wife swore up and down that he'd been with her."

"This was Lucy?"

"Yeah. Real jerk. I figured she was lying, but what're ya gonna do? We had no kid, no evidence, unreliable witness, nothin'. Tell me you've got a better case."

"Not really," Sam conceded as Willy wrote *Seamus?* on the pad she had before her.

"Our details aren't much different from yours," she went on, "except ours happened in Brattleboro, Vermont." She added, "Did you ever come across the name Seamus Kyle? He might've been a child of a servant or a playmate of your missing kid."

"Kyle? Nope."

"When you had Shaw under the microscope," Sam asked, "did you ever try to fit him for any other disappearances? Or anything involving anything sexual? We've got him at a strip club. Nothing illegal, but it seems odd."

"Male or female strippers?" was the response.

"Female. You think he was gay?"

"Just asking," Ryan answered. "If I'm right about him, his appetite is preteen boys. I'm no shrink, but I'm guessing strip clubs are a second-rate substitute. You met Lucy yet?"

"She's dead."

For the first time, Sam felt she'd brought Molly Ryan up short. "You're kidding me. He killed her."

"We can't say that. It's up in the air."

Ryan grew more animated. "No. That didn't come out right. He *killed* her. You get me? It's not a question. She had him by the balls. I'll give you a hundred bucks if I'm wrong."

"He's got an alibi. Claims he was in your town seeing his moneyman at Fitch, Mayhew. Had dinner with him, too."

"Give me that," Ryan demanded. "I'll talk to him myself. On the house. You won't owe me. You got somebody else looking into it?"

"No. Thank you." Sam gave her the date, along with the details she read off the business card Shaw had given her.

"I'll call you."

The phone went dead. Sam looked at Willy and said quietly, "Okay. Nice chatting. Have a nice day."

Willy chuckled and kissed her. "Whatever," he said.

CHAPTER TEN

James Hendrix, whom nobody, including his mother, ever called Jimmy, looked like a recruitment poster for the New Hampshire State Police. Tall, muscular, thin-waisted, close-cropped, and serious of demeanor, even dressed in civilian attire, as he was now, he'd been accused by others of never having had a choice of professions as a young man out of college—except, perhaps, a Navy SEAL.

In fact, he'd driven a truck and worked construction upon graduation, never liked the water, and hadn't become a cop until hitting his thirties. It seemed he was the last one to get the memo.

After that, watching him had been like taking in a fireworks show. His rise through the ranks had been blessed, unchecked, envied, and without mishap, ending with his arrival as commander of the Major Crime unit. There, he'd happily settled and seemed content to stay, as fit as ever, but now gray-haired, his face more lined than before, and his manner reflecting a calming maturity.

He knew about Joe Gunther through reputation rather than personal exposure, as he imagined was the case for many law enforcement leaders across northern New England. By accomplishments or pure longevity, Gunther had managed to become as well known in this highly specialized milieu as a superlative freelance bass guitarist might be to world-famous touring rock bands looking for local talent. He was the star everyone knew, but only within the profession.

Not that Hendrix was approaching this unofficial meeting at a Concord coffee shop with any degree of awe. In fact, he was at once curious and ready to be irritated, as he'd heard that Gunther, in a federal task force role, had been traipsing around Hendrix's state without much respect for local jurisdiction. His team, or whatever it was, had called on NHSP assistance a couple of times, which hardly qualified as a display of good manners.

So Hendrix was intrigued to know why the great man had at last chosen to reach out. Was it a too-little, too-late show of politesse? Or did he have something up his sleeve, specifically for Major Crime?

In fact, Hendrix thought as he pulled open the diner's door and entered its warm embrace of sweet and comforting odors, that if he were to be completely honest, he could understand an outside investigator avoiding the state police's bureaucracy. Having spent his entire career in its confines, Hendrix was the first to admit that thin skin and jealousy had not been relegated to the past, much as many struggled to put them there.

An older, kindly-looking man was sitting in a far booth, facing the door, his hands encircling a mug of something hot. Given the midmorning hour, the place was relatively empty, allowing for a quiet meeting.

James approached, his expression neutral. His host smiled gently and half rose in the booth, extending a hand. "James Hendrix? Joe Gunther."

Hendrix slid in opposite him. "So I heard."

That having been said, he immediately followed with, "Didn't mean to be snarky. Sorry," which was not a word he overemployed.

But Joe gave him a sympathetic look. "No need. I know a few people are probably thinking my small unit has been playing fast and loose. We're not, but I could see that."

"It's not so bad," James reassured him, slightly embarrassed. "There're always a few bitch-and-moaners. Part of the job."

"We do it, too, west of the river," Joe said. "I was in at the creation of the VBI. Those early days were tough, especially before the state police figured out how to work with us."

"I heard most of your ranks consist of ex-troopers," Hendrix said.

"They do," Joe admitted. "Which I think pissed off the brass even more at first. Now everybody's settled down, more or less."

A waitress appeared and asked if James wanted a coffee or anything else. He settled for the drink only, which she produced on the spot before fading away.

He took a sip, settled back more comfortably, and stated, "I doubt this is a social visit."

Joe liked that. It confirmed what he'd heard about the unusually named James Hendrix, that he was honest, direct, and a solid cop.

"I'm not sure what it is," Joe told him. "It might end up being a dead end, but I hope not. In the rumors you've heard about us over here, did you pick up on a knock-and-talk we'd planned on a guy's house in Gilsum, named Lemuel Shaw? State police was a part of it."

"Vaguely."

"We were told at the door that Mrs. Shaw—Lucy—had died the same day, supposedly of natural causes."

James listened, knowing no case with that name had been reported to Major Crime. "Okay," he said.

"We suspect she was really killed because of what she knew about her husband."

"Which is . . . ?"

"That he may've recently killed a burglar named Don Kalfus,

in Vermont, and also played a role in the disappearance of a boy in Brattleboro named Scooter Nelson, years ago, along with another, more recent one, in Boston. And therefore maybe others as well."

"I remember Scooter Nelson. Cold from day one, no?"

"Like the Boston one, except that Scooter's old cell phone was among the items found with Kalfus's body. We think the phone might have originally come from Shaw."

"Huh."

"So," Joe wrapped up, "this meeting, social or otherwise, is to let you know that, while we've got nothing in hand, we have high hopes for a break of some sort."

James nodded formally. "In that case, I thank you for your courtesy. Where would the break come from, do you think?"

"Fingers crossed, from Shaw's factotum or confederate, Seamus Kyle. We're not sure what he is. Shaw's got an alibi for the night his wife died, supposedly in her sleep at home, so I'm very curious about what Mr. Kyle might be able to tell us about that."

"Playing devil's advocate," James countered, "how do you know Lucy didn't die of a heart attack or whatever?"

Joe allowed for a small conspiratorial smile. "We used our own ME to do the autopsy at DHMC—Beverly Hillstrom. The big reveal was that she didn't find an obvious cause of death. Our whole theory is hanging on a single tiny piece of plastic bag found under one of Lucy's fingernails—along with a really high blood alcohol content. It opens the possibility that this death could've been caused by the administration of an inert gas, pumped into a bag covering Lucy's head."

"Could've, but not necessarily," James restated, although with no challenging inflection. He was used to theoretical spitballing. It helped avoid tunnel vision, sometimes, no matter how weird.

"Right."

"Did you confront Shaw with the cell phone?" James asked. "If he's been doing this for decades, and Lucy was in the know, why did he knock her off now?"

"No to the first question, and you're in good company with the second," Joe replied. "If we're right about this, somehow a trigger was squeezed—just before we could split them up and question them."

Hendrix was visibly underwhelmed. "From being a little pissed off at first, I'm now really happy you didn't ask for our help. Not to be disrespectful, but a little piece of plastic on an otherwise sick older woman? An ironclad alibi for a possible killer who's never showed any violence toward his wife in the past? That is correct, isn't it? Reading between the lines?"

"It is," Joe admitted.

"And you're hoping the lawn boy, or whatever he is, is going to hand it over like the ending of a one-hour cop show? Good luck."

Joe was not offended. "Sometimes," he said, "cases come out of the shadows; they build up logically. Other times, I think they're more like a crossword puzzle, where other words supply the letters you need to fill in the one you're really after. To my mind, that's what I got here. In some way I can't see yet, that last missing letter's going to fall into place."

"And eureka?" James asked, one eyebrow raised.

Joe smiled. "You can't say it's never happened to you."

James nodded. "No. I cannot. Well, when it does, don't be shy about calling again. Till then, happy hunting."

Joe poked his head through Fred Houston's open office door and located the tech wizard at the far end of his long, windowless, computer-packed work space—a far cry from Joe's own office in an ancient drafty building with an oversized leaky window.

"Hello?" Joe asked. "I never want to startle you when your thumb's poised right over the Delete key."

Fred shook his head and stood up from the stool he'd been occupying. "Doesn't work that way. Good to see you. You've been busy."

They relocated nearer to the door. "What've you heard?" Joe asked.

"That you had a drop-by at Shaw's house that went sideways."

"There's an understatement. In retrospect, a bad idea. I was hoping to shake him up, put pressure on her, and maybe get something incriminating to add to what we have."

"Scooter's phone?"

"Not only. I've also landed a silver ashtray anniversary gift from Shaw to Lucy, found in a storage shed belonging to Cheri Pratt. But that was all plan A."

"Did you manage to get something anyhow?"

"That's where the 'sideways' part came in," Joe explained. "At the door, we heard Lucy had died in the night and Lemuel was getting ready to have her cremated. That put Willy and me onto chasing the bigger issue, which was to preserve Lucy's body for an autopsy.

"The whole idea of going by their house was a mistake anyhow. I moved too fast with too little. What sticks in my craw is that somehow—assuming I'm right about Shaw killing his wife—he already knew to cover his tracks, meaning we wouldn't have found anything had we entered the house."

"Unless she just died like we all do," Fred suggested. "And there never was anything to find."

Joe got up and began pacing the length of the narrow computer lab.

"Goddamn it. Right now, I've got one guaranteed murder, one

incredibly suspicious, well-timed death, one revived missing child case—plus another connected to Boston—and poor little Angie Neal, who got caught up in the mix and, if she's lucky, will only spend the rest of her life talking to shrinks. I have also enlisted Christ knows how many people to help, invoked multiple magical law enforcement protocols to let me hunt damn near anywhere I want, and have my squad wandering across two states. All for what? A dead cell phone and an ashtray."

At the far wall, he turned, looked at Houston, and let out a sigh. "Okay. Maybe Lucy did die of natural causes right after opening a plastic bag of crackers. And maybe Lemuel is just a horny old rich guy who can't get any at home and fantasizes at the local strip club. But to me, that's like looking at a huge crater in the ground, ignoring the shrapnel and bodies around its edge, and calling it a hole. *Sure* it's a hole," he emphasized, "but something caused it. Something bad. And every time I get close to figuring that out, instead of proof, I find Lemuel Shaw claiming to be an innocent victim. It's driving me crazy."

"And you're here now because . . . ?" Fred asked quietly.

Joe smiled despite himself. "Because my squad already knows all this, because I just met with James Hendrix but had nothing to tell him, and because I wanted you to know that I'm still fighting the fight."

"Joe," Fred said. "We got Trevor Buttner for Angie. Your guy Kunkle tied the bow on that. It was a job well done and totally justifies creating the task force, which is not that big a deal anyhow. Not only that, but you've brought Scooter's very cold case a little closer to the heat, regardless of where it leads. From my perspective, from ICAC's perspective, you've got nothing to worry about. Some success is better than none, and most sex cases in my experience are dicey to start with. More often than not, there's always a lack of proof early on."

Joe sat back down. "Thanks."

"So why else are you here?" Fred continued. "Sure as hell nobody has ever confused me with a wailing wall. I'm not that good a listener."

"Don't sell yourself short," Joe argued, admitting, "but you are right. I want to talk about Seamus Kyle."

"What about him?"

"That's my question," Joe replied, producing a copy of the picture snapped of Kyle on Shaw's doorstep. "Who is he? Where did he come from? How long has he been associated with Shaw? If we're right about Shaw's popping up everywhere not being pure coincidence, then I'm thinking he can't be acting alone. Lucy was either a co-conspirator or a witness, theoretically. Now she's gone and we suddenly have Kyle. A replacement for Lucy? A benchwarmer who's been moved into Lucy's spot?

"Here's what's rattling around my head," Joe kept going. "If you're up to no good, the best way to beat nosy people like us is to create good camouflage. You set up phony alibis, you create false identities, you hire people off the books to work for you. You do not commit a crime and then cover it up. You reverse the pattern—you *only* commit the crime once the cover's been created."

"Until you get surprised by something out of left field," Fred said, studying the photo. "Like Kalfus stealing your car."

"Or a witness thinking he saw Shaw grab a kid in Boston," Joe agreed. "But here's the catch: you make a habit of this sleight of hand. Whether you're up to something or not, you've always got a fallback story. All the time. You make it a norm."

That caught Fred's attention. "What're you saying?"

"The strip club. If Shaw's into kidnapping boys of a certain age and making them disappear, what's he doing staring at third-ranked adult female strippers in rural New England? What's that do for a dedicated pedophile?"

"You're saying he's been laying down a false trail all along," Fred stated.

"Believable, wouldn't you say?" Joe responded. "You hear about men with multiple families, like that CBS reporter who broadcast from the road all the time, or Charles Lindbergh. Why not someone with a secret criminal life? He moves back and forth between them, each one having a complete cover story."

"You're asking about Kyle because he might be from Shaw's other life?"

Joe heard the reserve in Fred's voice. "I know it's out there. But what've I got to work with? I'm building a picture here with pieces of confetti scattered all over the street."

Fred took that in, thought a moment, and then lifted his chin slightly. "Okay," he said. "Got it. Let me poke around a bit. That work?"

Joe rose and laid his hand on Houston's shoulder. "Yes. Absolutely. Appreciate it."

Susan Spinney looked up from enjoying her beer on her back porch in Springfield to see Willy Kunkle standing on the lawn, taking her in.

Startled but not upset, she raised her bottle in greeting and said, "Is being a deeply creepy man natural, or do you work at it?"

"Me?" he asked.

"Most people ring the doorbell. You case a joint like it was an enemy pillbox."

He approached the porch at her gesture to join him. "Hard habit to break," he said. "And I don't see any really good reason to do it. Is Les around?"

"Depends," she said, sliding a seltzer bottle toward him from the assortment by her side. The day had been unusually warm, and while she was still wearing a coat, she hadn't been able to resist tacking some afternoon sunshine onto an official day off.

Willy placed the bottle between his thighs and unscrewed the cap with his right hand. "I want to talk him into a little scouting mission."

"Will this risk his career, like most of your schemes? He'll probably love it."

She took another sip of beer before rising to open the back door and yell, "*Les!* The Prince of Darkness is here."

Lester appeared in under a minute, wiping his hands with a dish towel. "Hey," he said, surprised. "That's my seltzer. What's up? Everything okay?"

Sue took advantage of his arrival to head inside, saying, "I bet that depends on what you agree to. I don't want to be a witness." She paused at the door and blew Willy a kiss. "Love you, Kunkle. Return what's left of my husband in one piece, please."

This time, Willy raised his own bottle—or, more accurately, Lester's. "Will do, kiddo. Love you, too."

"What's goin' on?" Les asked, sitting down and opening a bottle of his own.

"You talk to Joe this afternoon?"

"Nope. I was going to check for messages in a bit, see if the case file's been updated."

Willy pushed out his lips slightly before saying, "Won't find much. He's circling a notion like a dog does a hydrant, but he's not putting anything on record yet."

"What notion?" Lester asked reasonably.

"In a nutshell? He's wondering if Lemuel Shaw isn't an avatar—a manifestation of somebody who's not what he seems."

Lester followed the premise. "Making him who, in reality?"

"Jack the Child Grabber, if the boss is right," Willy said, taking a swig. "Joe thinks that *maybe* Shaw's two people in one: a local boy done good who moved back to the neighborhood, and a well-heeled pedophile with a *very* covert second life."

"One his late wife knew about?" Lester asked, closing the circle.

"That's the theory."

"You agree with him?"

Willy made a face. "Dunno. That's kinda why I'm here. Joe's chasing down the usual stuff—background checks and past involvements. I'm all for that, of course."

Lester laughed at the uncharacteristic largesse. "But . . . ," he suggested.

Willy gave him an apologetic look. "Okay, okay. It's just that we've been chasing this case for a while now and getting nowhere fast. It might not be the worst idea to tweak procedure just a bit."

"Here we go."

"Yeah . . . Well, come on, Les. You know how much those background searches dig up. Little to nothing. DUIs, past addresses, most of them wrong, criminal records that only show when the guy got caught. Hit or miss, mostly miss."

"Ah," Lester said, his eye widening. "I got it. You want to kidnap Shaw or Seamus Kyle and torture one of them. Cool. I've never done that before."

He interrupted himself theatrically by slapping his head. "Wait. That's right. That's illegal. Phooey."

Willy pulled again on his seltzer before putting the bottle down. "I want to tail 'em."

Lester's face fell. "Oh, shit, Willy, Joe's never gonna go for that. It's the definition of labor-intensive. Plus, I've still got more retracing of Kalfus's route to do. That's taken *way* more time than we expected. What you're pitching is worse than a procedural violation. It's a budget buster."

"Think of it," Willy continued as if Lester hadn't spoken. "Both Shaw and Kyle are in motion. If we're right, they just knocked off Lucy and they know we're suspicious. They've *got* to be busy hiding their tracks, covering up—going places, meeting people, doing deals. Now's not the time to collect computer data and wait for something to happen but to slip in behind them and dog their heels."

"Sniper-style," Lester suggested neutrally.

Willy tilted his head. "Exactly."

Lester went on. "Without authorization, without backup, and without pay, if I'm reading this right."

Willy's enthusiasm was unaffected. "Yup. Sounds like fun, don't it?"

"And Sammie's on board with this?"

Willy was coy. "She'll appreciate the childcare money saved after you and I are suspended."

Lester passed his hand over his face. Rationally, he knew it wouldn't get nearly that bad. But it wasn't good practice. It was precisely the kind of cowboying Joe disliked, and if anything did go wrong, the lack of backup would be a real consideration, for Lester at least. Willy was better suited for the maverick role and might have even been missing it.

Les had no similar itch to scratch.

But he wasn't immune from the double stimulants of frustration and a thirst for action. As Willy had eloquently put it, they were strictly following the recipe book at the same time the bad guys were kicking into high gear—assuming they *were* the bad guys.

Which Willy's proposal might settle one way or the other.

With Sue's fatalistic last words echoing in his head, Lester gave his partner a nod. "Okay. How do you want to work it?"

One of the lesser-mentioned associations common to law enforcement is the oft-repeated relationship cops have with funeral home personnel. As is true between shop owner and UPS driver, the two professions meet up regularly. It creates a camaraderie that Joe now decided to exploit, especially after learning that the firm handling Lucy Shaw's "details"—as the euphemism went—was owned by an old high school pal of his, Barbara Mahoney.

Joe and Barb had attended school in Thetford, Vermont, where both had been reared. Later, Barb had met and married Dennis Mahoney and become swept up in the funeral business. Now located in Claremont, New Hampshire, just across the Connecticut River, and widowed ten years before—Dennis having been overly fond of cigarettes, fast food, and beer—Barb was still at it.

It hadn't been the most varied or effervescent of lives, but useful, lucrative, and happily predictable, mirroring the girl's appetites that Joe had known decades ago.

Not surprisingly, funeral homes present themselves in imitation of the upstairs/downstairs portrait known to American viewers of British movies, with a fancy, sober façade masking some very prosaic inner workings.

Joe thus avoided the ornate and imposing main entrance of Mahoney's for where he suspected he was likely to find someone alive and receptive.

What he didn't expect was Barb herself, in the open garage, vacuuming out the front of one of her vans.

"*Joe Gunther!*" she exclaimed as she caught sight of him through the windshield, cut the machine, and stepped out of the vehicle. "My God, I hope I don't look as old as you do."

She walked up to him, put her arms around his neck, and kissed him on the lips, laughing afterward. "I always wanted to do that when we were in school. One more off the bucket list. How the hell are you?"

He stood rooted in place, his astonishment plain, revising his first plan to reintroduce himself after such a long time.

He laughed and ran his hand through his hair. "Damn, Barb. No wonder you've made such a success of yourself."

She was also, he thought, accurate concerning her appearance. Whether it was genetics, cosmetics, clean living, or all three, Barb Mahoney looked twenty years younger than he knew her to be.

In silent exchange for his appraising glance, she suddenly became serious, watching his face carefully. "Shoot," she said. "I should've asked if everybody was okay. Your mom? Your brother, Leo?"

He quickly put her at ease. "Oh, no. Barb. I'm sorry. Understandable, but no. That's not why I'm here." He turned and indicated the open garage door. "I was hoping my choice of entrances would take the edge off that."

Her features relaxed again. "Well, they did, in case you didn't notice, but I had to ask. You know how it is."

"I do, I do. And don't misunderstand. I appreciated the welcome."

She gave him a leer. "Least I could do. You still a cop?"

"Oh, yeah. Kind of a habit I couldn't break."

She nodded. "I know the feeling. Still single?"

"Only legally."

"Oh." She rolled her eyes. "Too bad, but good for you, not that I'm surprised. Wild guess is you're not here for social reasons, anyway. Am I right?"

"True, but it is nice to see you again."

She turned at that and beckoned to him to follow her through the back door, into the building, proper. "There's a line. Always the diplomat."

He seriously doubted that, recalling his awkward teen years, but he let it go and let her lead him first into a storage area, then a lab of sorts, complete with operating table, surrounded by some scary-looking and invasive equipment, and finally to what appeared to be an employee lounge, with TV, couch, coffee machine, and scattered magazines. It was as informal and lived-in as the front of the building most emphatically was not.

"Sit," she ordered him. "In one of the armchairs if you're protecting your virtue. You never know what I might do next."

He chose the couch, partially as a show of trust. When she joined him after pouring two cups, she sat at the other end, pointing her finger at him and waggling her eyebrows. He'd forgotten what a character she was. Or, how well she and his younger and more adventuresome brother, Leo, had gotten along.

"Okay," she said. "I'm actually on a tight leash, all kidding aside, and I gotta get cracking soon. What brings you to Claremont?"

"Lucy Shaw," he said bluntly.

"We got her. She rob a bank we don't know about?"

"I don't think so, but I am curious about the company she kept."

Barb sampled her coffee before replying, "Don't know. I never heard of her before they wheeled her in. She's from Gilsum. I met her husband, if that helps."

Joe played it neutrally. "What's he like?"

"Thinks he's cool, but doesn't carry it off. He also put out some weird feelings about her. I couldn't tell if he was relieved or sad. It seemed to come and go, depending on whether he was being watched or not."

"I take it he looked relieved when he thought he was alone?" Joe asked.

"Yeah. I left him with her for a few minutes of quiet time. Standard stuff. They usually cry or talk to the body, maybe touch a hand or something. It can be sweet. Anyhow, I poked my head in when he wasn't watching, and he was checking his phone. Couldn't have been less involved with her. I even tested it, for fun, by making a little noise before I walked in. The phone disappeared, and he was pretending to wipe an eye. Pretty slimy, I thought, which didn't improve when I caught him checking out my boobs. I mean, I'm used to that in the real world. What woman isn't? But here? You know him?"

"Barely," Joe said. "Did anyone else come by?"

"The usual friend types, trading stories about high times. All women."

"Family?"

She paused to consider that. "No. I asked the husband, Lemuel. Funny name. He said she had a sister down south but that they'd been estranged for years." Barb almost interrupted herself to add, "There *was* somebody you might ought to talk to. She came in alone. Really nice, but quiet. Dr. Pat Glowa. Another odd name. She was different from the others."

"How so?"

"Thoughtful, respectful. She was the only one I felt showed that she'd actually lost someone. Everybody else was either like hubby and the creepy guy with him, or the women, who might just as well've been on their way to the mall."

"You know what Glowa's story was?" Joe asked. "How was she connected to Lucy?"

"That was another interesting thing," Barb answered, quickly checking her watch and putting her mug down on a side table. "She made a comment that sounded like Lucy had been her patient. I might've gotten that wrong. I can't swear to it, but that was the feeling I got."

She stood up and smoothed the front of her jeans. "Well, I'm afraid that's it, Joe. I gotta run. God, it was great seeing you. A real treat." She approached him as he also stood, but simply gave him a quick hug, cocking an eyebrow as she pulled away, and said, "Scared ya, didn't I?"

She then reversed course and led him back through to the garage as he asked, "Did you get the name of the creepy guy with Lemuel?"

"Yep. Seamus. I heard the old guy call him that. We were never introduced. There was a very clear pecking order between them, where Shaw was the boss. But Seamus was like two people in one. I barely got a word out of him, so that part seemed shy and uncomfortable. But he also gave me the willies, like he was dangerous or something."

They reached the garage, and she repeated the quick hug. "I'm probably just making it up. Too many late-night Netflix movies. Don't be such a stranger, Joe, and think of me if you and that girlfriend you don't talk about ever break up, okay?"

CHAPTER ELEVEN

It wasn't difficult finding a name like Dr. Patricia Glowa on the internet. She purportedly had an office right across Route 120 from Dartmouth-Hitchcock Medical Center in Lebanon, New Hampshire. Joe didn't know the details of her relationship to Lucy Shaw or the nature of her practice, but he'd been pleased by her immediate receptiveness on the phone when he'd called out of the blue, suggesting a meeting.

He was surprised by the address she gave him, which turned out to be a modest, modern-looking business block, set to the rear of a high-end development park. There was no sign on the door she'd told him to use, and a pile of empty cardboard boxes were stacked just outside.

As instructed, he poked his head in the doorway and quietly called out, "Dr. Glowa?"

"Back here," came the response. "Keep on coming."

He entered a front office, with chairs pushed haphazardly around a central conference table covered with more boxes and pieces of office equipment, and worked his way to a rear door that led to a smaller room overlooking a patio and a discreet wooded area. Here was a large desk, more chairs, a few plants hoping for sunnier final perches, extra boxes, and a just-visible woman on her knees before an open filing cabinet, partially behind the desk.

"Grab a seat, Mr. Gunther," she said. "I just have to find one thing before I forget about it entirely. Bear with me."

"Take your time," he said, choosing a chair by the sliding glass doors.

Less than a minute later, the woman rose, triumphantly brandishing a file, circled the desk, and proffered her free hand in greeting.

"Mr. Gunther. Pat Glowa. Nice to meet you."

She had short, white hair, a great handshake, and was dressed in jeans, which he hadn't expected—not that he harbored many predictable expectations anymore.

She cleared a seat opposite him, plopped the file down on the crowded desk beside a forlorn plant, and blessed him with a radiant smile. "So," she said. "Lucy Shaw. What would you like to know?"

He raised an eyebrow. "No opening disclaimers about patient confidentiality?" he asked.

"The woman's dead. I'm a pragmatist."

"You are a medical doctor, though, correct?"

She waved a hand vaguely. "I can dig out my degrees if you'd like. Might take a while. But yes, I was Lucy's personal physician, and I am an M.D. This mess around us is because I'm segueing away from clinical medicine and pursuing a new ambition that I've aspired to for decades. I won't bore you with the details, but it involves public health and consulting with state and local government on how to improve policy. There's much more to it, but as I said . . ."

"You don't want to bore me," he finished for her. "I'd probably be a terrible audience anyhow. Can I start right off and ask if you attend the wakes of all your deceased patients?"

"In a moment, you can," she replied, crossing her legs and adding, "I would have offered you something to drink, by the way, but I don't have anything set up yet, and I don't even know if the building has a soda machine."

"I'm fine, thanks."

"Excellent. First, I have a question for you, Mr. Gunther—"

"Joe," he interrupted.

"Joe—all you said on the phone is that you were a policeman investigating Lucy's death. Could you perhaps give me a bit more than that, without crossing any lines? I know you folks value confidentiality as much as we do."

"Sure." He removed his credentials from his pocket and showed them to her. "I work for the Vermont Bureau of Investigation, and I'm temporarily assigned to a federal task force, working on a case spanning both Vermont and New Hampshire."

"And Lucy's a part of that?"

"We think so. The tricky part in these things is that names crop up all over the place, and we have to figure out how, if, and where they fit."

"Persons of interest."

"Right," he confirmed. "That's what she is right now."

"Did any of that play a role in her death?" Glowa asked.

Joe showed his surprise. "You don't think she died of natural causes?"

"I don't know. She could have. She certainly had the right preconditions."

Joe frowned. "We heard her PCP had filled out her death certificate, which is why we almost missed having an autopsy."

"That would have been the practice I just left," Glowa explained.

"That certificate was produced by one of my old colleagues drawing from the medical files I left behind."

"You wouldn't have certified her death like they did?"

"I don't know. What did they list as a cause?"

Joe tried to recall. "If memory serves, hypertensive and arteriosclerotic cardiovascular disease, diabetes, obesity, and hypercholesterolemia. I think that was it. Was that wrong?"

"Not necessarily. It sounds about right for a million death certificates. A very common litany of ailments."

Joe scratched his head. "I'm confused. If that sounds right, why did you imply it wasn't?"

"I didn't," she corrected him. "What were the findings at autopsy?"

"The pathologist found all that, but none of it was severe enough to be an obvious smoking gun."

Glowa jutted out her chin in a gesture suggesting agreement. "There you have it, then."

"What?"

The woman took pity on him. "I'm sorry, Joe. Welcome to the real world of medical diagnosis. You must be constantly assaulted by people accusing you of not doing your job and letting guilty people go free, all because of a supposed lack of evidence. Physicians get the same treatment—'You knew he was sick. Why didn't you fix him?' The problem, as in your case, is a matter of degree. How sick is too sick? How guilty is guilty enough to file charges? Lucy Shaw was not a healthy woman. But she wasn't at death's door. She was compliant with her medicines, good about coming in for visits, and even eliminated certain behaviors that, over time, were definitely going to shorten her life, like smoking."

"So you wouldn't have signed that death certificate like that."

"I have an academic background, as well as a clinical one," she answered him. "I would have pushed for an autopsy—a private one if the state's OCME had demurred. So I'm delighted you ordered one, and I'd love to see the results, if possible."

"I'll see what I can do," Joe said. "The tox results are pending, as usual, so it'll be a while."

"I understand. Thank you."

"Okay," Joe said. "Let me try this from another angle—call it a more global one. It goes to why I think you attended her wake, which I suspect you don't do for all your deceased patients."

She allowed that he was right with a smile and a nod.

"What was it," he continued, "that merited the extra attention? Friendship or concern?"

"Are you good at your job, Joe?" she asked. "I'm getting the feeling you are."

He didn't respond, waiting patiently.

"I would imagine," she began, "that in your work, you get your fair portion of cases that can't be landed for one reason or another. Am I right? The hoped-for solution hovers just beyond your reach."

"No argument."

"We do, too. Most of the time, it's diagnostic. Patients come in, complaining of one thing or another, and we simply cannot identify the source or treat its symptoms. Or we know what it is but can't do anything about it. We live with that. It's even partly why we do this work. If everything was a laceration, where a Band-Aid would do the trick, things would quickly become stale."

She shifted in her seat. "But once in a while, you get a patient where the physical aspects of her health run second to her emotional and psychological presentation. That was Lucy. She was my enigma, the riddle I couldn't solve. I loved having her come in, but not for the checkups and blood tests and culture smears. I looked forward to trying to dissipate the smoke screen. I wanted her to trust me enough to tell me what she was shielding."

"And did you?"

"Never to my satisfaction."

"What did you suspect?"

"Abuse. Not physical. Not while she was with me, anyhow. This was deep-seated and soulful. What most people might have seen as snobbishness or aloofness, I sensed was the result of trauma, probably dating back to childhood."

"She told you this?"

"Not in so many words. She slipped occasionally and gave me enough to believe I was right."

"How about her husband?" Joe asked, his interest growing. "Was there any mention of abuse from him?"

"Only indirectly. It was a battle royal for me to get her to drop the cigarettes. The drinking and junk food were two goals too far. And honestly, the reason I didn't push too hard was I think she used them to blunt the pain. None of this is uncommon, but I was nevertheless fascinated by her, I think in part because of her intelligence. I sensed that despite her situation, she might have been willing and able to help herself."

"The situation being Lemuel," Joe suggested.

"I thought so. It's commonplace for someone with an abusive upbringing to end up in a similar place as an adult. It sounds self-destructive, and that can be the end result, but it's much more complicated than that. It often boils down to their choosing companions whose behavior mirrors all they've ever known. It sounds perverse, but it ends up becoming almost a comfort zone for them."

"Beating substituting for love?" Joe asked.

"Simply put, yes. But the beating need not be physical. My feeling was that Lemuel fit that category—the hyper-controller. Her options, as she saw them, may have been to adapt or die."

"He told my colleagues that they'd stopped having sex," Joe said. "He used that to rationalize his going to strip clubs."

Glowa gave that a moment's consideration before saying, "Could be. But if I'm correct about the marriage's dynamics, he would have been the one to cut off intimacy. If she'd tried it unilaterally, he would have simply raped her."

Given his own suspicions, Joe kept his next question straightforward and neutral. "Why did he break off relations, assuming he did?"

"Specifically? I wouldn't be able to say. More broadly, sex is frequently a tool of power, whether administered or withheld. It could even be that he did both to her, at different times."

"They did have kids together."

"I heard that," Glowa acknowledged. "Boy and a girl. Estranged, from what I gathered. That, too, would fit what we're talking about."

"You think Lemuel abused them?"

"Broadly speaking, he could have."

"Does any of this fit the profile of someone who stalks and kidnaps children? Preteen boys?"

She considered that before asking, "Is that what you're investigating?"

"In part, yes."

"If you're asking if such a man could have a wife and kids, the answer is, you bet. They aren't all creepy guys living alone with bodies under the floorboards. John Wayne Gacy was married and had children. These are often psychopaths, Joe—clever, likable, chameleonlike in society. They're hard to spot."

There was a lull as Glowa's words sank in.

"But Lucy never mentioned anything to you?" Joe finally asked.

"No," was the answer, followed by, "I only knew a woman I suspected was haunted by devils. What those were, I was never told." She sighed. "I think that's why I went to her wake. To apologize for not pushing harder."

"You do realize how many nights we'll be doing this," Lester suggested.

Willy, in the passenger seat, plucked the bag of chips off his lap. "Could be a few," he agreed airily, digging in. "Sue already complaining? This is our first night."

"She mostly works nights anyhow," Les countered, pulling to the curb and killing the headlights. "I bet Sam hasn't even noticed."

Willy paused, his chip-laden hand halfway to his mouth. "You could be right. But you know—and don't give me any shit—I miss Emma at night. Kid's really grown on me."

Lester kept a straight face as Willy started chewing. Willy would be the last to admit a love affair with his own family.

The two of them had first discussed tailing Shaw and Seamus Kyle separately, keeping in touch by phone. But it didn't appear Shaw was going anywhere, choosing to hunker down at his house, so on the off chance that Kyle might meet someone deserving to be followed, Les and Willy had teamed up.

At the moment, they were glad for that. Now back in Keene, they'd followed Seamus to one of the town's poorer sections and seen him leave his car and enter a former old factory, now converted into apartments.

"Interesting gesture," Willy remarked through his mouthful.

"Locking his car? Yeah, I noticed that, like he's gonna leave it for a while. You wanna watch the back or should I?"

Willy opened his door, which, as with most unmarked police cars, did not trigger the dome light. "You're driving. I'll go." He waggled his phone in the air as he moved. Lester understood and switched his own phone to intercom mode, the current replacement of the clumsy walkie-talkies of yore.

It didn't take long. Under four minutes after Willy vanished around the edge of the building, his voice quietly filled the car. "He's comin' out the back with another guy—Caucasian, black puffy parka, red baseball cap, jeans, white sneakers. I took a picture. Swing around the south entrance of the alley and pick me up. Looks like they're aiming for a pickup at the other end. Keep your lights off."

Lester found his partner blending into the shadows. Together, they entered the narrow back street in pitch darkness, at a snail's pace, watching for movement.

"There," Willy said unnecessarily as twin taillights came on ahead of them. He snapped a shot of the registration.

Lester slowed. The pickup's headlights came on, allowing the two cops to see silhouettes of two men in the cab.

"What do you think?" Lester asked.

Willy understood. "Depends. If Seamus is after a lot, they'll probably head out. If he's just scoring, they could do the deal right here."

"Want me to pull back?"

"Nah. Why did he turn on his headlights?"

True enough, the truck began moving, with Lester not far behind.

Reflective of the region, the trip did not proceed to an even worse neighborhood. It took them out of town instead. The northern New England world of drugs, guns, and illicit behavior was just as likely to occur in the country as a metropolis. Policing was a thinly populated profession up here, its officers more concentrated in urban areas. It made sense, assuming any degree of self-preservation, for crooks to practice their dark arts far from the glow of streetlamps.

Fortunately for Lester, the moon was near full and the cloud cover scant, because the farther this two-car caravan proceeded into the surrounding woods nearby, the more he had to drop back, his headlights still off, so as not to be spotted.

Some five miles outside of Keene, the pickup's brake lights burned brightly before veering left off the road, indicating either a side road or a driveway.

Tucking into a shallow pull-off, Lester killed the engine and pointed through the undergrowth to where they could just see the twin red dots—like a fantasy animal's glowing eyes—abruptly wink off. "Time for a little recon?" he asked his partner.

Willy had already opened his door. "Absolutely."

Unlike Lester, who'd been trained by the state police to function in an overt capacity, Willy was back in his element, at night, undercover, proceeding stealthily. Lester honored the man's comfort level and quietly slipped in behind him, working hard to emulate his way forward.

It was easy enough at first, walking down the road to the cutoff. But there, after cautioning, "They might have video," Willy headed not up the drive, but in among the spectral trees alongside, right beside a clearly posted No Trespassing sign.

It was a black-and-white world, the moon robbing everything it touched of color. Traveling through an old photograph, the two men slid forward, placing their feet gingerly, their toes reaching for the soil beneath any fallen branches or brush, to avoid the telltale snap of a twig. Ahead, emerging with gradual clarity, a small hunting cabin distinguished itself beyond the pickup and a second vehicle beyond it. The building's two windows were illuminated, and, helping the two cops, the steady throbbing of a muted generator filled the silence.

Lester's heart was pounding, his eyes so wide he had to remind himself to blink. Had the roles been reversed, wouldn't he have put out a dog? Or rigged an alarm system? Or motion-detecting lights?

As if in answer to his concerns, Willy reached back and placed his hand against Lester's chest. Without a word, he pointed at his feet, unknowingly and ironically putting Lester at ease. Strung between two tree trunks, all but invisible except to an eye like Willy's, was a thin electrical wire.

Lester bent close to Willy's ear. "Grenade or something else?"

Not looking back, Willy whispered, "Who cares? We step over it."

Which was why, Lester thought, you let this man take point.

At last in the cabin's dooryard, Willy surprised his partner again. As Les moved toward one of the windows to look in, Willy produced his phone and dexterously took a series of flash-less pictures of the vehicles, their plates, and the building before sidling up beside Lester to photograph what was happening inside.

There were four men sitting around a table in the middle of a central room. Beer cans, handguns, and packages of opioids littered the space among them. There was laughter and easy banter going on. One of the four, facing the window, was Seamus Kyle.

Willy pocketed his phone and quietly stepped back.

Lester gave him a raised eyebrow, to which Willy responded with a thumbs-up.

No explanation was needed. As Lester well understood, they'd gained a hold over Seamus, not to mention the beginnings of identifying his companions. It wouldn't bear legal scrutiny. They were trespassing here, taking pictures on private property.

But Seamus wouldn't necessarily know that, and if Joe's instincts were right, a little dope peddling on the side was going to be the least of Seamus's concerns.

The two cops retreated, taking care to step over the mysterious wire on their way out.

Sammie pulled into the shopping mall parking lot, found a space close to her destination, and cut the engine before consulting her list against the business name across from her. This was the fifth party store she'd visited over two days, and she was beginning to lose heart. If their theory was right about Seamus Kyle having purchased nitrous oxide or helium to kill Lucy Shaw, Sam was having a tough time proving it. Both gases were easily available, including through the internet, making potential outlets almost too numerous to count.

She crossed to the store's entrance, a file folder in hand. She'd not only been checking retail outlets, but hospitals, ambulance services, and medical supply houses, among others, all in the hope that Seamus had followed a course of least resistance and done his shopping locally.

"Hi there," was the greeting as she exchanged the cold sunshine outside for the warm interior.

"Hi yourself," she addressed the bald man behind the counter. "I'm hoping you can help me out."

He gave her an affable nod. "I'll try. What d'you need?"

She displayed her credentials, which immediately cooled him down.

"Uh-oh. What's going on?"

"Nothing too bad, I hope," she replied easily. "Just crossing t's and dotting i's, as they say." She opened the file and spread out five photographs of young men, including the one of Seamus taken at the Shaws' front door. A so-called photo array of this type was usually restricted to connecting a suspect to a proven crime. But despite her not having anything that solid, Sam liked to be thorough and avoid possible accusations later of coaching witnesses by feeding them one picture only.

She therefore asked the counterman, "In the last few days, has any one of these men come in and purchased gas?"

The response was both astonishing and rewarding. Following only a casual scan, the man tapped Seamus's with his finger and said, "Yup. Him. It's slow this time of year. I've haven't sold any in almost a month—except to him a few days ago. A small tank of helium."

A few years earlier, Beverly had purchased a tiny jewel box of a home on the edge of a small lake in Windsor, Vermont. The town marked a convenient midpoint between her second job at Dartmouth and Joe's place in Brattleboro, but that, she'd maintained, had merely been an additional benefit.

Her primary residence was a wedding cake of a McMansion south of Burlington, far to the west, purchased by her ex-husband at the peak of his hubristic success as a lawyer. This far humbler Windsor abode, tucked away, modest, as shy as a colt finding its footing, had won her heart as the place she wanted to enjoy with Joe, even knowing that their times here would be few and brief.

It was with that love and contentment and past life experience that she greeted him that evening, leaning against the open front door as his car pulled into the yard.

"Hey, sailor," she said as he came in for an embrace, sighing deeply as her arms slipped around his neck.

"Hey, you," he replied, muffled by her neck, recognizing in this woman the oldest and best friend he'd ever had.

"How're you holding up?" she asked, dropping one arm to around his waist and accompanying him into the house.

"Good, especially now," he said. "Even if it's been a curious last few days."

"More fallout stemming from the late, perhaps unlamented Mrs. Shaw?"

"Fair to say," he agreed. "Although her death could be the pro-verbial tip of an iceberg."

He eased off his coat and jacket and draped them over the back of one of the armchairs in the living room. "You," he said, kissing her properly, "have been hard at work in the kitchen, I smell."

"I have," she admitted happily. "I know your druthers are prob-ably for sardines on Wonder Bread, but I have conjured up what I hope will be an acceptable alternative."

He touched the side of his nose. "If this is right that it's your world-famous spinach lasagna, then you're on."

"It is and you're welcome. Step right this way."

They ate on the screened-in back porch overlooking Lake Runne-mede, which the locals have the sense to call a pond. The end-of-day peacefulness allowed them to sit quietly at the table, enjoying their coffee in the dying light, and soak in the meager warmth of the day. This transition from winter to summer remained almost lyrical to most New Englanders, who, while stalwart about their abil-ity to brave the cold, are never proud enough to deny spring's life-saving infusion.

"So," Beverly finally said, reaching out to hold Joe's hand. "Tell me of your journeys and travails. I sense you are burdened, if not troubled."

"Not troubled yet," he agreed. "But definitely burdened. This case has pivoted, and you were there when it did. We've gone from the quirky discovery of a dead thief in the trunk of the very car he stole to something darker, more elusive, and a lot more complicated."

He paused to watch the shadow of a long, low-flying bird skim across the one remaining ice patch on the water's smooth surface, far away.

"It's got to be the same for you," he resumed. "Every time a body bag is opened at the morgue and you set your eyes on its contents. All those impressions at once—clothing, condition, gender, odors, facial features. You have to sort through a flood of information. For me, the phone ringing is that starter's pistol.

"Except I usually start with nothing. Especially with homicides. They're more like algorithms that spread out in widening circles. Family, friends, associates, enemies. Routinely, it doesn't take long to find blood on somebody's hands. The bad guys make it easy and make us look smarter than we are."

"But not this time," she suggested.

He paused, not wanting to sound melodramatic. What was truly bothering him had less to do with facts. He was haunted by Kalfus's curled-up body, little Angie's betrayed innocence, Lucy's nakedness, stripped of all high-fashion defenses under Beverly's autopsy light. Which didn't include the ghost of Scooter Nelson or the nameless Boston boy.

"No," he conceded. "Something truly evil's going on."

Fred Houston hesitated at the door of the VBI office on the second floor of Brattleboro's municipal building, peering in to see who might be there.

"Hello?" he called out.

The answer came from behind him. "Hello yourself, Fred."

He whirled around to see Joe in the hallway with a pitcherful of water for the coffee machine. "Damn. Don't you make any noise when you walk?"

Joe patted his shoulder as he preceded him into the office. "I used to. Hanging around Kunkle cured me of it. I think he's got us all tiptoeing like cats by now. There's got to be some herd behavior explanation for that. What're you doing on this side of the river?"

Fred instead looked around the small, cluttered office, its four desks almost precluding passage among them. "I thought I had it bad," he said. "At least I'm behind a locked front door."

Joe was tending to the coffee machine. "We tried that, briefly. None of us liked it. And the rest of the building has to stay open for the public anyhow. So far, either nobody knows we're up here or they don't care. You want some java? Proof positive it's fresh."

"Sure," Fred replied, sitting at Spinney's desk, being careful not to disturb his array of stork artifacts—accumulated tributes to his birdlike appearance and his nickname at the police academy.

"You here for us?" Joe asked. "Or were you in the neighborhood?"

Fred produced a thin folded file from his coat pocket. "Special delivery. Plus, I did want to get out of my office. It's nice to see what the weather's doing every once in a while. I don't have one of those." He indicated the window.

Joe took the file and opened it, glancing at its contents, or at least its title. "Seamus Kyle," he recited. "What did you find out?"

"Well, that's the wrinkle," Fred reported. "There is no such person."

Joe looked up, his eyebrows raised. "Far out."

Fred smiled at not just the quaint expression, but the equanimity behind it. "That's it?"

Joe checked the coffee machine. He began to ready two mugs. "Honestly? There's less and less about this case that surprises me anymore. In a way, finding out Seamus is an invention is more helpful than not. Seems like everything in Lemuel Shaw's world is out of whack, so why not his right-hand man?"

CHAPTER TWELVE

A tolerant and forgiving man, Joe was finding his patience tried as he sat watching the oversized flat-screen monitor on the office wall, listening to Willy explain the slideshow illustrating his and Lester's midnight high jinks.

Sensing his disapproval brewing, Willy concluded by saying, "Messy, unorthodox, and illegal, I know, boss, but investigative only. Not anything we'd move on. I just wanted to get *something* on the son of a bitch we could use as leverage."

Joe glanced at Spinney, who wisely stayed silent. As did Sam, whose expression only spoke of concern for her partner and fear that he might have finally pushed their leader too far.

But Joe didn't react, aside from asking Sam, "You?"

"Right," she responded. "It's pretty much what I filed in my report. I linked Seamus to the purchase of a small tank of helium. In and of itself, not much. He could just tell us he has a balloon fetish, but combined with what Willy and Lester got, it does add up to something odd going on."

"You read what I learned about Shaw from Dr. Glowa?" Joe asked them.

All nodded but Willy—forever the nonconformist.

"Well, add to it that Fred Houston just dropped by with his background check on Seamus."

"This should be interesting," Sam said.

"Yes and no," Joe replied. "He doesn't exist."

"No shit," Lester said excitedly. "Same as what I got from the fusion center. I was going to resubmit because I figured I had something spelled wrong."

"Apparently not," Joe reassured him.

"We've already asked this question," Willy said, introducing a change of topic. "But why did Lemuel Shaw kill his wife now—or have her killed?"

The apparent non sequitur prompted a pause before Joe replied, "You have a suggestion?"

"No," Willy said, an unusual admission from him. "I can't figure out if we're right and he's burning bridges to slow us down, or he did it for reasons we know nothing about. If it's the first, how the hell did he know we were considering him a person of interest? To my memory, we hadn't tipped our hand before Lucy was announced dead. We were *about* to, but not yet."

Lester suggested, "We showed up in force for that second interview at his house, where we first met Seamus and found out Lucy had died. Could someone have let him know we were coming?"

"One of our bunch?" Sam asked.

"Rich man," Lester said. "Influential, affable. If he is a crook, it makes sense he'd have someone on the inside, just as a friend, not necessarily a bad cop—maybe a part-timer or a constable."

"We'll probably never find that out," Joe said. "Could be, though. It wouldn't be the first time."

"I say we go back," Willy stated. "With a warrant this time. We have enough for probable cause now. Seamus claims Shaw's house as his personal address, doesn't he?"

"Far as I know," Joe agreed. "Although convincing a judge to let us in is going to take one hell of a persuasive affidavit."

They didn't invoke a show of force like last time. Joe was as sensitive to not acting high-handedly on foreign turf as he was to enlisting help once too often. As a result, only Fred and a few of his fellow deputies had been invited.

That being said, they did have a warrant based on the probable cause they'd built against Seamus, combined with Cheri's stolen ashtray. However, they didn't get a response when they reached Shaw's residence later that afternoon. It didn't affect their action. They could still enter the place. But one of the primary incentives had been to corner Seamus and perhaps Shaw and use the circumstances to ramp up the pressure against them.

But the place was empty and, as they discovered, seemingly abandoned, with cleaned-out drawers, tidied-up bathrooms, and a garage devoid of vehicles.

It also contained no drugs, signs of drug use, or anything else pointing to criminal activity. It was just an enormous, echoing, oddly cold showboat of a building, as reflective of its owner as any high-end commercial resort.

A few hours after their arrival, and following the departure of their companions, Lester approached Joe with the obvious conclusion. "They knew we were coming."

"Again," Sam added, flopping down in one of the overstuffed armchairs in the cathedral-ceilinged living room, surrounded by mounted animal heads, rifles on racks, and painted scenes of peerless hunting.

Joe pursed his lips in thought, wandering over to the wall of

French doors leading out onto a large deck. "I would love to know how."

Willy appeared from the kitchen, fresh from the outdoors, and contributed, "I may've found one way. Probably not the only one, but I bet it was their first heads-up."

"What?" Sam asked.

Willy's expression showed only empathy when he pointed to her and Lester while answering, "You two. I found a couple of wireless cameras at the bottom of the driveway, trained on the road. Nice units, very high-tech, virtually invisible. My bet is they run nonstop and most likely record what they see."

Joe caught where he was heading. "And they saw Sam and Lester driving by days ago, when they were following Kalfus's travel log."

"Not only," Willy continued. "I'm thinking they had a movie of Don ripping them off before, too. That, together with you two sniffing around later—not to mention our ordering the autopsy as confirmation—was all they needed to beat feet."

Sam didn't hide her frustration. "We didn't find any recording equipment just now. Or any cameras anywhere."

Willy agreed. "They took everything with 'em, maybe for use elsewhere. I only found the two outside based on a hunch. They either forgot them, didn't bother collecting them, or ran out of time. They would've taken some effort to remove, given how they're mounted." He gestured vaguely around the room. "Unlike what was probably hidden around here."

Lester shook his head. "Another sign they've totally cleared out."

Joe followed Sam's example and made himself comfortable in a matching chair across from hers. "Any ideas where to?" he asked them.

The other two chose the long leather sofa, Willy putting his feet up on the coffee table. It felt a little odd, setting up shop in someone else's mansion, evoking childhood chills of being discovered by adults and forced to move out.

"Do we have anything on Seamus beyond the pictures we took?" Lester asked. "In case we want to put out a public appeal? You know: 'Have you seen this man' kind of thing?"

"I'm hoping we won't have to," Joe countered. "Not to reward you two for pushing the boundaries, but we already have someone who knows him, assuming you and Willy can find the man in Keene who took Seamus to that cabin. Could be he knows where Seamus is hiding out, and, by extension, Lemuel Shaw."

"Or just grab the cabin owner," Les suggested. "We know where to find him."

Joe didn't agree. "Seamus drove to the apartment complex first, presumably from past experience. They went together to the cabin. The implication being Seamus didn't know the cabin owner, and vice versa."

Willy's response was immediate and unequivocal. "I'll find who you're after."

No one in the room doubted that.

Cody Wright was the name of Seamus's drug contact, which Willy got by visiting the Keene PD, locating the appropriate detective, and showing her the photo he'd taken of both the suspect and the truck's rear license plate.

"You got something on him?" she asked reasonably.

Reluctantly, Willy played coy, not wanting to go into details concerning that night. "I hope to get something on the guy he's with," he said instead. "He's the one I want."

"I know him?"

He saw no harm in that. "Seamus Kyle?"

She checked her computer before shaking her head. "Nope. Sorry."

"Yeah," he said. "I get that a lot about him."

It wasn't Willy's style to merely knock on a man's door and engage in conversation, at least not with someone he wanted to manipulate. There was the tactical aspect of gaining an upper hand in such an exchange, but with a seasoned, former sniper, it also boiled down to enjoying the chase.

As a result, it was late at night when—after tailing Cody Wright's truck—he reached a seedy, self-proclaimed "social club" on Keene's east side.

He wasn't surprised, having researched Wright's past misdeeds on the PD's computer, and had thus already selected some old clothes and a greasy ball cap from his back seat.

Watching his quarry enter the establishment, Willy waited fifteen minutes before exiting his car, giving his disguise a few final tugs, and following suit, mumbling and shuffling as he went.

The place was drab, bordering on the pestilent. The lighting was poor, the air worse, and the population of hollow-eyed, sallow-faced patrons deserving of its surroundings.

Willy spotted his target sitting at the bar, chatting up a female barkeep with a hard expression and a navel ring perched atop a beer belly under a sweat-stained crop top.

Willy chose a stool at the end of the bar, his shoulder against the wall. As a final touch, he displayed his trademark, propping his pale and withered arm and hand on the counter before him. It was and always had been his proof to all doubters that he wasn't an undercover cop.

Waiting for the bartender, he studied Cody Wright, who by now had started taking in his potential clientele. This is what Willy had been hoping for—an illegal transaction in full view.

While Cody scanned his opportunities, one of which was already rising from a corner booth to walk unsteadily toward a purchase, the woman tending bar slid over to Willy and more demanded than asked, "What d'ya want?"

"Budweiser in a bottle."

She openly stared at his exposed hand. "Our draft not good enough?"

"I like what I like."

"Ours is better."

"Don't worry about it."

She finally looked up into his eyes. "Whatever."

She moved away. Willy watched the exchange of money for a couple of baggies between Cody and his pigeon. The place had the usual barely audible canned music, and a muted TV set in need of replacement was wedged against where the ceiling met the wall above the cash register.

The bartender returned with a brown bottle, opened it before Willy, and said, "Four bucks."

Willy produced a five without comment. As she turned to get the change, he checked for anyone watching, before swapping her bottle, upright, for an identical one from his inner coat pocket.

He took a small swig of what was now water and settled down for the evening.

It was normally a game of chance, playacting a transaction with a drug dealer. You couldn't overdo your stay, you didn't want to appear too eager, you certainly didn't want your mark to run out of product and leave. It was subjective, gut-driven, and dependent on various factors. When Willy did make his move, he barely knew what prompted him, which of course was part of the art form.

But move he did, having made sure Cody had noticed him by then, and sidled up beside the younger man to quietly ask, his bad arm still in view, "What'll twenty get me?"

"What're you after?"

Willy kept his voice low. "Look like I care?"

"I know you?"

Willy used a couple of names he'd been given by the Keene cop earlier. "I know Benny Studin, who knows Connie Baxter. What d'you care?"

Cody's eyes dropped to the hand Willy had again placed on the bar. "You should put a glove on that thing."

"You should mind your own business."

Cody grimaced with disgust and took the bill Willy was proffering, giving him a baggie of pills to be rid of him.

Willy returned to his corner and his bottle of disguised water.

That was all he needed. He gave himself another ten minutes, made a show of emptying his bottle, and left the building.

He stood in the shadows, motionless, for forty-five minutes more. An interminable stretch for most people, an easy one for him. He'd stayed put for a couple of days in his prime, peeing where he lay, alternating between catnaps and a form of meditative wakefulness, all for the sake of a single rifle round into the right target.

Waiting for Cody Wright paled by comparison.

Cody never heard Willy slip in behind him as he finally drunkenly ambled toward his parked truck. Until, that is, the words, "Move and you die, Mr. Wright," enveloped him from behind.

Naturally, he did move, as Willy knew he would. People never did as they were told. Cody spun around at the words, allowing Willy to lightly tap the side of his head with his gun.

"What did I just say?" he asked, the gun now almost shoved up Cody's nose.

"What the fuck?"

"Go to your truck, legs spread, hands on the roof. Lean far enough in that you'd fall on your face otherwise."

Cody did as he was told, although Willy kicked his feet back to make him more dependent on the truck to stay upright.

"Who the fuck're you?"

"Cop."

Cody tried to turn to stare at him, but by now, he was too off balance to make it work. "The hell you are. You're a fucking cripple."

Willy tapped him again. "Respect."

"Ow. Damn."

Willy briefly tucked his gun under his armpit, quickly displayed his badge—not that Wright could read it—and then switched to slapping a pair of handcuffs around the man's wrists. It was an unlikely maneuver he'd practiced enough times to make it seamless.

He finished by spinning Wright around, hands now secured behind his back, and pushed him against the truck. The street around them was empty, dark, and quiet.

Willy eased his pistol back into its holster and quietly recited Cody his Miranda rights.

"You're no cop. I don't care if you do have a badge."

"Do you understand your rights as I've explained them?"

"No fuckin' way. That arm is *real*, man. They don't hire people like you."

Willy slapped him, not too hard, but enough.

"Ow. What the hell, man?"

"Do you understand your rights?"

"Yeah, I do. Shit. Stop hitting me. I'm not stupid."

"You're standing here in cuffs, Cody. That doesn't make you smart."

"This is entrapment."

"That makes you even dumber."

Cody was confused by that, visibly trying to figure it out, furrowing his brow. Willy smiled at the effort.

"What do you want?" the hapless dealer finally asked.

This time, Willy patted his cheek gently, making Cody flinch. "That's better. We may be getting somewhere."

"Where?"

"It's a who, not a where. Seamus Kyle. Tell me about him."

Cody's lack of a poker face betrayed him. As he opened his mouth to deny all knowledge, Willy slowly opened his jacket and made to remove his gun again.

"What're you doing?" Cody asked, interrupting his own response.

"Getting ready for you to be stupid again. Seamus Kyle. Talk."

"You can't do that if you're a cop."

"I'm an unusual cop. You said it yourself. I do all sorts of things I'm not supposed to."

The gun came all the way out.

Cody's eyes were glued to it as he asked, "What d'you wanna know? About Seamus?"

"Everything."

"Hey there," Sammie said softly, making room in the bed for Willy to slide in beside her. "How did it go?"

Willy kissed her ear. "Usual. Running gunfight ending with a high-speed car crash."

"That's sweet," she responded. "Your family appreciates your cutting back."

Willy slipped his hand under her T-shirt and fitted his knees behind hers, soaking up the sensation of her against him.

She placed her hand on top of his and snuggled in, sighing. "So you found him?"

"Yep. Made him an offer he couldn't refuse."

"About Seamus?"

"Yup."

"How 'bout Shaw? Anything there?"

"Nope. Cody never heard of him."

Sammie readjusted, bringing her knees up and smoothly removing her pajama bottoms. Willy was already naked under the covers.

"That's better," she said, curling up again. "So, what did he say about Seamus?"

"That he made him nervous. Cody called him a dangerous man."

"Really," she stated. "That's good for us, or at least it fits what we've been thinking."

She moved her free hand back and rested it on his hip. "He know where he might've gone?"

Responding to her caress, he began to slowly explore with his own hand, feeling her heartbeat pick up in return.

"Not in so many words," he whispered. "But he did say Seamus needed more product this time 'cause he was heading north for a while."

"Cool," she replied, moving slightly to allow him more room. "We should be able to figure that out."

"Yup," he agreed, before following her lead.

"North?" Lester asked, leaning back in his chair. "As in New Hampshire north?"

"Don't know," Willy admitted. "That's the impression Cody was left with, not that he's God's gift to insight. Still, it's not a stretch."

"How so?"

They were alone in the office, Sam delivering Emma to school.

"Human nature," Willy explained. "You don't run for the dark side of the moon when things get hot, far from everything and everybody you know. You just leave town and hunker down. Where better than your own state's barely populated north country? Who's gonna know? And up there especially, who's gonna ask? You know what they say about most folks living that far in the woods—skittish, sketchy, and scary."

"You should talk," Lester replied.

"The question remains," Willy went on. "How do we find the son of a bitch?"

"We ask the people most likely to know," Lester volunteered. "The local PDs and sheriffs."

"We already sent out a BOLO," Willy argued.

"Which got dutifully pinned to the wall where everybody ignored it. We need to bypass normal channels and make it personal. Cop to cop."

Willy didn't respond, watching him.

Lester took that as encouragement to proceed. "Piece of cake to identify every law enforcement agency above Franconia Notch, or whatever latitude you choose, and then reach out personally—phone, text, email, whatever, complete with any pictures. Let them know that finding Seamus, and Shaw, is a top priority."

"Shitload of work, and we don't have anything on Seamus beside a head shot. How d'you get around that?"

Lester shrugged. "We have Shaw. Right now, it seems wherever he goes, Seamus isn't far away. And as for reaching everybody, once you got the format down, it shouldn't be too hard. I'm betting it'll get noticed, too. How many times have *we* been approached for a BOLO in a way that wasn't same ol', same ol'? Basically, never, right? We all follow protocol till our eyes glaze over."

Willy didn't answer, well used to his colleague's enthusiasm for such projects. Lester was one of the few veteran cops in Willy's experience who rarely presented as wizened or weathered by his years on the job. Somehow, even suffering a few personal setbacks along the way, Lester maintained a resilience that the more burdened Willy Kunkle could only envy. Indeed, it was the man's genuineness that cut him slack in Willy's habitually skeptical outlook.

"What else we got?" he therefore agreed. "Go for it."

The return on Lester's investment came three days later in the form of a text from the Thomaston, New Hampshire, police department. Once more at his desk, Les consulted Google maps and pulled it up.

"Jeez."

Willy looked up at the wonder in his voice. "What d'you find?"

"Thomaston. You ever hear of it?"

"New Hampshire?" Joe joined in. "Somewhere near Lancaster. Almost to Canada. Is this in response to your BOLO on Seamus?"

"Maybe," Lester confirmed. "Officer Dillon Rowe just wrote that he doesn't want to get my hopes up, but he thinks he's got an older hit on Shaw."

"How much older?"

"Little vague there. Ten years, more or less, is what he says. They had a tech crash—his words—where they lost a lot of their data, so they're left with a mix of virtual files and old-fashioned paper ones."

"Jesus," Willy growled to himself, beginning to type. "Makes you wonder what he's not saying."

Sammie was looking up the Thomaston PD's website. "It's a

three-man department," she reported. "And Joe's right about the location."

"Rowe looks about twelve," Willy said, glancing across the room.

"What's Officer Rowe suggesting?" Joe asked.

"Short version," Lester replied, "he thinks he has something, but it'll take some effort to produce it, and he's not sure he's officially supposed to do that. He says he could do with some backup."

"An eager beaver," Willy commented. "And a lonely one with a big secret, from what it sounds."

"I like it," Joe said. "I think we should hear him out."

"Field trip?" Sam suggested, smiling.

Joe nodded. "Yup."

CHAPTER THIRTEEN

Much is made about the thinly inhabited, heavily forested northern belt that skirts the Canadian border from Lake Champlain to the Atlantic Ocean, eventually melding into where the U.S. yields to equally rugged New Brunswick. It is generally viewed broadly by outsiders, caricatured with references to lumberjacks, rough living, hostile weather, and funny accents.

As with most clichés, there is some truth to that, but mostly on the surface. The uppermost reaches of Vermont and New Hampshire do appear similar on the map—verdant and empty. Vermont is wide where its sister state is narrow, just as the reverse holds true for where they abut Massachusetts to the south. They each have colorful mountain ranges—the Greens and the Whites—that overlook the Connecticut River, and they both have access to water, in the form of Lake Champlain for Vermont and a bit of the Atlantic for New Hampshire.

But for travelers driving north along Interstate 93, heading for the top of the Granite State, their true differences start looming with the force of a spiritual realization. If the timeworn phrase "We're not in Kansas anymore" ever rang true, it's here.

Joe had always been hard-pressed to know how to capture the distinction between the two. But driving with Willy toward Thomaston now—since Lester and Sam still hadn't concluded their survey of Don Kalfus's peregrinations in Shaw's stolen Mercedes—Joe finally thought he'd hit on a reasonable descriptor: northern New Hampshire, unlike Vermont, was "muscular."

That didn't nearly capture it all, but it touched on how the forested peaks up here, unlike in the upper Green Mountains, looked bigger, taller, steeper, and more threatening. There was an ominousness to this region that had been smothered by the millennia just across the Connecticut River.

It wasn't headliner news, he realized. The peaks of the Whites *were* all those things. The second-highest winds ever recorded on the globe—including in the Himalayas—had been clocked on Mount Washington, and the death toll among hikers, climbers, and recreational day strollers was legion. Where EMS rescue teams elsewhere were occasionally called upon to enter the mountains and bring out the lost, injured, and dead, here they'd developed into highly trained, well-equipped teams that did little else.

And that didn't address the snow. Unlike atop the more worn-down Green Mountains, New Hampshire's Whites were still slathered in feet of the stuff. It loomed threateningly at the tops of cliffs and clotted ravines and streambeds to where an unwary person could vanish from sight, only to reappear weeks later as wrinkled remains.

Just as with human muscularity, the impact wasn't wholly negative. These ancient peaks also deserved terms like "majestic," "soaring," and "breathtakingly beautiful." Joe acknowledged those as perfectly true, but at the moment, he wasn't given to poetical flights of fancy. The impression of feeling encircled by snow and ice man-killers fitted his dark mood well.

This case had been cancerous, emotionally. Beginning with a homicide was never a high point, but the gradual descent here into kidnapping, domestic abuse, and who knew what still lay ahead had filled Joe with a dread he couldn't help projecting onto the towering, forbidding terrain surrounding them.

Thomaston didn't come to much when they finally reached it. Dwarfed by neighboring mountains north of the Presidentials, spared the commercialism of Gorham, Lancaster, or even hard-scrabble Berlin, it presented as almost endangered, clinging to its hilly edge like an uncertain notion—an exercise begun by humans who'd later moved on.

They hadn't, not entirely. There was a post office, a single-story municipal building, a volunteer fire department, and, as expected, a police station of modest scope, complete with one cruiser parked outside.

"They speak English?" Willy asked, looking around.

"You might not find out if you ask," Joe cautioned him. "The whole Live Free or Die thing really applies up here. They might not take to your natural charm like they do back home. I wouldn't expect them to see cops as more than government stooges."

"That's okay," Willy replied easily. "I am a government stooge, so we should get along."

Joe relented. "You just might at that," he said, bypassing the tiny, snow-clotted downtown to meet their contact as agreed farther down the road.

At the town garage, marked by its dome-shaped salt barn, easily the largest building they'd seen so far, he circled to the back of the structure and stopped near a cruiser parked facing them, but out of sight of the road. As they left their vehicle, a young man appeared from the barn, looking around warily as he approached.

"That's him," Willy said to Joe.

The uniformed officer took them in, especially Willy's limp left arm, before shaking hands and asking, "You from Brattleboro?"

"Joe Gunther and Willy Kunkle. Yeah," Joe told him.

"Dillon Rowe." He looked around again. "Listen, I'm not sure how thin the ice is under my feet," he said.

Joe gestured to the entrance he'd appeared from. "Would you like it better if we talked in there?" he asked.

The young man smiled thinly. "You mind?"

Willy bowed slightly and gestured that Rowe should precede them.

The three entered a building as high and empty as a small cathedral, its center dominated by a large but reduced pile of salt, still being put heavily to use against road ice during a winter that would hang around long after southern Vermont started sprouting crocuses. It was dark, mysterious, and resonant inside, lending to the conspiratorial mood of the meeting.

"No secret passwords?" Willy asked.

It was hard to interpret if Rowe was irritated or embarrassed by that.

"Why here?" Joe asked, shooting Willy a look. "Why the cloak-and-dagger?"

Rowe studied his polished black boots a moment, organizing his thoughts. "Your BOLO triggered a memory that could cause problems for me. I wanted to find out what you really wanted before I talked to you."

"We're after one definite homicide," Willy answered, "another probable, and some interconnected kiddie perv stuff. Major shit."

Not how Joe would have worded it, but it worked. Dillon Rowe nodded and asked, "And Lemuel Shaw is part of it?"

"He's a primary person of interest," Joe answered carefully. "Do you know Mr. Shaw?"

Rowe glanced out the open door at the expansive, empty parking area, dazzling in the daylight. "There's not a lot to do in Thomaston," he began. "There're three of us, counting the chief, and we stop the occasional speeder or DUI, we do VIN checks and warn folks about their inspection stickers. It's quiet. Most people drive somewhere else to get into trouble. They don't stop here."

Joe could almost feel Willy's patience wearing. "Okay," he said encouragingly.

"I told you, or somebody in your office, that we had a computer crash that fouled up our records. That's not exactly true. We have a really old system. Most of it's still on paper and in file cabinets. The chief has a computer he can barely work, but he doesn't have a choice if we want to communicate with anybody or keep up with state regs. But it's not ideal. Anyhow, part of my job is to upload our older files, which is how I came across your Mr. Shaw."

"And?" Willy asked bluntly.

That didn't hasten Rowe's narrative flow. "It was a funny coincidence, really. Just dumb luck. A few days later, or earlier, and it wouldn't've clicked in my head. But when I got the BOLO, on top of your phone call—it was me you talked to—the double mention of Shaw's name made me remember a file I'd handled a few weeks ago. It was one of those things, you know?"

Willy sighed and shifted his feet.

Rowe continued, "You read these things all the time—'At fourteen hundred hours, so-and-so did such-and-such to what's-his-name.' Or, 'I pulled over this vehicle at this location for this offense.' You know the drill, or I guess you do, going back to your uniform days."

Willy tried rushing him again. "And you stumbled over Shaw's name."

Rowe almost looked surprised. "Yeah. Just under a decade ago, one of the guys before me—no one stays here long, except the chief—noticed a car parked near one of the trailheads near here. That's no big deal. We get hundreds of cars lining the roads when the season's high and the hikers are like ants on sugar. There're so many of 'em sometimes I think they do more hiking to get to the trailhead than they do walking in the mountains. You know what I'm sayin'?"

Neither of his companions responded.

"The difference here was that it was night, and maybe the officer was bored, or something caught his eye. Anyhow, according to his report, he pulled over, walked up to the driver's side, and caught your man Shaw getting a blow job from a kid."

It was an effective punch line. He had his guests' attention now.

"How did he establish it was Shaw?" Joe asked ahead of Willy.

"Standard procedure. Asked for his license and registration. It's an unusual name, Lemuel."

"And the kid?" Willy wanted to know.

Rowe made a face. "Billy or Bobby Smith is what he said. The report had it both ways, so I'm not sure. No identification. There was no way to confirm it."

"That doesn't matter," Willy said. "No doubt something came up during processing. How old was Bobby or Billy?"

"Supposedly around twelve, but we never found out."

"What do you mean?" Joe asked, not liking where this was heading.

Rowe grew nervous again, moving to the door and looking outside. "This is where it gets a little hinky," he admitted, facing them again. "When I first found this file, which was buried where it made no sense, it struck me as wrong. I couldn't figure out why nothing had happened. The initial paperwork was there, mostly, and a case number was punched, which made it an official encounter, but there was a note saying, 'Referred to chief,' and that's where it ended. I knew there had to be more, like you're saying. Underage kid, sexual contact with an older man. But there was nothing."

"What did your chief say?" Joe asked, already suspecting the answer.

He didn't get what he expected.

"I didn't ask him."

Willy was less diplomatic. "What the fuck, man? Why the hell not?"

Rowe's cheeks flushed, but he answered directly, his eyes steady. "Because I need this job. I have a family. You don't know my chief."

Joe thought back to what Sam had read about the Thomaston department on the internet. "Clyde Herrick? That him?"

"Yup. Born and bred here. Been chief for decades."

"So?" Willy asked leadingly.

"So he's really old-school. Totally set in his ways. He doesn't like the boat rocked."

Willy was looking disgusted. "You let it drop."

Rowe's tone grew defensive. "Not entirely. I did ask him then about Shaw, to see if it rang a bell. I figured it had to, given the way this thing ended up."

"And?"

"I hit a nerve. I only asked if he'd ever heard the name Lemuel Shaw. I didn't mention the file. And he lit right up. 'Why d'you want to know?' he asked, immediately pissed off. I said I'd bumped into it somewhere. That it struck me as a weird name. He told me to forget about it. 'Nobody to you,' was how he put it, and I got the message, so I let it go. But when your BOL came in . . ."

He hesitated. Willy and Joe both gave him time to finish.

"I felt bad. That report, especially the way it'd been misfiled, I knew in my gut something was off, and Herrick's reaction drove it home."

Joe patted his shoulder. "Rock and a hard place, Dillon. You've done the right thing now."

Willy was less forgiving. "You're goddamn lucky you fessed up. You said this was years ago. How many?"

"Nine."

"What did you do with the file?" Joe asked, hoping it might still be available.

Reassuringly, Rowe smiled. "I put it back in a new wrong place, where nobody but me can find it, unless they tear the whole cabinet apart."

"Outstanding," Joe commented.

Willy merely nodded as he asked, "And nothing happened afterward? Life went on?"

"Far as I know. I never brought it up again, and he didn't either."

"Does your boss know about our BOLO?" Willy asked.

"I doubt it," Rowe replied. "He carries a flip phone and relies on me and my partner to man the computer."

"What about that partner?" Joe asked. "Did he see it? And what're his relations to Herrick?"

"The chief likes him less than me. Plus, I've never seen him *look* at a BOL. He's not that into the whole law enforcement thing, not like me. He mostly likes walking around with a gun."

Willy lightened up enough to comment, "You're clearly hanging with the wrong crowd, Dillon."

The young man looked at him unhappily. "Tell me about it."

"The BOLO also mentioned Seamus Kyle," Joe said. "You remember that?"

"I do, but it didn't sound familiar, and there was no DOB or anything, so I didn't have anything to work with."

"Yeah," Joe conceded. "We don't have one. We also doubt that's his real name."

"We passed a town hall on the way in," Willy said. "Would they have land or tax records where we could find if Shaw's on file as a property owner?"

Rowe looked momentarily nonplussed. "Sure. I guess. I mean, yeah."

Joe saw where Willy was heading. "We could pose as attorneys doing a title search. That shouldn't raise any alarms. Is the clerk a friend of your chief's?"

"Not that I know of," Rowe answered. "She's really old and reminds me of Yoda, and I've never seen them together. Nice lady. Very outgoing. You thinking Herrick and Shaw are connected?"

"Tell us about Herrick," Joe requested, neither answering nor airing his suspicions.

Dillon shrugged. "I don't know about anything criminal, but I wouldn't put it past him. Look, he's been in that position longer than God. At least it seems that way. But he's got nice stuff, gets a new truck every two years. I know what he makes. It's not enough to do that. And the way he handles the cases we bring in? Gary— the other patrol cop—he doesn't give a shit. But I see the boss playing favorites all the time. If you check with the county prosecutor, there's no way the numbers we bring the chief match what he's passing up the ladder. He cuts people slack all the time."

"And you think he gets paid for that?" Willy asked.

Dillon blew out a puff of air, his pent-up frustration having gotten the better of him. "I can't say that. It's just how it feels. But I got nothin' to prove it."

One hundred and fifty miles to the south, Lester and Sam were back in the car, running down the last few miles of Don Kalfus's recorded trip in Shaw's borrowed Mercedes.

They had done portions of this stretch before, primarily to compare the journey with various sightings of Kalfus on closed-circuit cameras or burglaries he was believed to have committed.

This time around, they weren't only looking for gas stations where he'd stopped, or pawnshops, or food stores, or people's houses. Now, in a concession to frustration and thoroughness, they were checking every stop, regardless of the apparent reason why.

Which brought them at last to a pull-off used by New Hampshire's department of highway maintenance, complete with a padlocked shed, a pile of broken asphalt, and two dumpsters.

"You sure?" Lester asked his partner, who had a computer tablet balanced on her knees, featuring the Mercedes's downloaded map.

"According to this. Time stamp has him parked here ten minutes."

Lester killed the engine. "Okay," he said, sounding bored. "Long enough to take a leak behind the shed."

They got out and looked around, finding little more than what they'd seen at first glance.

"Could he've broken in there?" Sam asked, seeing Lester studying the shed's lock.

"Not if this was closed. You never got a hit to your inquiry about break-ins concerning this place, did you? Or anything featuring the DOT?"

"Not that fit our time frame."

"Then I'd say no," he announced, releasing the padlock, which rattled against the hasp. "There're no signs of anyone monkeying with it. Anything in the dumpsters?"

She'd checked one and was peering into the other. "Both empty. What did you find?" she asked. He was on his knees, reaching under the shed's slightly raised northern corner, elevated to keep it level on the uneven grade.

He pulled out a two-by-four, about three feet long. "You have your blood testing kit with you?" he asked.

She crossed over and looked at the end of the stick he was studying. It was discolored by some rusty-looking dried liquid, familiar in appearance to both of them.

"Yeah," she said softly. "I do."

The test was fast, reliable, and designed to react only to human blood. This it did.

"Okay," Lester said, admiring the color change at the end of the testing swab. "We have a winner."

"How did you notice it?" she asked.

"A couple of inches were poking out as if somebody shoved it under there, but not far enough. Funny thing to do, I thought."

He looked around them, adding, "Where's a security camera when you need one?"

Suitably, given the purpose of this pull-off, there was a truck yard across the street, with garages, repair bays, a refueling station, and more, all belonging to a commercial haulage service.

"Ya think?" he asked.

"Worth a try," she agreed.

They carefully placed their find in a cardboard evidence box intended for long guns, took one last look around, and crossed the highway to the business's front office.

Expecting little, they showed their badges to the manager behind the counter and were led to a break room in the back—cluttered and dirty—where their escort showed them a small stacked bank of dusty recorders, along with one flat-screen monitor divided into eight video squares.

"That's it," he said. "Runs twenty-four seven. Saved our ass three years ago when a bunch of teenagers tore up the place with their pickups and you people were able to nail 'em 'cause of their plates. Other than that, I don't know. Nobody really looks at 'em."

"You save the footage?" Sam asked.

"Only for a month."

Relieved, both cops smiled.

"That'll do," Lester said. "Which of these is aimed at your front gate?"

The manager tapped one of the squares. "This one."

They were rewarded by seeing that the camera allowed for a glimpse across the street at its uppermost edge.

"That enough?" Sam asked, peering closely.

"Sure," Lester said. "You can't see the shed's roof, but the rest of it's there." He turned to the other man. "Is that pull-off lit at night?"

"Sure. So are we. It's a better deterrent than the cameras."

"You got your tablet?" Lester asked Sam.

She was pulling it from the bag hanging off her shoulder. She turned it on, checked the log, and recited the date and time stamp out loud.

"That's what we're after," Lester told the manager.

He opened a drawer, pulled out a keyboard, inserted it into one of the black boxes before him, and entered a command. They all watched as the picture before them sped backward through time, coming to an abrupt stop at the time Sam had recited.

"Cool," Lester said. "Hit Play."

The manager did so, and they next saw Shaw's Mercedes pull up before the shed, small and just barely within the top of the frame.

"That what you're after?" the man asked as the recognizable figure of Don Kalfus stepped out from behind the wheel and looked around.

"Sure is," Lester muttered, transfixed as a second car, a Jeep, appeared.

The Jeep produced two more people, a man and a woman.

"What the hell?" Sam asked, barely whispering. "That's Lucy and hubby."

They continued watching as the trio clustered together in a quick and obviously heated conversation, finishing with a shoving match between the two men, the older, paunchier Shaw being no contest against young Kalfus.

Until Lucy, ignored until then, stooped down, picked up the two-by-four, and landed a blow on the back of Kalfus's head worthy of Mickey Mantle.

"Holy shit," the manager said.

Kalfus collapsed, Shaw regained his balance, dropped to his knees, and checked his wife's handiwork.

They watched in silence as the couple briefly conferred over the still body, before awkwardly lifting and shoving it into the Mercedes's trunk.

At that point, ten minutes from start to finish, Lucy returned to the Jeep as Shaw got behind the wheel of the Mercedes, and both vehicles began rolling toward the far edge of the image.

"Pause it," Lester told their host.

The picture froze.

"Back it up in one-second increments, if you can."

"Sure."

"What did you see?" Sam asked.

Lester reached out one long arm and tapped the monitor with his index finger. "That."

"Damn," the manager said. "Somebody's riding shotgun."

There was the shadow of another person, briefly illuminated by a quick reflection, sitting in the Mercedes's passenger seat.

"Seamus?" asked Sam.

Lester kept staring, baffled. "It's the wrong car. That would make him riding with Don. How's *that* make sense?"

Sam paused before saying, "It wouldn't be the first time we heard of Don taking his girlfriend for an adventure."

Patrol officer Rowe had been correct about the Thomaston town clerk. She was short, round, and infectiously affable. She was also very helpful to the two gentlemen from out of town who wanted access to the public tax records, even making sure they had some privacy by setting them up inside the enormous vault at the back of the building, which, fortunately for her, had once been a bank.

Nevertheless, well attuned to the hearing within small communities, the men worked in silence or spoke only in muted tones as they pulled ledger after ledger and scanned the lines and columns for anything of interest.

It was a borderline fool's errand. They knew that. The connection between Shaw and Thomaston was tenuous at best, and it certainly didn't extend to his definitely owning property up here.

On the other hand, that was the nature of leads in this peculiar business. Sometimes, it came down to all scent and no sight in the pursuit of one's prey.

And—occasionally—instinct.

"Huh," Willy said, an hour into it.

"Find something?"

"Not sure."

Joe sidled over to see where he was pointing at an entry.

"Four hundred and eighty acres. Farquar LLC. That ring a bell?"

Joe nodded. "Vaguely. I just don't know why."

Willy pulled out his phone, laid it on the desk, and tapped out a message.

"Lester?" Joe asked.

"Closest thing to Siri we got."

Instead of a return text, Willy's phone vibrated within a minute.

He turned it on and adjusted the volume to its lowest setting, forcing both men to lean in to hear.

"Farquar?" Willy asked.

"Lucy's maiden name," Lester answered as they'd hoped he might. "But that's not as big as what Sam and I just caught. We got footage of both Shaws braining Kalfus and tossing him into the Mercedes, the same day we later found him in Vermont. And you'll love this: the late, lamented Lucille Farquar Shaw delivered the whack. With a two-by, no less. We're hoping for his blood at one end and her prints on the other. They chucked it under a shed, right across from a trucking business's surveillance system."

"God bless technology," Joe said, much as he regularly cursed it. "Nicely done."

"Why the question about Farquar?" Lester asked.

"We found a piece of land in Thomaston belonging to Farquar LLC."

"Ooh," Lester reacted. "How discreet."

Forty minutes later, Joe and Willy discovered how Shaw's interest in discretion wasn't restricted to a deed owner's name. They found themselves on a dirt road, high in the hills, looking at a chained-off driveway decorated with No Trespassing signs.

"So much for mistaking that for an unmarked country road and asking the homeowner for directions," Willy said.

Joe agreed. "Looks like we'll have to make any door-knocking a little more formal."

It took a couple of days to line up the needed warrants and man-power to approach Shaw's Thomaston estate in the manner Joe had proposed, during which time they studied their target from every angle, including satellite imagery off the internet, to gain some in-sight into its topography. They also made sure to keep things discreet, not being keen on having someone local phone the homeowner.

They even took time to locate the Massachusetts architect of the compound's primary structure and secure a copy of his floor plan. Not a standard precaution, perhaps, but one suggested by Willy af-ter seeing how vast a place was Shaw's home away from home.

The man trained to hunt humans was not comforted by what he saw.

"In military terms," he told them on the day before their pro-posed visit, "it's a defensive, possibly armored building, like a fort. It's got the look of a country home, but built to hold off people like us, with exposed approaches, cross-fire zones, entanglement areas, and that's without knowing how he's rigged the inside. Looking at this"—he tapped the floor plan—"you might only think of a jacked-up version of your average family home, but I'm telling you, all I see are a series of positions designed and laid out to be defended room by room against an assault team."

"We're not going in with an assault team," Joe pointed out.

"More's the pity," was the warning.

CHAPTER FOURTEEN

The problem with Willy's alarmist appraisal of Shaw's country estate was that Joe knew his colleague to be naturally paranoid. That
didn't mean Willy was wrong about the building being built like
a fortress, but no one could assure them that Lemuel Shaw was in
residence. Staging a military-style attack on an empty building was
not appealing.

Their approach, therefore, equipped with search and arrest warrants, was a nod to reasonable compromise. Joe and Willy drove up
to the house along its long, twisting driveway, but with the ubiquitous Fred Houston and a backup tactical team positioned a half
mile down the road.

The house was of staggering dimensions, in tune with what
they were used to from Gilsum. There, the architecture had been
extroverted—big windows, multiple decks, porches, and balconies,
a sweeping vista of the valley at its feet. Here, while the construction material was also logs, the mood was utterly opposite. This was
a hulking, Nordic, walled off, blank-faced monstrosity with few
windows, no decking, zero view, and the aura of a wooden factory
building straight out of Dickens.

In Willy's wording, as they rounded the last forested corner and saw the place looming ahead, "Cozy."

Joe stopped the car some three hundred feet from the traffic circle before the entrance. "It's got a Hitlerian Wolf's Lair look to it, don't you think?"

"I do," Willy agreed. "You notice the cameras and sensors on the way in?"

"I noticed some. I don't have your eye for them."

"Six, not counting those." Willy pointed to the two corners of the house ahead, where the walls and roof met.

"Think he knows we're coming?"

Instead of answering, Willy speed-dialed his phone and said to whoever answered, "A heads-up: this is better rigged with cameras than a movie set. You might want to start sniffing for electronic signals, just for laughs."

"Fred?" Joe asked, his eyes ahead.

"Yeah."

Joe hesitated before proceeding. "You still good to go?"

Willy's enthusiasm was evident in his response. "No bullet holes in the windshield yet."

"Swell," Joe replied and slowly brought them the rest of the way.

Under their coats, they were wearing ballistic vests, which Joe revealed to one of the cameras as he rang the doorbell. "Mr. Shaw?" he said loudly. "It's the police. We have a warrant. Open up."

Willy was standing to one side, as watchful as a hound on the hunt.

"Try the door," he suggested after a minute of utter silence.

Joe followed his body language, pressed his own shoulder against the wall, and reached over to twist the large knob, keeping himself clear in case a heavy-caliber round came crashing through the door.

None did, and the door swung open without complaint or resistance.

Joe glanced at his partner opposite, who braced himself, drew
his handgun, and prepared to enter in tactical mode, moving low,
fast, and to one side.

Once in, crouching with their backs against the log walls, all
they saw was an overarching lobby with a hallway beyond. It was
well furnished and appointed, in masculine hunting lodge fash-
ion, with rough wooden chairs and tables and heavy, rough rugs.
There was an oversized antler chandelier overhead.

"This is the police," Joe tried again in a loud voice. "We have
a warrant."

"Come out, come out, wherever you are," Willy chanted under
his breath. "Boss," he then said, his voice still low.

"Yup?"

"Work yourself around the edge of the rug to the door. Stay on
the hardwood."

"You see something?"

"Not yet. Don't want to, either."

Joe understood his concern. People with Willy's background
were more attuned to detail than the average observer. But they
were also familiar with hidden explosives in an unusual way. Willy
had often rigged what were known in his trade as "access denial"
devices—antipersonnel charges designed to defeat anyone creeping
up behind him as he lay motionless, hidden, and vulnerable, seeking a quarry.

Willy was a man with an eye for covert ordnance.

The interior of the house was as he'd described it from seeing
the plans, with clear lines of sight and strategic ambush spots as they
went. And yet, there was no opposition.

At least, not in human form. At each doorway, Willy conducted an assessment, and in almost every instance, there was something—a camera, a sensor, a pressure plate under a rug. They didn't know if these were attached to surveillance, alarms, or explosives, but given the silence so far, the first seemed the better bet.

Until Joe heard Willy calmly say, "Shit," and freeze in place.

"What?" he asked.

"I missed one." He pointed to something on a far baseboard Joe couldn't even make out.

"Okay. We're still here."

"That's the catch," Willy explained. "We're also not getting out without help. We triggered a safe-arming device. I heard it snap into place. If this is even close to what I would've done, it means our way in is now closed behind us."

Joe stared at him. "I don't understand."

In another context, Willy's response would have been short and acerbic. Now, he was patience personified. "All those traps we by-passed? I was hoping they were just to track our progress. This one, I think, is rigged to explosives. It's like a master switch opening all the circuits in the house. If we go back, half of those we passed will now blow."

Joe absorbed that before asking, "What d'you want to do?"

Willy held up his phone. "We're now in a Cat A situation. We tell the others what we got and keep going. We don't have much to lose."

Joe was of two minds concerning that, but he was curious, too, about what might have been prepared for them—unless Lemuel Shaw routinely left the house like this, as other mortals simply lock the front door.

By now, he seriously doubted that.

Willy ordered up a hasty team on his phone, exceeding what they'd set in place down the road. In their vernacular, a "hasty team" was more than just tactically trained, forced-entry people. It included at least a couple of bomb techs—specialists trained by the FBI in Huntsville, Alabama, and, because of their limited number, always on call via mutual aid agreement across Maine, New Hampshire, Vermont, and Massachusetts. Someone, from somewhere, would be here to help fast, but it would still take time.

Ergo, Willy's suggestion that they keep going to find out what Shaw had prepared.

They found it near the rear of the house. A large room, outfitted as a library, lined with books and comfortable reading chairs situated by a few windows. In its center, as a distinct counterpoint to the room's peaceful intention, was a man sitting on a folding metal chair.

It was a wide-eyed Seamus Kyle, wearing an explosive vest crisscrossed with electrical wires.

"Nobody move," Willy said from the door.

Nobody did.

There's a dilemma in these situations that most action movies skip: Is the person in the vest friend or foe? Given their belief that Seamus had followed Shaw's orders in eliminating Lucy, there was no obvious way for Joe or Willy to know if this situation reflected a choice on Seamus's part or something else. Was this a blastoff moment for a greater cause? Or had the young man been as manipulated as the two cops in creating this quandary?

First things first, Joe therefore thought, and asked, "Seamus? Without moving your head or any other part of your body, can you tell us if you're okay?"

"What do you think? I need to pee."

Good, Joe thought. *Humor.* "We've got a team on the way right now that's trained to get those things off safely. Shouldn't be too long. You been here awhile?"

"I don't know. I woke up in this thing."

"How did you know not to stand up?" Willy asked.

"He was here. He told me."

"Shaw?"

"Of course, fucking Shaw. Who else would it be?"

Joe followed his instincts with his next words. "I thought you two were tight."

"You're not the only one."

Joe was still puzzled. "How did he know we'd be coming? Today? Now?"

Seamus looked stunned. "Really? In this town? You're kidding me."

Willy slowly approached Seamus, saying, "I'm not gonna touch anything. I just want a closer look."

To keep the young man focused, Joe continued, "You have a falling-out? I don't understand."

Seamus scowled. "What the fuck you think? Are you supposed to be the smart one?"

That's where Willy usually would have slapped him. Instead, he silently crouched and began studying the vest.

Joe stayed on track. "Just hoping to save your life. Are you worth the effort?"

That brought Seamus pause. His mouth partly opened in confusion before he asked, "What're you saying? You can't leave me here."

Joe shrugged. "From where I'm standing, you're hardly a model citizen. We know about Lucy."

"Like you know a movie from the ads. I don't think so."

"Educate me, then," Joe urged him.

"You've got time," Willy said softly, still scrutinizing the wiring. "Trust me."

"You think she was just a fat old broad who liked everything white and gold and ate too much chocolate. She was a cold, manipulating bitch. She deserved what she got."

"What you gave her," Joe corrected him.

Seamus's mouth tightened. "Whatever," he said.

"How did you administer the gas, by the way?" Joe asked, feigning curiosity, when what he truly wanted was an admission of fact, before a witness.

Seamus was dismissive. "Easy. Got her drunk. There was a challenge. Then put the bag over her head, pumped in the gas, and presto. Shaw told me it would be quick, but I was surprised."

"He knew how to do this?"

"He called it tried-and-true."

There was a chilling glimpse. Joe kept on track. "She didn't fight back?"

"A little. I was pinning her down. Lying on her. I always thought that part surprised her, having a man on top of her. I thought about doin' her, just for laughs. Such an ice queen. But I changed my mind."

"Sounds like Lemuel's pretty cold, too."

Seamus straightened with anger, causing both other men to lean backward in alarm. "Shithead."

"Easy," Willy said calmly.

Joe kept going, not seeing many options. "What happened between you two?"

Again ignoring caution, Seamus shook his head. "You people did."

"How so?"

"You're here, aren't you? Suckered in here by me as bait. That son of a bitch doesn't miss a trick. I shoulda seen it coming when he had me whack Lucy. It's always take care of number one with him. This way, we all go up in flames and he gets off."

"What was Lucy's sin?" Joe asked. "Surely she knew all his warts already."

Seamus shook his head again. This time, Willy barely noticed. "There you go again, thinking she was some ditzy arm candy. She was like his Bonnie What's-her-name."

"Parker," Willy filled in absentmindedly, still lost in his analysis. "What?"

"Bonnie and Clyde?" Joe asked. "She and Lemuel were partners in crime?"

"Yeah."

"What sorts of crime?"

Joe felt as if he'd suddenly shouted in church. Seamus fell silent, seemingly shrinking into himself. *Ouch*, Joe thought. *Time to back away from that.*

"How did you and Shaw get together?" he asked instead. He stole a look at his watch, praying the missing members of the hasty team had been located and were nearby. Now that he and Willy had tripped the safe arm, assuming that's what they'd done, the need for bomb technicians was not debatable.

Unfortunately, Joe's foray into a new direction didn't work. Seamus appeared beached against a growing gloom.

"Shaw worked in Boston, didn't he?" Willy chimed in helpfully, rising at last and resuming his earlier position.

"What did he do there?" Joe followed up.

"Money stuff. I don't know," Seamus answered dully.

"But he did well. Rich guy."

"He could buy all this," Seamus made to sweep his arm through the air.

"*No!*" Willy ordered him.

Seamus froze, brought out of his funk by the yell. His eyes widened with fear, and his face showed its youth for the first time. "Are you gonna get me out of this?"

"We're working on it," Joe reassured him.

Time, distance, shielding, Christian Mock repeated to himself. Time, distance, and shielding. The holy trinity for tactical bomb techs, or TBTs. One or all three can kill you or save you, depending on how they played out. Speed but not haste, despite the "hasty" in their title; distance spoke for itself, except the Remotec robots that gave you the safest separation were too slow in a Cat A emergency; and shielding, meaning body suits and barriers, which didn't even apply here.

The traditional eighty-pound bomb suits were too cumbersome to move in quickly and of no use anyhow in a proximate, atomizing pressure blast. For that matter, the all-cotton, nonconducting vest Mock was wearing now, as he walked "in the stack" with his three TAC team members—each holding the back of the vest of the man before him—only carried the tools of his trade. When disarming a device, he actually took it off and spread it out to have what he needed immediately available. If something went wrong, all TBTs knew there was no saving them anyway.

The holy trinity, in responses like this, boiled down to time alone, aided only by training and good luck.

The two detectives preceding them had left the mansion's front door open, for which Mock was very grateful. He knew Gunther and Kunkle. Mock was a Vermont trooper himself, the nearest responder when the mutual aid call went out. The irony was that he did not know his hasty team colleagues, all from New Hampshire.

They had the same education, however—in frequent, repetitive, grueling doses—and so could rely on equally acquired skills over personal familiarity. Many lives had been sacrificed over time to fine-tune what they were doing now.

The division of labor was a crucial aspect of this. TAC people were hunters, trained to react to movement and suppress human threat; tactical bomb techs were problem solvers, analytical more than reactionary. Mock was there not just to disarm, but to spot, as Willy had earlier, potentially lethal anomalies. Was there fresh paint on a wall and nowhere else? A carpet unusually skewed? Any oddly half-open drawers? Any light switches, TV sets, motion detectors, or wall sockets that looked peculiar?

And that addressed only the visible. Heat sensors, motion detectors, hidden pressure plates, and so-called PIRs, or passive infrared sensors, also had to be considered. In a setting like this, the TAC people became Christian Mock's devoted bodyguards, keeping him alive so he could return the favor.

If everything worked out.

"Tell me more about Lucy and Lemuel," Joe urged Seamus, hearing over his earpiece that the hasty team had entered the building.

"What d'you mean?"

Joe was candid. "When we first heard of him, he was just the owner of a stolen car, taken by a guy named Don Kalfus. That name familiar?"

"Nope."

"We found him dead in the trunk of the same car, and now we have evidence that both Shaws played a role."

Seamus didn't respond.

"I'm guessing you do know something about that," Joe suggested.

After a further pause, Seamus asked, "What's up with your backup? You said somebody was coming to get me out of this thing."

Willy answered, "He said they had training for that. Chances are they'll fail and you and us are gonna die. You wanna come clean, now's the time."

Seamus's mouth fell open at the change in tone, his eyes widening. He swallowed hard before saying, "What the fuck, dude? I might as well take you losers out with me right now."

Joe followed Willy's lead. "'Chances are' is not a guarantee. Otherwise, we wouldn't be here and a disposal team wouldn't be in the building, making their way here." He stepped closer to Seamus, increasing the intimacy between them. "You know who put you in this thing, Seamus. You know he wasn't screwing around. This is no game. But here we are anyway, risking our lives to save you."

He crouched before the young man, getting eye to eye. "We're a team here, man. We've been working this since it started, putting the pieces together, figuring out who's who, connecting the dots until they took us right here, right now. We're going to do everything possible to get you out of this, but we need your help to put Shaw where he belongs. Please tell me you're good with that—that you don't want him getting away with it."

To Joe's surprise, it seemed to work. Seamus's shoulders relaxed, and his expression calmed. "You won't leave me?" he asked.

Joe shook his head. "No way. You're stuck with me." He gestured over his shoulder at Kunkle, adding, "You're probably stuck with him, too, but that's because he's a crazy bastard, in case you hadn't guessed."

Seamus actually chuckled at that.

Joe dragged over a small armchair from near the window and sat on its edge, a few feet before the bomb-shrouded source of the information he was after—fully conscious of his own vulnerability. For the moment, neither he nor Willy had a choice. They were trapped by the trigger they'd inadvertently set off. But Joe also knew that in due course, the hasty team's bomb expert would create a so-called booby trap lane through which safe passage would be better ensured. That would be his and Willy's chance to hand the scene over to those better equipped to handle it.

But he knew something else, too—that what he'd just told Seamus Kyle was no lie, and that for whatever strange reasons, both Willy and he would in fact stay put. It was in their natures to do so, in their DNA as first responders. The adage has it that firefighters enter places others are running from. Cops of their pedigree are no different.

Without giving any of this thought, Joe leaned forward, his elbows on his knees, and quietly said, "Okay, Seamus. Tell me what I need to know."

Christian Mock and the others were making headway. The balance to these operations was to quickly and cautiously mark a route of least resistance and maximum safety. Each room was entered carefully, checked electronically for radio signals, studied through special goggles for infrared beams, accompanied by prayers that nothing more sensitive—like covert, less defeatable PIRs—was lurking in the mix.

What gave Mock hope as he progressed was that he *was* locating traps. Not taking the time to disarm them—this is where the compromising nature of his role came in—he either marked them with colored "bypass" indicators as he went, or simply avoided them by leading his teammates along another route.

There was a lot of talk throughout. These high-risk entries tended to be noisy, if only marginally comprehensible. Two major pitfalls in such tense environments were that people got too quiet, or, if they spoke, used misleading language. The solution, again reflective of training, was to use coded words, virtually nonstop,

identifying problems tersely and with clarity, and presenting solu-
tions everyone understood. For example, instead of "Look out," or
"Be careful," the word used was "Bosco," since in and of itself, it
could neither be mistaken for anything else, nor uttered by anyone beyond these four to confuse them. Less playful a word—
which none of them wanted to hear—was "Avalanche." As the
word implied, it meant all else had failed and that you were free
to save yourself as best you could—usually against all odds.

"They grabbed kids," Seamus explained. "Boys. They'd been doing it for years. That's what this place is for. It's a fuckin' torture
chamber."

Joe frowned. "Together? The two of them?"

Seamus's tone was matter-of-fact. "Like I said, Bonnie and Clyde.
It was sick."

"But you helped them."

"I didn't help them with *that*. They did that shit on their own.
But yeah, I took care of stuff, mostly around here. You know, maintenance, chores, running errands."

Joe proceeded carefully, not pushing too hard, too fast, and certainly not driving home that Seamus had murdered Lucy Shaw.
"Okay. I don't want to put words in your mouth or suggest anything
that didn't happen. But what do you mean they grabbed boys? Give
us details. It might help us find Shaw so we can hold him account-
able for what he did to you here."

Seamus's anger flared. "That'll be the day. You won't catch him.
What do you not get, anyhow? He liked boys. She liked boys. They
grabbed 'em, used 'em, and killed 'em. That's where he came up
with the plastic bag trick."

"For how long?"

"Years. I don't know. Before I got hired."

"And nobody got wise?"

His answer was simple. "Money, baby. What d'you think? If they did, they got paid off. Or ended up like your dead car thief."

"I don't get why Shaw wanted his wife dead," Willy said.

He was interrupted by a man in black appearing in the doorway. "Hi, guys," he said pleasantly, his soothing tone contrasting with his helmet, pushed-up goggles, vest, gun, combat boots, and equipment.

Joe studied him for a split second before saying, "Monk? Christian Monk?"

"Mock, sir," Christian corrected him, duly impressed. "I can't believe you came that close. What've we met? Twice? If that?"

Returning to business, he addressed Seamus, whose almost relaxed body language had completely tightened up again. "Hello, sir. My name is Christian. What's yours?"

Mock was approaching as Kyle barely said, "Seamus."

The bomb tech began spreading out his vest on the floor, chatting easily. "I'm here to see if we can get you out of this pickle. I'm assuming that's okay with you?"

Seamus nodded.

"First things first, then," Christian said, his voice more serious. "I gotta ask you to stay absolutely still and focus only on me, okay? And just to explain things a bit, I have a microphone and a camera rigged to this thing around my head, along with the light. That means I'll be talking to a buddy of mine who's in a van outside. He and I like to talk things out, now and then, sort of problem-solve, if you get my meaning. So, there'll be some of that as we go. You got that? Just answer. Do not nod your head."

Seamus nervously said, "Yes."

Christian then turned to the others near the room's door. "Probably best you give us a little space, to cut down on distractions. Would you mind?"

It was a nice way of suggesting that if not all of them wanted to die in an explosion, now would be the time to leave.

Seamus stiffened, his eyes glued to Joe's, who responded without hesitation, "I'll keep Seamus company, if you don't mind. I think he'd like that."

Christian understood and appreciated the gesture. It had happened before, that a hostage in similar straits had wigged out and made things difficult.

This was Willy's moment to also volunteer to stay. He'd even anticipated it himself, almost heard his own voice issuing the predictable one-liner.

But he froze.

Joe, at the same moment, looked at him, instantly recognizing what was at stake. "Willy," he said easily. "I don't think Emma would appreciate your staying. I know what I said before, but this is an order: Leave. Now. Please."

Willy felt almost ill, his body suddenly flooded with conflicting emotions. Joe had put his finger on it, as usual, and Willy, also predictably, had completely missed the obvious emotional weight of a parent's commitment. He struggled to maintain a cool demeanor as he replied, "I'll split the difference with you. I'll be right outside, in the next room." He gestured to the door.

Joe nodded and returned to Seamus.

Willy slipped out the door, turned the corner, and pressed his back against the wall, struggling to control his breathing.

One of the TAC team members placed a gloved hand on his shoulder. "Come on. I'll guide you out."

"I'm staying," Willy said without explanation.

The man caught his eye for a second, before dropping his hand and moving away. These situations bred odd reactions in people.

Joe was still on his chair, crowding the field. He raised his eyebrows at Christian Mock. "This all right with you? I don't want to be in the way, but I'd like Seamus to know we're in this together."

"Yeah," Seamus said softly, his situation once more clear to him. Gone was the distraction of discussing Shaw and the recent past. It was all about the here and now. For all of them.

Mock seamlessly slid into professional mode, gently and progressively exploring the wiring maze before him. Using his light, a dental mirror, even a tongue depressor once, probing with his bare hands, speaking regularly to Seamus and to his colleague in the van, he worked smoothly, carefully, and quietly to reverse engineer Shaw's infernal machine. Wire by wire, one detonator at a time, he deconstructed it, often using a pair of sparkproof ceramic scissors. Throughout, he updated his audience on his headway, reassuring them as the challenge became increasingly less lethal.

This was no straightforward vest bomb. Even Joe could see that. In the same way that the house had been rigged with safe-arm devices and multiple redundancies, the envelope around Seamus was a road map of Shaw's combination of sadism, control, and mad intelligence—commingled with his engineer's knowledge of electronics and explosives. It was yet another example of how much could be missed in a police background check of a person's history.

With all of Christian Mock's poise and competence, he clearly was working at his outermost limits. Rather than a single bomb rigged to a trigger, this was layered, interconnected, and riddled with false leads and booby traps.

Mock was not alone in his tension. Seamus Kyle was running low on reserves. Despite the bomb tech's display of calm self-assurance, and Joe's ongoing, quiet, and distracting conversation, the young, fragmented, increasingly sweat-soaked subject of this attention was beginning to lose his composure. He had nothing to do except sit and wait for a split second's insight—if he got even that—announcing the end of his life.

Even Willy, as the minutes stretched toward an hour, forced himself back into the room, albeit behind a blast-deflecting barricade that the TAC team had unobtrusively built near the door. He watched with growing fatalism the opposing forces of Mock's and Joe's composure against Seamus's swelling hysteria. The young man was as fixated on this eerily quiet scene as he might have been watching an anaconda slowly strangle a pig.

It couldn't stay unresolved. The warring dynamics took on a force of their own, with Seamus's anxiety as the inevitable catalyst. In the end, there were two bombs in the room, and Mock and Joe found themselves spending almost as much time stopping Seamus from exploding as Mock was on defusing the vest.

The spark, however, when it came, was neither Seamus nor his vest, but the most benign of muttered comments that Mock made to his colleague over the radio. He had successfully navigated almost every layer of Shaw's handiwork, when he gingerly felt along Seamus's spine, and discovered a final small detonator—what he later admitted thinking Shaw might have thrown in as an afterthought.

"Found another one," he relayed in his usual soft monotone. "Might be motion-activated."

That was all it took. Wide-eyed, his face contorted, Seamus twisted in his seat, stared down at Mock, and screamed, "*What?*" and leaped to his feet.

Mock reacted like a dog to a whistle. Without thought or warning, he yelled, "*Avalanche!*" sprang from his crouch, tackled Joe head-on, and knocked them and Joe's chair over backward, just as the entire TAC team hit the floor behind their barricade, taking Willy down with them.

The noise, when it came, proved anticlimactic. A muffled thud, like a heavy book hitting a rug.

But no less effective for that.

Finally standing, dangling a fringe of spaghettilike strands of cut wire, Seamus straightened at the muted blast and momentarily froze. He then coughed once, producing a spray of blood from his lips, and collapsed.

With one last detonator to go, Lemuel Shaw had achieved his goal.

CHAPTER FIFTEEN

On the face of it, Seamus's death should have been the day's main feature. The fact was that, as dramatic as it had been, it didn't mean the survivors were out of danger. Shaw's behemoth of a building remained full of devices—some disarmed, others bypassed, and, quite reasonably, many as yet undiscovered.

That was not lost on Christian Mock, who raised himself off Joe Gunther, politely said, "Sorry about that," and immediately began coordinating the extraction of nonessential personnel.

Joe lay on the floor a moment longer, his legs still entangled in his chair, gazing across the carpeting at Seamus's lifeless heap, and working to put the past hour into perspective. Joe's life had been full, varied, and inordinately eventful, including combat exposure in military service.

But this had been a corker.

"Taking a little 'me time'?" Willy asked, looking down at him.

Joe turned his head to take him in. "How 'bout you? You okay?"

Willy frowned and reached down. "I'm not the one staring at the ceiling. You hurt?"

Joe accepted the help to stand up, where he found his legs to be surprisingly wobbly. "No . . . I'm fine. Not an everyday experience, you know?"

Willy compressed his lips doubtfully. "The day's still young," he said, and escorted his boss toward the door.

The way out was like following a demented version of Twister, where the targets for your feet were as just convoluted and challenging, but the area expanded to one room after another—a long, meandering journey where a loss of balance ran the real risk of bringing down the roof.

Seamus was abandoned where he lay. Until the building and what remained of his vest were thoroughly vetted by a team of bomb techs, no peripheral activities—including a body retrieval—would be allowed.

That level of caution was evident even outside, where Joe and Willy met with Christian Mock and others who were directing everyone to leave the property entirely, all the way to the highway beyond the gate.

"That much of a concern?" Joe asked.

"We found a couple of nonactivated det cord traps, designed for approaching personnel if needed. God knows what else this nutjob has rigged. Your ICAC pal in the van says he picked up radio signals right now coming from somewhere off-site."

Joe shook his hand as he prepared to leave. "Thank you, Christian, for landing on top of me. It was unexpected and much appreciated."

Mock brushed it off. "Pure instinct. Probably born of a simple mind. That's what my wife tells me. I'll look forward to seeing you back in Vermont sometime, hopefully under more pleasant circumstances."

He wandered off to wrap things up with his colleagues. He'd be leaving for Vermont almost immediately, his hasty team role completed. New Hampshire's bomb squad would take over cleaning up the Shaw property from here on out.

Joe and Willy made Fred Houston's van their destination upon reaching a highway clotted with official vehicles stretching for half a mile, most of them flashing strobe lights unnecessarily.

As they walked up this line, Joe asked Willy, "You okay after all that? Any combat flashbacks?"

Kunkle's honest response surprised him. "Worse than that."

Joe paused to study him. "What happened?"

"I froze."

"What d'you mean? You were right there. I saw you."

"Still. I wanted to leave you high and dry."

Joe tried to process Willy's obvious distress. "For crying out loud. That's perfectly reasonable. What the hell? You really think that's a bad thing? It's not like we were surrounded by bad guys, shooting it out."

"It's never happened before."

A vehicle was heading toward them, and Joe steered Willy between two cruisers to avoid it.

"You were never a father before. What d'you think? That's why I mentioned Emma when Mock was rolling up his sleeves."

"You got Hillstrom," Willy pushed back as the vehicle rolled by and they resumed walking toward Houston's van.

"That's different," Joe replied. "You know that. Kids are a part of you. You don't think of Sam every time you get in a jam. And I bet she doesn't worry about you then, either. But Emma? Get used to it. And pay attention, too. You owe her that."

"I feel like I let you down."

Joe shook his head and grabbed Willy's good arm, stopping him again to emphasize, "You never have and you never will."

Willy smiled, if begrudgingly. "I have more times than either of us can count."

Joe resumed walking. "Ancient history. Different circumstances."

Houston looked up as they slid open the side door and stepped inside. "I think I've got a fix on him," he said as a greeting.

As usual, he was seated before a bank of monitors, one of which had a map of the surrounding area.

"Where?" Kunkle asked.

Joe sat on a bench to Houston's right and looked over his shoulder at the screen.

The ICAC man tapped on a blinking dot. "Right there. He was either monitoring what you were doing inside or manipulating things somehow. Whatever it was, he was accessing the internal routers via Wi-Fi. I got hold of the port logs to grab his IP address. That gave me the subscriber information for this guy." He hit a couple of keystrokes and brought up Clyde Herrick's name.

"That mean anything?" he asked.

"It does," Joe told them both. "What's that location?" he asked, indicating the flashing dot.

The Thomaston police chief, not surprisingly, lived on a dirt road, now paved with snow and ice. Located on the other side of the township from the Shaw estate, it was deep in the woods, on steep terrain, but fortunately approachable from two directions, allowing Joe and Willy, accompanied by the still available TAC team, to approach discreetly and from all sides. For local knowledge and to show his appreciation, Joe had invited young Dillon Rowe to join them.

One final addition to their operation was an associate attorney general for New Hampshire's Department of Justice, one of which routinely kept company with the New Hampshire State Police's Major Crime unit on high-visibility outings. Of the many and varied differences between this state's law enforcement model and Vermont's, having your own prosecutor on hand—complete with a laptop to secure warrants and a cell phone to reach a judge—had some real advantages.

From outward appearances, Clyde Herrick presented as Lemuel Shaw's polar opposite. His property was as run-down and poorly maintained as Shaw's was immaculate and upscale, reinforcing the notion that the latter had formed a relationship with the former solely based on his law enforcement and local bigwig status. Reflective of what Rowe had said about his boss, salted here and there were jarring icons of excess cash—a late-model truck and a shiny Kubota tractor among them.

Joe's approach resembled their first of the day, with the added presumption that their nemesis knew they were coming. As before, Joe and Willy made the initial contact, climbing Herrick's cluttered, rotting porch, sagging under piled cordwood, and knocking on his door, but this time with people forming a tight cordon around the house.

A large, unshaven man with bloodshot eyes opened up. "What do you want?" he asked in a hostile voice.

Both VBI men were wearing the labeled armored vests identifying them, prompting an already taxed Willy to ask, "Really? That makes you the only cop in the county not hanging around your pal's house. Nice leadership."

Joe spoke directly, privately praying that Houston had led them to the proper address. "We want Lemuel Shaw." He proffered a document. "Here's the warrant."

Herrick looked genuinely surprised, to Joe's satisfaction, and shouted over his shoulder down the hallway, *"We got company!"*

If he expected either man to respond like an unleashed hunting dog, Herrick was disappointed. Instead of pursuing some unseen quarry, Willy reached out, grabbed his arm, calmly said, "You're under arrest. Turn around," and spun him on his axis as Joe pulled out a pair of cuffs.

Toward the back of the dark, evil-smelling hovel of a building, Lemuel Shaw heard the warning and looked up from the laptop he'd been using to monitor the alarm and surveillance systems at his home across town.

He did react as if to a starter's pistol, slapped the computer shut, leaped to his feet, and bolted to the back door overlooking the rear deck. As he stepped outside, a heavily armed New Hampshire state trooper dressed in Ninja black appeared as if from nowhere and grabbed hold of his shirtfront. "Lemuel Shaw," he said through his ski mask. "You're under arrest."

Shaw didn't miss a beat, despite his earlier panic. His body relaxing as he spread his arms wide, revealing only the computer and no weapons in hand, he replied, "Lawyer."

"What we got," Willy Kunkle told his boss, "is a dog's breakfast. Tons of circumstantial junk, basically not a single smoking gun, the world's most convoluted story line, and nobody talking."

They were still on Herrick's front porch, watching the owner and his tight-lipped guest being escorted to separate cruisers. The property was alive with cops, searching for, collecting, and documenting evidence.

"Maybe," Joe answered placidly.

Willy was incredulous. "What do you see I don't?"

Joe gestured toward the vehicle holding Herrick. "He hasn't invoked a lawyer yet, has he?"

Willy gave that a moment before saying, "He knows the system from the inside. You think he's hoping to make a deal?"

"I'm willing to listen if he does."

They chose the most imposing building they could think of quickly—the federal courthouse in Concord, New Hampshire, named after Warren Rudman and, although built in the 1990s, looking like a throwback to the art deco thirties. The U.S. Marshals had office space there, where Joe and Willy brought the increasingly beleaguered Clyde Herrick. All three of them ended up in yet another bland room, equipped solely with a table, chairs, and a video recorder. The intended impression of its being in a structure designed to decide people's fates had apparently reached home. Herrick was ready to talk.

Joe slid the Miranda form across the table for openers. "You know what this is, Clyde. It's your choice—right now, right here—to either work with us or invoke your right to remain silent. You know better than anyone where you rank in all this. I recommend you choose wisely."

Herrick didn't hesitate. He pushed the form back. "I wanna deal."

"For the record, you are refusing your right to remain silent? If so, sign here."

The police chief scribbled illegibly at the bottom, repeating, "Do I get a deal?"

"You get us to listen," Joe replied.

Herrick was petulant. "I incriminate myself, on the record, for nothing?"

"Or you say nothing," Joe countered, "and the United States government incriminates you on what we know, which is not in your favor. Right now, Clyde, you are a coconspirator to terrible things. I leave you to imagine how that's going to go down if you don't speak on your own behalf."

In fact, they knew little of Herrick's involvement with Lemuel Shaw. They had suspicions, coincidences, reasonable leaps of logic, and a recent trove of relevant findings from Shaw's house. But few things helped more than a confession.

This was the moment when—unconsciously or not—Herrick could believe he controlled his own fate. In fact, whatever he said wouldn't necessarily help him out. Where he ended up at the end of this judicial journey, nobody could say at this stage. If he threw in with Joe or clammed up like Shaw, there were no guarantees. But the artifice of self-destiny was what Joe was counting on.

An impression that finally held sway.

"Okay," Herrick said as if in charge of events. "I'll play. But you'd better treat me right."

Joe sensed it was all Willy could do not to burst out laughing. Treating Herrick "right" had nothing to do with this.

By contrast, Joe's response was bland, bordering on bored. "Fine. Let's step away from all the recent drama, then, and begin at the beginning. When did you and Shaw first meet?"

"Maybe twenty years ago or more. When he came up to build that thing he calls a home."

"What were the circumstances?"

"What?"

Willy crossed his legs impatiently. Joe rephrased, "How did you meet?"

"Oh. He bought my truck."

After a moment, Joe prompted him. "Tell us about that."

"He needed a truck. He bought mine."

This time, Joe stayed silent, forcing Herrick to fill the gap.

"I thought it was weird at the time," he expanded. "He's this superrich guy from away, and my truck was hammered. Fact, about a year later, he got rid of it. And he paid big for it, double what it was worth."

"You weren't suspicious about that?" Joe asked, pretending to be taking notes and not looking up.

"Why should I be? Man's entitled to be stupid if he wants. Plus, that was his style. He bought other stuff from me. Always paid top dollar. I got used to it after a while. You seen his house, right? The man spends money. It's what he does."

"He did this all over town?" Joe asked, surprised.

Herrick's eyes widened. "Oh, no. Nobody knows anything about him. That was his biggest hang-up. He made that clear as day: I was to keep who he was under wraps."

"Why?"

Herrick put on a small show of bluster. "Everybody's entitled to some privacy, aren't they? I'm not gonna mess with 'em just 'cause they wanna be left alone."

"That's commendable," Joe commented. "Tricky, though, given that he bought a huge estate and had a mansion built. No one ever set eyes on him or dealt with him directly?"

"They didn't have to," Herrick said. "He had his own people, and I played interference now and then. He made it worth my while to moonlight a little. It helped move things along."

"You ever meet his wife?"

The answer was curt. "Sure."

A topic Joe planned to return to. "Tell us," he requested instead, "what Shaw was doing at your house when we arrived."

Herrick relaxed again as he feigned ignorance. "How do I know? He had a computer. I know squat about those. Ask my guys. They'll tell you I avoid 'em like the plague. Shaw came by, asked if he could use my living room. I said sure, and then you people showed up in town, and he told me to stay put. That's why you found me at home. I have no clue what he was doing."

Joe nodded silently, allowing Willy to speak. "You're fucking lying," he said quietly. "How long you been on the job?"

Herrick flushed but answered the question, pointing at them as he answered, "Thirty years, so don't think I don't know good cop, bad cop when I see it. I might as well've written the book."

"Comic book is more like it," Willy countered. "You don't think we didn't tear your poor excuse of a police station apart before this sit-down? First rule of interrogation, Clyde: do your homework. What we got against you'll put you in jail for decades, and that's *before* we hit you with all the shit you pulled with Shaw. You don't have to cooperate right now. You can pretend you're God Almighty and flip us off." Willy leaned forward to emphasize, "But we will bury you if you do."

"Oooh," Herrick mocked him. "Now I *am* scared."

Joe spoke as if nothing had been said. "Nine years ago, Clyde, one of your patrol officers—now long gone to another agency—stopped Lemuel Shaw as he was receiving oral sex from an underage boy." Joe slid a document across the table from a folder before him. "This is an affidavit from that officer, attesting to the fact that he later submitted that report to you for processing, and that you told him not to worry, because you would do the rest."

"Nine years ago?" Herrick asked, his forehead suddenly shining in the bright overhead light. "How'm I supposed to remember that?"

"Do you know Dillon Rowe?" Joe asked.

Herrick hesitated.

"Careful," Willy cautioned. "Could be a trick question."

The chief glowered. "He's one of my officers. Not a good one, but he has a pulse."

Joe presented a second document. "This is another affidavit, written by Officer Rowe, stating how he discovered the paperwork about that stop nine years ago, tucked out of sight and never acted upon, presumably where you'd put it to keep it available but out of circulation."

Herrick pretended to look baffled. "This is crap. I know nothing about it."

"We wondered," Joe continued, "why you did that, instead of just destroying it, but then it became obvious. You wanted to keep it for a rainy day—to remind Shaw of the favor he owed you."

"You ever use it?" Willy asked.

Herrick tried pushing back. "I don't even know what you're talking about."

"That's curious." Joe said, holding another sheet of paper, which he added to the collection before their increasingly nervous guest. "This is a lab report on the original citation—a citation with your fingerprints on it."

"You were getting nervous, Clyde," Willy said. "Were things weird enough between you and Shaw that you wanted a smoking gun always available—and maybe it was time to use it?"

"You were scared Shaw might be going off the rails," Joe proposed. "I don't blame you. It was time for a little insurance. If we hadn't knocked on your door, you were probably thinking about using it, weren't you? The guy is completely nuts, after all."

"But your timing sucked," Willy said. "And now you're screwed."

"Not necessarily," Joe argued. "You know a lot. You've got more than just proof of a little illegal sex." He suddenly saw a possibility, as could happen in the middle of such conversations, where a moment's clarity presents like a bright light. "For example," he added, "I bet you can name the young man your officer found in that car, can't you? That's why the report was so red-hot. Especially now. Go on, Clyde. I'm right, aren't I? That's why you played dumb when Dillon Rowe asked you about Shaw." Joe laughed. "Come on. Prove me right."

Herrick couldn't resist. "Seamus Kyle."

Joe lightly punched Willy's arm, who was impressed by this bit of deduction. "You dog, Clyde," Joe complimented the man. "It must've driven you nuts, knowing Shaw was about to kill your golden goose. Did you and Seamus ever discuss how you knew it was him in that car, so many years ago?"

Old trick, Joe knew, but it worked now. "Nah," Clyde confessed. "He was clueless."

"It must've amazed you, when Seamus began working for Shaw. Did you see that coming?"

"No," Clyde admitted. "But he was different from the others. He ended up like Frankenstein's right-hand man."

"Igor?" Willy suggested.

"Yeah. Right. Him. But like brainwashed, you know? Creepy. A horny old man who treated him like shit, and he acted like he was God."

"What happened to the others?" Joe asked casually, again reading between the lines.

Clyde immediately stilled, watching them carefully. Satisfied that he'd played out enough slack to the man, Joe decided to tighten the rope. He began laying out documents from his folder as if dealing from a deck.

"Turns out you weren't the only one taking out insurance, Clyde. Shaw didn't trust you, either. You knew his place was rigged with booby traps?"

"Sure."

"Well, he relied too much on them to cover his tracks. After Seamus was killed, we had a bomb disposal team disarm the entire building. This is their all-clear report, including Shaw's office and his personal safe. Did you know about the safe?"

A growing apprehension grew in Herrick's eyes. "No."

Joe showed him a photograph. "Big unit, also rigged to self-destruct, and containing lots of interesting items, some of them featuring you. Are you absolutely certain you don't want to make a clean breast of all you know? Right now? Prosecutors pay attention to that. You know they do, along with any help you throw in for good measure."

To bolster his pitch, Joe added a picture of a dozen thumb drives, all secured from the safe. "Did you know he was as handy with covert video equipment as he was with explosives?" he asked. "You won't be surprised to hear we have some embarrassing footage of you."

Herrick's earlier red face returned. "I didn't do boys," he protested. "I don't do that shit."

"A man of principle," Joe said. "I should have known. Still, you'd better start talking about what you did do, unless you want the people coming after us to throw the book at you solely based on this." Joe tapped the photographs.

"It was part of our arrangement," Herrick said dully, his voice a monotone.

"Details, Clyde," Willy threw in.

The man wiped his forehead. "The sex. That was part of the deal. I gave him protection for what they were doing, but I didn't do boys. I'm no fag."

Joe worked not to show his disgust, although the scope of what these people had cooked up was filling his brain like acid. "Tell us what you know about Lucy."

"She was part of it. She did those kids, too."

"And . . . ?" Joe raised his eyebrows encouragingly.

Herrick's anger flared briefly. "Yeah, yeah, yeah. Fine. She had a thing goin' with me, too, for a while, and she supplied me with a woman now and then, too."

"A woman?" Joe challenged him. "Or a girl?"

"They didn't have driver's licenses, okay? I didn't know how old they were. We're only talking about a couple, anyhow."

Joe could sense Willy's inclination to simply shoot the man. "How did it work, Clyde?" Joe asked, before someone—himself included—could interrupt the confessional momentum. "How did they satisfy their appetites?"

"With the boys? They were never from around here. I saw one once—a hitchhiker—I thought would work, but Shaw said, 'Never fish your own pond.' I remember that. He got 'em from cities like Boston or Lawrence or wherever. I don't know details. They just showed up. The girls they gave me were hookers, I think, or paid-for trailer trash."

Joe put out a few more photos. "He kept them in these rooms? We found five of them in the basement, all looking like cells."

Clyde studied those more carefully than he had the others. "I guess. They're nice-looking. I never saw 'em. No windows, huh? I wondered about that."

"What do you mean?"

"He kept some of the kids a couple of years. I didn't know how he could do that." He pointed at the pictures. "Guess that's my answer."

"How many were there, grand total?" Joe asked, as shocked by Herrick's tone as by what he was saying.

"I don't know. Not a lot. Maybe three at a time, tops. Seven? Over the years? It wasn't a huge thing, like you're thinking."

"You have no clue what I'm thinking," Willy muttered, his emotions less restrained than Joe's.

Herrick didn't notice. "Seamus took care of them," he said.

"Tell us about that."

"It's what I meant about his being Shaw's weirdo sidekick. He starts out one of 'em, like I said, and then he becomes their jailer? How twisted is that?"

"You saw a lot of Seamus?"

"Off and on. I'd drop by to see how he was doing. Find out when the Shaws might be coming up. Keep in touch."

Keeping your thumb in the pie, Joe thought. He placed another picture on the table, this one of the long-missing Scooter Nelson. "You ever see him?"

Herrick peered at it without interest. "Maybe. I guess so. He's not one of the recent ones."

Joe moved on. "Lemuel and Lucy fell out toward the end," he said. "You know why?"

Herrick shook his head. "I didn't see her as much as the two guys, and not at all toward the end. I was surprised she'd died. You saying that wasn't natural?"

"One last question for now, Clyde," Joe asked, not answering. "Then we'll take a break. Were there any other people, besides Lucy, you, and Seamus, who were part of the inner circle? Anyone Shaw trusted like he did you three?"

"Not that I know," Herrick replied, the living embodiment of the banality of evil, in Joe's eyes. "Course, I never traveled south to their other place. This was my patch, and I stuck to it."

"This confirms it," Sammie announced, holding up a fax back in their Brattleboro office. "According to prints filed with the National Center for Missing and Exploited Children, Seamus Kyle, aka Thomas Nesbitt, disappeared without a trace nine years ago, from Leominster, Mass."

"Score one credibility point for ex–police chief Herrick," Willy said from behind his desk.

"And," Sam went on, switching to her computer monitor, "preliminary reports from the cadaver dog team in Thomaston indicate five skeletons in five separate graves, some still with plastic bags over their heads. One was also wearing a ring and had dental work matching Scooter Nelson's. It's looking like it might be the oldest one of the bunch. He could've been their first."

A silence settled over them at that, which Joe tried to lighten.

"You hear Dillon Rowe was made acting chief?" he asked.

Lester tried to help. "Good for him. God knows I wouldn't trade places with him, but to each his own, I guess."

"What's left of my brains would rot," Willy agreed.

"Speaking of brains," Joe asked them all, "is any one of you satisfied with the way things rest with this case?"

Lester, by character more inclined to coloring within the lines than the rest of them, reacted on the bright side. "It's looking good," he said. "We got Lucy killing Kalfus, Seamus knocking off Lucy, and Shaw blowing up Seamus, along with thumb drives, fingerprints, physical evidence, and Herrick's testimony to support it all. We're close to solving several missing kid cases, we connected a string of burglaries across southern Vermont and New Hampshire to the man who did them, found two small warehouses full of stolen items to be redistributed to their owners, and have two people behind bars for felonies ranging from murder to kidnapping to sexual assault on a minor, among other things. And we did it all as part of a federal task force where I don't think we pissed off even a local deputy. That may be the biggest accomplishment of all."

But his effort went for naught. Predictably, the others were focused on Joe's implication that too many loose ends remained.

"Why was Lucy killed?" Joe asked as an example.

"Why did they kill Kalfus?" Willy joined in. "He was just a thief."

Sam added, "And why did Shaw do Seamus and not Herrick?" she asked.

Joe pointed at her. "I like that. What else?"

Lester joined in, if tentatively. "Why the fight between Kalfus and Shaw at the strip club?"

"Another good one," Joe said. "And what about the passenger at Kalfus's murder scene? Riding in the Mercedes with him? Who was that?"

He returned to Sam and repeated, "Why Seamus and not Herrick? What threat did one hold over Shaw the other didn't? They each had long histories with both Shaws."

"Geography," Willy suggested. "Clyde told us he'd never been to the Shaws' Gilsum house."

"Seamus killed Lucy," Lester said. "Clyde knew nothing about that side of things. It's like the Shaws had two lives running in parallel—one involving stolen kids in Thomaston, the other more in plain view in Gilsum."

"Seamus is the bridge between them," Willy suggested. "Once a stolen boy, now a cat's-paw of the lord and master, sidling up to an unsuspecting Lucy and killing her. If we'd been able to get hold of him before he went boom, he could've exposed everything."

Joe picked up that. "Okay," he said. "But by 'everything,' there's more than what we're seeing. To Lester's point, there's that fight between Shaw and Kalfus at the club. We never answered that adequately."

"I was never satisfied Robin Whiteman was being straight, either," Sam said. "She lied to us once, remember, when she first claimed she knew nothing about Don's burglaries. Why not again? He did take her on one of his sprees. She could have been the mystery passenger in the Mercedes. If I'd been her, I wouldn't have confessed to that trip."

Joe was nodding as she spoke. "But then explain the body language. She's on a joyride, like before, only this time, her boyfriend gets murdered by two people who meet up with him at a pull-off? And she stays in the car, even after one of them replaces Don behind the wheel and drives off? That doesn't sound likely."

"Not for the Robin Whiteman we've got in our heads," Sammie argued. "But what if she's playing a really dark, deep game? There may be a shitload more to that girl than we figured."

"As there might be to Melissa Monfet," Willy said. "Anybody remember her? She was having it all sorts of ways—screwing around with Don, looking away from what Buttner was doing to her own daughter. If anybody was designed to stay cool while her boyfriend's beaten to death by a crazy old lady with a two-by-four, I say it's Melissa. Could be she, Buttner, and the Shaws are *all* connected."

"Okay, okay," Joe responded, holding up both hands. "I like it. All of it. And it opens up the notion that the Shaws lived on *three* parallel tracks, not just two. But does any of it alter what we've got so far? Does it change any of our results?"

Again, there was silence in the room, but contemplative this time. Raising his hand halfway, as in school, Lester asked, "I hate to say this, but while we have video of Don Kalfus being knocked out and stuffed into the trunk, we don't really have proof that he died there. It could be the mystery passenger is more than just someone along for the ride."

Willy laughed. "Jesus, Les. Nice. That's outside the box. Can I add that Seamus murdering Lucy is totally circumstantial? Even with what turned out to be his dying confession, some lawyer could argue he was actually taking one for the team."

"A team that put a bomb on him," Lester protested.

"Hey," Willy pushed back. "Old hat for Seamus. Didn't they also kidnap and abuse him as a kid? How did he react then? He became one of them. If you can't beat 'em, join 'em. Drill sergeants have known that for centuries."

"Hang on," Joe cut in. "I know I'm supposed to say, 'Enough, back to the case,' but we're onto something here. We're talking about what may be crucial missing pieces. What if they go to the essence of what we already got in hand?"

"The psychology behind the hard evidence?" Sam asked generally.

"Kind of," Joe replied. "People do what they do for a reason. Could be logical, could be impulsive, and, to your point, Willy, could also be the result of brainwashing. We got this far chasing stolen property, helium rental forms, watching videos, connecting tax records to suspects, and a bunch of other good police work. It's great and we have people in jail, but what about the driving engines behind it all?"

"The why instead of the how?" Lester asked.

"Right. We're told not to worry much about motive. Stick to the facts, build on the evidence, let the prosecutors earn their bucks. But we *always* wonder about the why. It's human nature to ask, 'What the hell were you thinking?'"

He rose and stood looking at them. "I'll tell you what's been bugging me from the very start of this investigation. It's the same thing Willy said a few minutes ago: Why was Don Kalfus killed? It might've been Scooter Nelson's phone, but Don was like a vacuum cleaner. He stole everything. He wouldn't have cared. Why not just buy it back? Or steal it back? Less muss and fuss. Less heat from the likes of us. It doesn't make sense unless we can find the reason behind it."

"Don was a fall guy," Willy suggested.

"That's what I'm wondering," Joe agreed. "He ended up in the middle of something way outside his ballpark."

"Which got him killed," Sam said, almost to herself.

"And leaves us where?" Lester asked.

"In an unusual place," Joe suggested. "With the prosecution happy and high fives all around, we need to quietly review everything that led us here and figure out if we got it right. That includes rechecking the evidence and extracting fingerprints and DNA across the board, regardless of the suspect's current importance. For example, Shaw's Mercedes—we had prints there we never ran because our theory held water. Let's run everything now, especially around that passenger seat."

"Better us than some defense lawyer doing it later and making us look like idiots," Willy restated, forever the pragmatist.

Joe pointed at him approvingly. "If that's your motivation, then exactly right."

CHAPTER SIXTEEN

A local Vermont joke counters, "How's your job?" with, "Which one?" Barely funny, and often evoking an appreciative look from people in the know. Of the many things associated with the state, "upward mobility" is rarely one—especially among those in Robin Whiteman's income bracket.

As a result, Joe did not drive to Taco Bell to find her at night, but to one of Brattleboro's supermarkets during the day, where she worked as a bagger. This was a job with which he was familiar, if only because more than one cop had moonlighted at such places for extra cash. Pride of social stature was not a broadly practiced regional affectation.

He'd called ahead, knowing how disposably management saw such positions, and not wishing to get the poor woman fired just because he pulled her aside at the wrong time. He therefore went straight to the break room at the prearranged time and found her sitting down at a small table, a mug of coffee in one hand, the ubiquitous smartphone in the other.

"Miss Whiteman?" he asked, sitting opposite.

She nodded, midway through her first sip. "Yes," she said, wiping her lip with the back of her hand.

"Sorry," he apologized. "Joe Gunther. I called?"

"Sure. This about Don again?"

"It is. You may know that we sometimes conduct follow-up interviews, especially on big cases like this."

"Sure. Whatever," she said without interest.

"You told my colleague Special Agent Kunkle that you'd known Don a few months, had ridden in the stolen Mercedes at least once, and had even been to a house in Stratton that he burgled."

She put the mug down, frowning. "Am I gonna get in trouble for that? I didn't do anything."

"We know that," Joe reassured her. "What we're less sure about is whether you told us everything you did with him."

She looked startled. "At that house?"

"No. In total. I suspect you might not have been quite as bored by that experience as you said and that you may have joined him on a shopping spree more than once."

Her mouth tightened slightly before she said, "I told you what happened."

Joe placed his forearms on the table and leaned in for emphasis. His voice was too quiet to be overheard by the two other people sharing a table in the far corner. "Miss Whiteman, we don't usually ask questions we don't know the answers to. We ask them to confirm what we've learned and expose who we're talking to as a liar."

It was a Kodak moment, as the saying once had it—her chance to either burst out in outrage and stomp off, or admit defeat and cooperate.

She thankfully chose the latter.

"What do you wanna know?" she asked, her voice flat.

"Did you ride with him in the Mercedes on any other occasion?"

That, she obviously wasn't expecting. "In the Mercedes?" she asked. "I told the other guy—the one with the funny arm—we took a quick ride north of Putney once, to Windsor. But the car was hot. Don wanted to impress me, but he didn't want to get busted, either."

"But you did go on other trips with him, just not in that car?"

"Yeah," she admitted, looking down.

Joe removed several pictures from his pocket and placed them faceup before her. "During your time with Don, did you ever see any of these people?"

She studied them, which was unusual in Joe's experience. "No," she said.

"How about the names Lemuel Shaw, Lucy Shaw, or Seamus Kyle?"

She shook her head. "Nope."

"Does the name Melissa Monfet do anything for you?"

"No. Sorry."

"How 'bout on the night Don was killed. Where were you?"

"Working. At Taco Bell."

"And after your shift?"

"Home. You can ask my parents. They're always up late, so we watch TV together."

That didn't mean she didn't sneak out afterward, but Joe had gained access to her phone records through a warrant and hadn't found any activity after 2:00 A.M.

"Did you ever meet his mom?" he asked, shifting directions slightly, seeking to confirm what Cheri had told Willy about never having met Robin.

"She's dead," she answered quickly. "So, no."

That caught him off guard. "And the name Cheri Pratt?" he asked in the same voice.

"No."

"What did he tell you about his mom?"

"That she died when he was little. He was a foster kid. Moved around a bunch."

"No permanent home? No one he thought of as a mother?"

"Not that he told me. It sounded bad, like people took him in for the state benefits, until he acted up enough that they got rid of him. He said he grew up feeling like a bad used car. A what-d'ya-call-it."

"A lemon?"

"Right." She flipped her phone over that she'd placed beside her coffee and checked the time. "I gotta get back," she announced. "We done?"

"Yes," Joe replied, waiting until she'd left before updating the others via text.

It was after dark when Willy Kunkle saw the lights go on at Cheri's house. He'd seen her enter her driveway minutes earlier and weighed ambushing her there or waiting. He was looking forward to this. As with so much else since the discovery of Don Kalfus's unexpected death, things had shape-shifted considerably, introducing a host of unexpected characters, turning victims into perpetrators and mourners into something much darker. The traditionally straight line between a thief and his consequences had taken some serious twists and turns.

Riding on his earlier rapport with Cheri when he'd first met her with Ron Klecszewski, Willy had opted to come alone. A rationalization, not to mention a violation of safety protocols. Willy was the first to admit how often he took advantage of Joe's forgiving nature.

He waited further to see just one sign of movement across a curtain, ensuring that Cheri hadn't repaired to the bathroom upon her return, before he crossed the street and rang her doorbell.

"You again?" she asked upon opening, a cigarette in hand.

"You know how these things go," he told her. "They take a lot of digging and a lot of time. Can I come in?"

She shook her head wearily and stepped back, leaving the door wide and commenting, "I never know why you people bother askin'."

"You could say no," he reminded her, stepping in.

She was walking ahead of him toward the kitchen. Given the bedlam of the rest of the house, he guessed it was the only place left with space enough to sit.

Which is what she did upon entering, settling before a cup of coffee he couldn't imagine she'd had time to pour.

He sat across the chipped and cluttered old metal breakfast table in the room's center.

"What d'you want?" she asked, not making eye contact.

"I don't know how connected you are to the internet and the news," he began, "but you might've heard some buzz about a man killed by a vest bomb in northern New Hampshire."

"Nah. Don't care about that."

"Don't blame you. It's relevant, in that the dead man was connected to Lemuel Shaw, who you knew, it turns out."

She blew out a cloud of smoke. "Oh, yeah?"

"Yeah. Remember that silver ashtray you claimed you knew nothing about, from him to his wife, Lucy?"

"Vaguely. That was Donny's shit. I told you that."

"Well, yes and no," Willy corrected her. "We've been filling in some holes in this case, making sure everything's tucked away, and we found you'd been a lot more active in Don's life lately than you said. Your fingerprints, for example, were everywhere in that storage shed and elsewhere."

"That doesn't prove anythin'."

"It does get you closer to colluding with a criminal enterprise, to put a legal slant on it."

"You must be desperate. That enterprise is history. Donny's the one you wanted, and he's dead."

"Yeah," Willy drawled. "Poor old Donny. He was another bump in the road for us."

He let that dangle, causing her to catch his eye for the first time. "What's that supposed to mean?"

"He wasn't really your son, was he?"

"Close enough."

"And the box we found you holding in the storage shed?" he asked, moving on. "Lighter, jewelry, ashtray?"

"I told you. All Donny's."

"Without a single print of his on any of it. Just yours."

"I'd been lookin' through it."

"Not when we grabbed you. You'd just walked in."

"Earlier."

"How about Shaw's car, where Donny was found dead? We found your prints there, too."

She flared. "That's bullshit."

Willy tilted his head. "Nah. You tried to wipe them away. Movie stuff. People never remember what they touched. We missed them the first time." He held up his hand, adding, "But not the second time."

Her response caught him by surprise, which later he ruefully admitted. For all his renown as a human predator, no one was infallible, and hubris, along with a creeping gentleness, had dulled his edge.

In a single unexpected motion, Cheri swept up the coffee mug by her hand and launched its cold contents into his face, simultaneously upending the kitchen table on top of him and sending him flying onto his back.

But he was faster than she'd anticipated, and rolled with his own momentum, breaking free of the table and rising to his knees, close to the door leading toward freedom.

Cut off, Cheri veered away as he regained his footing, made for a door behind her, and, through it, ran upstairs.

Willy gave pursuit, but only as far as the turn in the stairs, where, glancing up, he saw her swivel on the top landing, grab a shotgun leaning against the wall, and level it at him.

He ducked back just as the double-aught round exploded into the wall by his head.

Joe was still at the office when his phone vibrated.

"Hey, boss," Willy said calmly. "Wanted to give you a heads-up. Got a situation over at Cheri Pratt's place."

At Willy's urging, Joe showed up only with Sam in tow, Lester already being back home with his family. They parked quietly on the street, entered the building, and found Willy in the kitchen, sitting again at the resurrected kitchen table.

"Hey, guys," he greeted them.

"Cute," Joe replied, taking in his stained shirtfront. "What the hell've you done?"

Willy pointed to the doorway with the stairs. "She took exception to my line of inquiry."

"And?" Sammie asked.

"She took a shot at me when I followed. Check out the hole in the wall."

Joe took a couple of steps to inspect Cheri's handiwork, keeping clear of the actual doorway. "You sure she's still up there?" he asked, sensitive to the fact that under normal circumstances, the building should've been surrounded by the police equivalent of an armed battalion.

In response, Willy yelled, *"Cheri?"*

"What?"

"Joe's here!"

Willy smiled at his boss.

"You're kidding me," the latter said in an undertone, now at the bottom step. "Hey, Cheri," he called out in a normal voice. "We got a problem here?"

"Not with you, I don't."

"Why don't you come down so we can talk?"

"You come up."

"I would if it weren't for that shotgun. Judging from what I can see, you're pretty good with it."

"I won't shoot *you*," she protested.

"I appreciate that, Cheri, but I doubt Kunkle thought you were going to shoot him, either."

That brought a chuckle from Willy, but in fact, Cheri responded, "Nah. I just got scared."

"I don't blame you," Joe said. "Things have gotten out of hand."

She seemed to absorb that.

He suggested a compromise. "I'll head up there, Cheri, but you have to do me a favor."

"What?"

"Unload the gun and prop it against the wall where I can see it. Will you do that?"

After a telling pause, they heard the classic mechanical slap of a shotgun being cleared.

Joe cautiously peered around the corner and saw the gun's barrel being leaned against a doorframe at the top of the stairs.

"We good?" he asked.

Her response was noncommittal. "Bring my cigarettes."

As he climbed the steps, she slowly came into view, from the top of her disheveled head to her crossed blue-jeaned legs. She was sitting on the floor, her back to the wall. She looked tired. He glanced at the shotgun, whose chamber was locked open, further evidence of its being empty.

Joe sat on the landing and handed over the pack of smokes. "Been a rough haul," he commented. "You must be wiped."

"I been better," she admitted, extracting a cigarette and lighting up.

"I bet. It's hard enough just goin' along, without more crap coming down on your head."

"Yeah."

Joe reached out and tapped her skinny knee lightly with his knuckles—a show of support. "I am sorry things soured between you and Donny."

It was a gamble. He was making presumptions. But there had been truths not acknowledged by this woman from the start, and he wanted her to open up.

Her eyes narrowed. "How the hell?" she began before lapsing back into silence, her cigarette forgotten between her fingers.

"Cheri," he said, an angler teasing a fish to bite down. "People like me have been at this a long time. We're not bad at finding things out."

She sighed, took a drag, and filled the air above her head with smoke. "Wish to hell I'd seen some of it comin'. I mighta been able to duck it."

Joe nodded as if this were all old news. "It's not how it works, though, is it? Do me a favor, just because so much else has been hitting the fan?"

"What?"

"Tell me how it started. I mean this whole mess. We know how it ended, but not the beginning. But what was the first domino to fall over? It got lost in the drama afterward."

She answered casually, disarmed by his supposed knowledge of the facts. "Oh, yeah, well, nobody would know that. Not really. It was too many years ago. Hell, Lemuel and I woulda been in god-damn high school, weren't we?"

Joe hid his surprise with a knowing smile. "Long time ago."

"No shit."

He gave a small tug to the hook—another guess disguised as old news. "But you weren't in the same school."

"No, course not. He went to Keene. Back in the day, that was the big city for some of us, and he really caught my eye."

She seemed momentarily lost in the memory, blowing another plume into the air.

"He must've been a lot different back then."

She laughed slightly, ending in a smoker's wet cough. "No kiddin'. Tall, skinny, built like an athlete. He could go all night. I couldn't believe it when I saw him again. I had to ask if it was really him, he'd gotten so old and fat. I know I got some wrinkles on me," she added proudly, "but I still look pretty good, right?"

"You do," Joe said agreeably, adding, "When was this? That you met again?"

"Oh, I dunno. Maybe a year ago? I was in Keene, like usual, and there he was. Just walkin' in the street."

"And the fire was still burning?" he asked, digesting how the commonplaces and coincidences of small-town living could trump the detachment of a larger world.

She flashed a little slyness. "It didn't take long to relight."

"But . . . ," he suggested.

She sighed. "Yeah. Wasn't the same."

"What went wrong?"

"What didn't? Donny, Lem's wife, life's complications. You name it."

"Seems like things got more than just complicated between Don and the Shaws," Joe said.

The look of reverie slipped from her features, replaced by the hardness he was used to. "No shit. The one thing I forgot about Lemuel was why we broke up the first time."

"Which was . . ."

She stabbed the cigarette out angrily onto the wooden floor. "He was one of the meanest pricks I ever knew. Whatever he saw, he wanted, and whatever he wanted, he got."

Joe suggested, "And you fell for it twice?"

She gave him a nod and admitted, "I know. Stupid. You wouldn't understand. You're a guy. You get to do whatever you like. But Lemuel could be like a hot pan to butter. I didn't remember any of his crap when we met again. I was rarin' to go—the old days, all over again. He had a hold over me that made me feel like I had no control."

"So what did he take from you this time?"

She looked surprised by the question, if less by its nature than the enormity it represented. She caught her breath briefly, passed a hand across her forehead, and half opened her mouth at the depth of the recollection. It seemed as if she'd held off putting her loss in true perspective until this moment.

"Everything," she finally got out, before beginning to weep.

Joe waited, using the time to sort through not just his inventory of loose threads and its implications, but the enormity of some of the betrayals he'd recently been exposed to. From the snatching of young boys to the creation of an assembly line of sexual abuse and murder, Joe and his colleagues had been witnesses to a landslide of depravity, none of which they'd had time to absorb and process.

After Cheri had calmed enough to wipe her nose on her sleeve and free up another cigarette, he asked, "What was behind Don's argument with Shaw at the strip club?"

She stopped in mid-gesture. "You know about that?"

"Like I said, Cheri."

Without lighting up, she leaned her head against the wall. "Oh, hell. Two cocks in a henhouse. Where better? I told you how grabby Lemuel is. He'd been buggin' me to cut into Donny's business."

Joe hid his surprise by asking, "Oh, yeah—you said you'd stopped all that. Were you and Donny still working together?"

"Kinda," she began, tacking on, "not really." She waved her hand before putting her lighter to the cigarette and taking a drag. "I went along on trips sometimes, for old times' sake. I really loved those days, and Donny and I were still a good match."

"Until Shaw got into the mix," Joe said.

"Lem and I were hot and heavy again, like before. He found out about the stealin', liked the danger of it, the thrill. Bein' rich didn't make any difference. He took chances his whole life. Now, he was bored, feeling old, sick of his wife, gettin' his rocks off with me. Pulling jobs with me kept the excitement goin'. But it got tough for me, jugglin' the two of them at the same time."

Her turn of phrase caught his attention, and given everything else that had gone before in this case, an uneasiness began to creep up on him. "And then Don found out somehow," he said, following the notion to see where it led.

"Yeah. He got jealous. I mean, he was screwin' Robin on the side. What did he expect? But it led to him pickin' up that I was operatin' again, with somebody else, *and* takin' things from his storage units and sellin' them, which I probably shouldn't've done. Between that and the sex, it was a double whammy to his ego."

Joe was impressed by the easy duplicity of it, but more so by having his suspicion confirmed about Cheri's true relationship with Don.

He worded his next question carefully, although still casually. "When was it you and Donny went from mother/son—which I know wasn't biological—to being a couple?"

His matter-of-fact tone was taken at face value. "Yeah," she admitted. "Sounds weird, I know, but it felt really natural. You know how it is: You spend a lotta time together. One thing leads to another. He was almost sixteen when it happened, so it wasn't *that* big a deal, and like you said, it wasn't like we were related."

"No, no, no," Joe said soothingly. "It explains a lot more about the fight at the club, though."

Her face grew solemn. "I still can't believe he stole Lem's car. Poor old Donny had no clue who he was messin' with. Course by then, he'd turned into an asshole in my eyes, so goin' after Lem was just par for the course."

By now no longer sure what to expect, Joe asked, "When did Lucy come into it?"

Cheri glowered at the mention. "That pig. What the fuck he ever see in her?"

"Shaw?"

"Yeah," she confirmed with emphasis. "That woman's a monster."

He caught the verb tense. "You know she's dead?"

Cheri eyed him carefully. "Really? Good. I hope somebody killed her."

"What did she do to you?"

"She poisoned everything. I coulda handled things if it wasn't for her."

Joe couldn't help thinking that by this point, Lucy was only trying to catch up. "Does this connect to why your fingerprints were on that ashtray and lighter?" he asked. "You broke your own rule about not stealing things with inscriptions."

Her smile was grim. "I wanted to prove they weren't the only ones who could push people around. I stole that stuff when Lemuel told me Lucy went ballistic after hearin' he'd stepped out with me. Typical that he told her. Still, I wanted her to know it wasn't just her husband I could take, but her personal junk, too, right out from under her nose."

"So it wasn't Don who stole them?"

"Nah." Another deep drag.

Joe was fighting the image of a lost-on-an-island reality show, where no one has a conscience, and everyone betrays everyone else. "That didn't work out too well, did it?"

"Not really," she conceded.

It was time to bring up one remaining key piece of missing knowledge. "Tell me about that last night," he requested. "When you rode passenger with Don."

Her cigarette had grown a long ash, which she flicked onto the floor before taking another drag. "That was Lem," she began. "He said he needed to talk to Donny, to work things out with him."

"You didn't know what was going to happen?"

She shook her head, her gaze straight and unfocused. "Maybe I didn't care. Things were getting too fucked up."

"Why did you stay in the car? It was two against one."

That caught her attention. She stared at him. "How did you . . . ?"

"It was caught on tape, Cheri. From across the road."

He stayed silent, letting his previous question come back to her.

"Lem told me to stay put."

Joe pushed her. "So what? They were fightin'."

She flared a little. "Donny had pissed me off, okay? He was being a prick about Lemuel. He'd already dumped me for that girl. He was treatin' me like shit, even though I taught him everything—about stealin' stuff and what to do in bed, even. Anyhow, he agreed to meet Lem at the pull-off, but he was being a horse's ass about it. What did I care about the two of them gettin' into it, finally? Male shit. Let them work it out. Not my circus, not my monkeys."

"Lucy hit him with a two-by-four, Cheri," Joe insisted, replacing his earlier affability with something sterner. "This wasn't a schoolyard squabble. They killed him. They set him up and killed him, and you played along."

She slowly closed her eyes, slumped her shoulders, and dropped her hands to the floor, where Joe reached out and removed the cigarette from her fingers. She seemed drained of energy, almost of life itself.

"They didn't kill him," she said, almost inaudibly. "I did."

Joe had no counter to that. The experienced and stoic interviewer in him yielded to simple incredulity. "What do you mean?"

She explained without inflection. "We drove to Vermont to dump the Mercedes in that ditch. They'd already reported it missin', so they couldn't take it home. When we got there, Lem opened the trunk and forced me to look at Donny."

She took a ragged breath. Once more, tears began coursing down her cheeks. "He was all bloody from where she'd hit him. Lem made me feel Donny's pulse—the big one in the neck."

"Why?"

"To prove he was still alive. And was breathin', too. I could see it."

Joe encouraged her gently, the final horrifying ingredient of an endless nightmare being added to the mixture. "Okay."

"He told me Lucy had hit Donny to teach me a lesson. You steal from me; I steal from you. That's how Lemuel put it. But she'd failed, and it was up to me to finish it. He said if I wanted him and me to be together, he'd take care of her if I did in Donny, right then. It would be the glue that kept us together."

Everything Joe had learned tonight filled the gaps they'd identified. But this, he hadn't seen coming. He'd thought Shaw had ordered his wife killed as a result of that night. By striking Don Kalfus, she'd become a liability to Shaw—yet another fall guy—which her jealousy over Cheri hadn't helped. But this cold-blooded addendum of committing his lover to a blood oath?

"How did you do it?" he asked quietly.

"Lem said if I didn't, he'd claim I'd done it anyhow. 'I want you where I can find you,' he said. He told me I didn't have a choice. I had to do it so we were all in the same boat. Everybody with blood on their hands."

Joe sat utterly still, the cruelty of what he'd heard escalating to a near-biblical vision of sacrifice, orchestrated by a puppeteer of monstrous dimensions.

"He said Donny was finished anyways. His head was crushed. He may have been breathin', but he was dyin' anyhow. Lem reminded me of what a turd Donny had been. He made it sound like no big deal, finally."

"So, what did you do?" Joe asked, sensing he already knew the answer.

She confirmed it. "I used a plastic bag," she replied. "There was one in the trunk, with some things in it. Lem emptied it and had me put it over Donny's head. He didn't struggle. He just stopped breathin' after a while."

She stayed silent after that, inert and closed down, emptied out.

Joe steered away from the black hole of such perversion and

concentrated on the facts. This confessional moment with Cheri—complete with a shotgun resting against the wall—was never going to be repeated. He fought to put himself in the moment she'd just described, of a manipulated woman given to impulse, now a victim of her own unharnessed appetites, and thought of one outstanding detail—the piece of evidence he and his squad had used to open the case at the very beginning.

"Why did we find that old flip phone in the car?" he asked.

Her eyes opened. "You found that?"

"Yes."

"It helped?"

"Yes. It was very important. But if Don didn't rob the Shaws, you must've stolen it."

"It was in a glass case," she explained. "Really weird. An old, dead phone, like a trophy or somethin', labeled '#1,' with a bunch of other strange junk—a pocketknife, a comb, I remember there was a hat. They all had different numbers. Number one had to mean something, so, I grabbed it. And after Lem made me kill Donny, I took it out of my coat pocket, where I always kept it. I knew it was important. I dropped it into the trunk, hopin' it might cause him some pain."

She reached out and put her hand on Joe's arm. "You tellin' me it worked?"

He didn't answer.

Her face was transformed by wonder. "I'll be damned."